Fire Warriors
on the Mountain

TJ Withers-Ryan

Book 2 in the *Fire Dancers* series

First published 2021 by TJ Withers-Ryan

Produced by Independent Ink
independentink.com.au

Cover design by Daniela Catucci @ Catucci Design
Edited by Michele Perry @ Wordplay Editing Services
Internal design by Independent Ink
Typeset in 12.5/17 pt Adobe Jensen Pro by Post Pre-press Group, Brisbane

 A catalogue record for this book is available from the National Library of Australia

ISBN 978-0-6451467-3-8 (paperback)
ISBN 978-0-6451467-4-5 (epub)

Disclaimer:
This is a work of fiction. Unless otherwise indicated, all the names, characters, businesses, places, events and incidents in this book are either the product of the author's imagination or used in a fictitious manner. Any resemblance to actual persons, living or dead, or actual events is purely coincidental.

To Zoe, for a child's love,
and to God, who showed me unending love first.

Contents

Chapter One

Spring was breaking over the southern ocean; the wind off the water held a biting chill, but nothing like it had at the start of our journey. The Tokseng *junk* ship chopped its way through the waters with the constant slap and thud of water against the hull. Its fan-like sails filled, dragging us to our destination – the Golden Islands.

On deck, lanterns lit the night with a golden glow edged with rust. The scent of the salty sea and fried food filled the air. Crew and passengers alike were dancing and clapping to the music of a pair of fiddles. We were a ragged bunch, with people from all over the continent and the islands.

Our voyage from Gabon to the Golden Islands had taken a full month, and we had all been busy. Those of us from the caravan troupe were technically just passengers, but we had all spent hours each day changing the rigging for the sails, or mopping salt water away from anything that could rust, or helping Cook in the galley of the ship, or even polishing the *junk*'s two cannons. It actually wasn't such a strange way to spend a month, since we were used to constantly setting up and packing down a circus most nights.

Even I had been able to do some of the tasks, with the help of Cook's anti-pain herbs. My hands were still bandaged because of my burns, and I was glad I'd been able to help a little during our voyage. It was my first time on a boat, though, and those first few days of seasickness had been unpleasant, to say the least.

But now land was nearly in sight, barely a day away. Everyone deserved a night of celebration.

Bear and I stood to the edge of the crowd, watching everyone's antics. He laughed every now and then at something the others said or did, but he stayed with me rather than join in. He'd grown a short beard along his stubborn jaw, and it tickled when he brought his face down near mine as he laughed.

It had been weeks since I'd last laughed. This whole voyage, I'd found myself standing at the edge of everything, as if I was looking in at everyone else's conversations from the outside. While the people I worked alongside joked and laughed, I just listened. Where I used to laugh, there was a big hole of emptiness. I kept hoping that hole would fill up so things could get back to normal, thinking surely one more day would be enough.

Every morning, I tried to jolly myself into feeling something – anything – positive to start my day. But I couldn't seem to pull myself up out of that hole.

There was too much between me and the hole for me to approach it. Too many memories of everything that had happened since I was kicked out of my tribe, being forced to leave my family. And while finding these new people to join had been a step in the right direction, I still wasn't sure of my place within their circle. Discovering there was a fire burning inside of me that needed to be released had been amazing and wondrous – but I'd been burned by that fire the instant I began to trust and rely on it. Then the attack … I'd fought to protect the others – me, who'd never wanted to fight anyone in my life. I'd thrown fire at other people. I'd heard their screams.

I'd killed a man.

And what hurt the most was that my actions still hadn't been enough. People I cared about, members of my new family, had been hurt.

I knew most of what had happened wasn't my fault, knew I'd done everything I could, but knowing that didn't seem to take away my feelings … or my nightmares. I desperately hoped that with training from people in the islands, I could rebuild my whole self, not just gain some more self-control of my abilities.

As another jig started up, Bear slipped one arm around my waist and pulled me with him, out of the crowd. 'Come away with me?'

I nodded without hesitation. We'd barely had any time to ourselves in this month-long channel crossing. There were always people around, no matter where we went on the ship.

Bear tugged me towards the hold and practically leapt down the ladder into the lower deck. I descended the ladder with more care. My hands still hadn't healed fully since the fighting more than a month ago in the desert. I hated that every time I held Bear's hands, I felt the weight of the bandages and the sting of unhealed skin beneath.

Away from the crowd and the music, I could hear the constant shushing of the waves against the hull and the creak of the wooden ship itself. Every board and rope seemed to be continually shifting back and forth under the strain of carrying us. In the pitch black, Bear and I moved slowly until our eyes adjusted.

We were in the passengers' quarters, but we could hear the

animals in their section of the hold. Just a few yards away were the sounds of sleeping horses. We hadn't brought the goats, instead leaving the herd with a shepherd in Gabon until our return. So I was here only as a dancer, not a goatherd.

Of course, I wasn't allowed to fire dance, just normal dancing. Until Ebony – my dancing mentor – and our caravan leaders, Ayita and Grey were satisfied that my fire magic was under control. Really, it was Ayita's decision, as she was the matriarch, but she often shared her authority with Grey.

Bear's muscled arms slid around my side and tugged me down the side of the hull towards the sleeping bunks and hammocks. He stopped at ours – it was the same size as everyone else's, but we both had to fit in it. I knew what he wanted. My body thrilled, leaning towards him without conscious thought. In the dark, his lips found mine, brushed my cheek, my neck, and sought my mouth again.

I gasped, overwhelmed with desire. After a month of only holding hands and a few furtive kisses in the corner when we weren't helping the crew or our fellow caravan members, every kiss was intense. Like an explosion of liquid fire, hot and fierce. He kissed me like I was the only thing he needed right then. My legs melted against his, barely holding me upright. His strong hands slipped under my shirt. My fingers fumbled with his belt buckle. I couldn't catch my breath. Every touch felt magnified by the time we'd spent *not* doing this.

Between kisses, I managed to get out, 'What if someone sees?'

He grunted. His lips moved to my collarbone. 'They're all dancing and drinking; we've got a fair while yet. And if I'd known this voyage would mean a month without ye, I never would've walked up the gangplank!'

I smiled. He didn't mean it – the caravan was his life, and he would never have stayed behind while they travelled to the islands. 'You just wait till we arrive,' I said. 'Ayita said we'll have a hut all to ourselves. Think of that.'

He growled and ran his hands down my sides. I shivered and closed my eyes in pleasure, then pushed him up against the wall of the bulkhead, pressing myself against him. It felt like my heart was trying to escape my chest as I moulded my body to his. He was so close, so hot, so clearly everything I wanted.

I felt the familiar sparking sensation a moment too late. The flames licked straight up my arms from my fingertips, burning me every inch of the way. My bandages and shirt caught fire in an instant and swept more flames onto Bear's shirt.

I leaped back with a cry of pain and fear. Bear made a shocked noise and began ripping off his burning shirt. I slid out of my own shirt more carefully, as I had to avoid lighting my own hair on fire, then unwrapped my ruined bandages as gently as I could. Looked like I'd have to make new ones again. Since the start of our voyage, my emotions had taken to reigniting my fire powers without me consciously activating them, and I couldn't work out how to stop it injuring me each time.

The flames lit our faces in a strange glow as we stomped the shirts out on the floorboards. I slapped my arms vigorously to douse the flames, then gasped as the floorboard beneath my feet lit up. A spark must have fallen from me.

I tried to call the flames back into myself, like I had in the desert after the fight with the hecklers. But it didn't work. I bent to slap the boards with my ruined shirt and panic rose within me as the scent of burning wood filled my nostrils.

Bear kept his head better. He ran to the corner of the hold, where a jug sat atop a keg of water, and sloshed the full jug over the floorboards. The flames flickered and drowned.

Finally, we sank into darkness again, all the darker because we had temporarily had light. As the light faded, I caught a deep flash of fear on Bear's face. I blinked. Was Bear afraid of me, just like all the rest of them?

'*Tairneach*.' It was a Grimsall swear word he had taught me, meaning 'thunder clouds'. I knew he wasn't swearing at me but was shocked and concerned for me. 'Fern, are ye all right?'

I shook my head even though he probably couldn't see it. 'My arms,' I said, and stuck my hands in the rest of the water in the jug. It stung, and I hissed in pain and shook my hands.

He made a sympathetic noise. I was still aware that we were now both shirtless, so I fumbled on the dark floor until I found my shirt. It looked pretty much ruined, with ragged burn holes and stinking of smouldering cotton. I gave up and reached into our bunk to grab my other shirt, wincing as I pulled it on over my stinging arms.

I checked my wrist for my handfasting bracelet, the outward sign of our engagement. Thankfully, it was only a little blackened on one edge, not burned too badly. I smiled faintly and said, 'Sorry. I don't know why this keeps happening. Before we got on the boat, I wasn't making fire at all anymore! Not since the riot on the border.'

The instant I mentioned it, I was back there. I remembered the flames, the smoke, the people screaming and running. Striking down attackers by throwing balls of fire. Prickly heat raced up my forearms. My gut lurched, afraid it could happen again at any moment. I couldn't believe I was burned again – not that my skin had been healing, anyway. I'd been catching fire too often for the burns to heal properly. I shuddered, and hugged my arms gingerly around my waist as if to protect them. I looked up at Bear miserably in the gloomy darkness and tried to pull myself back together.

But I wasn't the same young woman who had stood up to the

bullies in Nurahadi or the race riots on the Deridai-Gabon border. I was a shell of myself. Why was I such a failure? I couldn't even kiss my betrothed without nearly burning the ship down.

As my eyes adjusted to the darkness and pain once more, I caught an odd look on Bear's face – pity. It made my gut twist again, not in fear this time, but in disgust at myself. If even the one who loved me felt pity for me, how pathetic I must be. How could he even still love me? I wasn't worthy of that love. Maybe he didn't even feel it anymore. Was he just pretending, because he pitied me that much?

But that was just it – his love, given consistently over the months since my fire powers had shown themselves, was the only thing that had held me together so far. I didn't know what I would have done without him. My throat closed over as I fought back tears.

Bear gathered me into the circle of his arms. '*Dinnae* fret, Fern,' he murmured into my hair. 'We'll be there soon, and ye can get the training, find out what ye need to, to make it stop. They'll know what to do.'

I didn't feel entirely comforted. What could they do? In the riots, I had intentionally hurt people, and if I'd hurt myself in the process, maybe I didn't deserve help. Maybe my arms not healing was my body's way of punishing itself for my crime, whether it had been committed in self-defence or not.

He tried to start kissing my neck again, but although he was still shirtless and pressed against me, I couldn't bring myself back into the moment. I pulled back and clung to him, gasping for air as if I was drowning. He sighed, and just held me while I sobbed into his shoulder. It felt hopeless. Bear's arms around me were my only light in the darkness.

Chapter Two

'Land, ho!'

The call came late the next morning. The end of our voyage had arrived, and we would land in the Golden Islands later that afternoon. All the crew and passengers were a little the worse for last night's celebrations, except for Bear and I, who hadn't been drinking. They'd spent most of the morning staggering about or laying listlessly at their posts, holding aching heads or staring blankly with bleary eyes.

Our circus master, Grey, kept moaning that he couldn't wait to get off the ship. 'Land that stays put!' His usually caramel-coloured skin looked washed out, and his words were muffled by the hand that he kept clutched over his mouth. 'That's all I want.'

At first, the island was just a speck of citrusy green on the horizon. It emerged gradually as we all peered fixedly at it. It turned into a tree-covered island with two massive, jade mountains.

I blinked in surprise, seeing that one of the peaks was smoking. I nudged Ebony's arm and pointed. 'Should it be doing that?'

She laughed, her coiled braids jiggling, teeth grinning white against her dark skin. She was someone who only spoke when she had good reason to, so I was surprised when she bothered to explain for me: 'Most of the Golden Islands have an active or dormant volcano, hey. Aiatal has one of the largest active volcanoes in the world.'

'Isn't that dangerous?' I couldn't help asking. 'To place your main dwelling on a simmering cauldron, just waiting to boil over?'

This time both she and Bear laughed uproariously.

'It's fine, lass,' Bear told me. 'We have volcanoes in Grimsa, too. You'll see, if we ever take the caravan there.' He nudged my shoulder. 'Or we could go there on our own, sometime. Ye could meet my family.'

I had mixed feelings about that idea – trepidation and excitement merging about meeting his family, and doubt that a smoking mountain could ever be 'fine'. Of course, I'd heard of volcanoes before, but all the tales seemed to involve whole islands and villages – even entire civilisations – being destroyed and lost, buried under rubble and ash. That sounded like something to avoid, but I should have expected that the promise of fertile soil would win people over.

We put down anchor before we reached the reef. We would have to take the ship's smaller longboat over the shallower waters, to save the hull of the larger vessel from being torn to shreds on the coral and waves. The longboat could carry a few of us at a time to the strip of white sand that wrapped around the island's edge.

But as it happened, we didn't have to wait for the longboat to be free, because as soon as someone spotted our ship, the Islanders gathered along the shore and got into their own canoes to escort us through the waves. Their dugouts could fit six of us plus the man who was paddling each canoe. They were no ordinary canoes, though. They each had a thick balancing pole floating on either side, about six feet out from the hull. They looked like waterbugs crawling over the surface of the swell. The paddlers were tan and well-muscled men – no women, I noted. Many of them wore the 'hundred braid' hairstyle Ebony favoured, and a woven, flax loin-cloth decorated with colourful beads and embroidery.

When a canoe came alongside the ship to meet us, I followed Bear down the ship's ladder and he held my hand as I clambered down into the canoe. It had wide boards for seats, and Bear and I sat side by side on one. I was more nervous than anything else, but as we pulled away from the ship and our paddler manoeuvred us out over the reef, I began to feel excited as well.

The paddler of our canoe smiled widely at us and said, '*Fa ora, afio maligayang Aiatal!*' I blinked as he added in perfect – if accented – Trader's Talk, 'Hello, and welcome to the island of Aiatal.'

I smiled politely.

'Thank you,' said Bear.

'I am Tau Lemaota,' our paddler said. His eyes caught on mine, and he paused, smiling again. Every part of him radiated arro-gance, from the way he held himself to his bold gaze and tone of voice. Still, I had to admit he was a good-looking man. His muscles gleamed with every stroke of the paddle, his skin a deep, golden brown. I wondered if he polished his body with oil or whether a lifetime of sea spray imbued that gleam. His hair was shorn almost to his scalp, but he had some untamed stubble to make him look strong, as if the muscles weren't enough proof of his manliness. I couldn't stop myself from staring at the black and blue tattoos that twined all over his bare upper body from throat to wrists.

We each introduced ourselves as we approached the shore. When my turn came, I gave them my name in Trader's Talk, Fern, rather than my Batherden name, Julei.

From the seat in front of us, Ebony said to Tau, '*Faafeyai. Trader's tauta leleiya, eh.*'

He bowed in his seat, then grinned and continued paddling. He and Ebony carried on a smooth dialogue the whole way, and every now and then I would catch a word of Trader's Talk – Ebony talking about the purpose of the caravan's visit. Tau didn't even seem out of breath from what must have been back-breaking work; he made it look easy.

No wonder he seemed so brazenly confident, with that kind of physical strength. Most of the strong men I'd met acted fairly self-important. Unnerved by my mix of attraction and annoyance at his self-assuredness, I couldn't wait to get off the boat and put a little distance between myself and him.

I looked down over the side of the canoe at the coral of the reef, easily visible through the brilliantly clear water. The coral was a mass of colour – underwater plants I didn't recognise, blue sponges, green mop heads, and creamy antlers. And all of it was sparkling and teeming with schools of red and gold fish. I gasped as a manta ray soared a few feet from us, like a giant, grey, underwater bat.

As we approached the shore, even from such a distance, we could see circular, brown huts made of grass and palm wood. Children were running around, splashing in and out of the shallows. A drumbeat picked up and the music carried over the water to pound in our ears. People began dancing in a line along the shore, in a way I'd never seen before.

'The hula,' Ebony shouted from behind me.

Beside her, Dakota chuckled at her lover's excitement. Her long curtain of straight, black hair blew wild in the wind off the ocean. I was glad to hear her laugh; she hadn't been herself for a while now. Her clothing was still as colourful as ever, but it seemed like the shine had gone out of her golden smile, and she wasn't as talkative as she used to be.

We three dancers admired the hula style together. It looked simple and innocent, yet also sensual, all rolling hips and arms. Dakota began swaying in her seat, mimicking their motion; a true dancer, she couldn't help herself. The hula dancers wore grass skirts and flower crowns, and a necklace of many colourful strands covered their shoulders. I blushed to see that most of them had bare chests or only a breast band.

The canoes slid up onto the shore, smooth and sleek as seals. After our month at sea, when I stepped out onto the bright sand, I staggered and nearly tripped over myself. Bear caught my elbow and I smiled up at him in thanks.

'You've lost your land legs, girl!' Ebony chuckled. She, of course, was striding over the sand with her usual graceful confidence. There was a reason she was the leader of our dance troupe; she never lost her grace.

The locals of the island of Aiatal, who called themselves the Aiatalei, were creating a shade cover along the beach by setting palm fronds over long bamboo poles. They milled around patiently, giving us curious smiles and chatting among themselves as they set up a feast under the shade. They'd arranged a grass runner and my mouth watered as I looked at the veritable feast laid out, of fruit, fish, and flavoured rice. Off to one side of the shade, the dancers kept dancing, smiling broadly at us as we made our way up the white beach. Everywhere I looked, the shoreline seemed dotted with yellow bushes covered in giant yellow flowers.

In the centre of it all stood a man who was large in every possible way, and a similarly proportioned woman. They wore twice as much clothing as anyone else on the beach, and jewellery as well – rings adorned every finger and toe, with bangles of bronze and copper on each arm and around their necks.

Tau led us over to the large man and woman and crouched in a quick bow. Rather than wait until our whole group was on shore, Tau began introducing us immediately. 'Chief and Mother, you know Ayita and Grey Mingan Kaw of Tallapoosa, leaders of the caravan. And this is some of their caravan troupe that has come this season: Ebony Tuitama of Fefine Mohe Island, Dakota Micasokee of Tallapoosa, Fern Batu-gerel of Bat-Erdene, and Bear MacRuairidh of Grimsa.'

I was amazed to hear he'd remembered each of our names perfectly from meeting us in the boat, with us having to practically shout our names above the roar of the surf. *Doesn't mean he's not still an arrogant jerk.*

Tau turned to us in the group. 'Please be introduced to Saulomone Lemaota, chief of Aiatal, and his wife, our island mother, Felesita Lemaota.'

We all bowed, and the chief and his wife nodded with raised hands – in the island fashion.

'*Afio maligayang Aiatal!*' said the chief. 'Welcome. It is a pleasure to meet you all, and I look forward to seeing you over the days to come.' The chief swept an arm to indicate the spread. 'In the meantime, come, eat, and drink! Please.'

We arrayed ourselves along the line of the grass runner, and the locals sat wherever they pleased alongside us.

The rich adornments the chief and his wife wore made me feel suddenly self-conscious of my ragged, mismatched clothing. I didn't have much clothing, but I didn't need much for travelling with the caravan – apart from my performing costumes, which all belonged to Ebony, anyway. But my fear around my failing powers was making me uncharacteristically cautious, even to the point of being shy about what I was wearing. A sense of my own shame was growing in my gut, making me afraid to show myself to others.

I have to shake this off, I told myself.

Chief Lemaota sat at the head of the grass spread and waved Ayita to sit next to him on the grass runner. She took his hand and gently pressed it against her forehand, an island way of showing respect. He smiled and pulled her in to press his nose against hers in a more friendly greeting. Her hair was almost like his: a mass of long, frizzy curls, although I was spotting more white among her curls recently. She had feathers woven into a braid down one side of her face today, keeping some of her hair out of her face.

The chief sat back happily and said, 'So! It's been a long time, no? How are things on the mainland?'

'Treacherous and beautiful in turn,' she replied. 'Just one reason I was so delighted to receive your invitation to come perform for Aiatal and Kamahimaihi.'

'Money to be made?'

'In some places. Less in other places than there used to be. Don't want to end up stealing from our savings. What am I to do? There are always other cities we can try, but where can I take my family, if nowhere is safe?'

Chief Lemaota nodded gravely. 'You need protection. You want me to ask if any of my warriors want to go with you?'

'No, no, I couldn't ask that of you. You'll need your warriors still. Weren't you having trouble with Lelena Island last time we spoke?'

It had been two years since the caravan's last visit, but the chief and Ayita made it seem as if no time had passed at all. They asked about each other's families, the health of their livestock, and how exports from the island were going. They spoke much like Ebony did – direct, with a slight inflection as if every sentence was both a command and a question.

The plan was to stay on the main island, Aiatal, for the first two months of spring. We would then transfer to the second-largest island, Kamahimaihi, for the last month of spring, before heading home. Ayita and Grey preferred to travel north during the height of summer.

While Ayita and Chief Lemaota continued catching up, the others of us sat there awkwardly smiling at the locals and eating whatever they passed to us on palm leaf plates. I was happy to see Ebony introducing Dakota to the few locals she knew from Aiatal. Dakota bit her lip with nerves, but she soon opened up as she usually did, making new friends easily. I envied her bright laugh. People responded to her as if she flattered them merely by paying them attention.

I couldn't help but marvel at how different these people were from me. They were so much bigger, with a larger bone structure and more natural padding. I also assumed, based on the feast before us, that everyone was fairly well fed. My athletic frame seemed tiny next to theirs. And while my skin was tanned a light, creamy brown from all our travel in the desert, the Islanders had a deep, golden tan ranging from ochre through terracotta to a tawny orange-brown. Bear's pale skin made him look like a ghost next to them. Their hair was dark like mine, but where mine was as straight as straight could be, theirs was a mass of curls when they let it spring about their head or tamed it back into braids large and small.

And their skin was decorated with swirling patterns of ink from nose to toes. I found myself staring as I admired all their beautiful tattoos: pictures of spirals and fish, flowers and sharks, mountains and oceans. I wished I had something like that. If I had a tattoo, I wondered what I would choose as the pattern or image.

The local woman across from me offered me a palm leaf with a whole fish on it. I smiled at her and took some, trying to look friendly and not like I was staring at everything and everyone around me. I felt terribly aware of every action I took, wondering which would be acceptable and which offensive to these new people.

On the ship, Ebony had taught us the law of reciprocity that people lived by in the islands, where if someone gave you something, you would owe them a favour in return. And while it had sounded simple enough when we were talking on the boat, I wondered what I could do later to repay someone feeding me at a lavish welcome feast. I didn't have anything that I could trade with – that I knew of, anyway. Hopefully favours came in many forms.

I broke off a piece of fish and ate it with my bare hands. Bear dug a shell cup into the accompanying rice bowl. The barbecued fish melted in my mouth, leaving tiny, black scales on my fingers until I licked them clean.

The simple act of eating made me feel a little more at ease, and it made me wonder. Had I felt so self-conscious on first meeting the caravan folk? I couldn't recall. I knew my self-esteem had plummeted, between my burned arms and my grief. Even when we left a month ago, I had been excited to come here. But now … I only had a desperate hope left that training my power to stay within my skin would restore my body and my mind to what it had been.

As if I had summoned the words, I heard Ayita saying to the chief, 'And if we could meet with your fire warriors, your trainers, it would be very important. One of our crew—'

Chief Lemaota waved a hand dismissively. 'We can talk about all that tomorrow. For now, we eat with you and your people. A toast!' He looked about him slowly. 'Where is that *hava*?'

'Careful,' Ebony whispered in my ear. 'We make *hava* from

fermented pepper plant. It's relaxing in small doses, but it'll numb your body and slow your mind if you drink too much.'

From the looks of things, the effect was much like drinking strong ale. It made most people happy and relaxed, but it made others melancholy and cranky. It made Bear nudge himself closer to where I sat and give me longing looks. As for me, the tiny sip I took was enough to make me feel heavy-limbed and sleepy. I couldn't wait for the ceremony to be over so I could take a nap.

While we ate, the others from the boat arrived on more of the island's waterbug canoes. They all enjoyed the same kind of welcome we had, and the same *hava* ceremony. The chief and his wife drank with them each time, but the alcohol didn't seem to catch up to them at all.

The meal took a long time, but eventually we were guided off the beach and into the jungle. These were well-worn paths, tracked by innumerable people over many years, with all the leaf litter crushed and a head-high clearance from the hanging vines and spreading ferns. I smiled to myself upon seeing my namesake everywhere. It was stretching up from the jungle floor, clinging halfway up other trees and blooming towards the canopy.

We were led into the main village on the island and past the longhut in the centre of the village, over to a gathering of small huts that were clearly unoccupied and were properly built just for guests like us. Some of the huts were joined to each other, while others were standalone individual huts.

Bear and I were pleased to see they'd gifted us with a hut to ourselves, as Ayita had expected. Before our guide had even walked away, Bear wrapped an arm around my waist and nuzzled his face into my neck. I chuckled and squirmed away just enough to grab his hand and pull him into the hut.

'Alone at last!' he murmured happily.

Inside, he collapsed onto the pallet bed with a huge sigh of relief. I knew it had been a strain for him, being around people every second of the day for a month straight. The ship had not been like life in the caravan, where Bear could disappear into his own van, or go for a ride on the horses when he needed some space to himself. As a horse trainer, he was used to spending a lot of time on his own with just the animals for company, and while he liked people … maybe not this much.

He rolled over for a nap and I tried to join him. But the second I lay down, the whole world began rocking from side to side as if we were still on the ship. I began to feel seasick, even though I'd rarely felt seasick on the ship itself. I stared at the woodgrain on the walls until I couldn't take it any longer.

I staggered outside and sat myself down in the shade of a palm tree. With my feet bare in the sand, the sun playing gently through the palm leaves above, and a rustling breeze cooling the sweat on my neck, I relaxed. In the distance, the ocean waves crashed on the shore.

Soon, the world stopped spinning. I closed my eyes and drifted off to sleep sitting up.

Chapter Three

That night, after a solid rest for some and a bit of exploring for others, we reconvened at a bonfire on the beach. The night meal was just as large as the welcome lunch had been, with roast meats, root vegetables, salads, fruit, fish, and rice. I didn't have room to eat much after such a large lunch, and I didn't know if it would be dreadfully rude to only pick at the feast before me. Actually, I was also wondering if eating so much fruit all the time would give me gas – but maybe everyone here was used to that? I wanted to ask Ebony, but she was seated farther down the row. So, I just filled a small palm leaf for myself and snuck anything I couldn't eat over to Bear.

Everyone now and then while we ate, Bear would reach over to hold my hand, sometimes giving it the little double-squeeze that we'd given meaning. 'Love.' *Squeeze.* 'You.' *Squeeze.*

It was such fun simply to be together – eating new foods, absorbing a new culture. Eating together as a couple was still a wonderful novelty; after all, we had only been handfasted less than two months. When he held my hand, it felt like my burns and their pain faded, and my awkwardness at being in a new culture seemed less important. Instead of noticing those things, I felt aware of everywhere he touched me, from his fingers on mine to his thigh pressed against my knee, to the stir of his breath on my neck when he looked at me. He leaned in to kiss my cheek, and I smiled, thinking he smelled like sweet fruit.

As the bonfire climbed higher, the hula dancers again took to the sand, tattoos and flowers waving gracefully. After a while, they beckoned for everyone else to join them. *At last!* Something I enjoyed. I jumped up and took Bear's hand in mine, tugging him towards the dancing.

I soon found the style was harder than it looked. It looked so simple, and anyone could imitate the moves enough to join in, but it required keeping your knees constantly bent, with your core muscles activated to keep a straight torso over bent knees. I could tell that if I weren't already a dancer, I would soon be getting blisters from the twisting feet movements against the sand.

Only the hula dancers showed the beautiful, smooth grace of years of practising this art form. Their hips swayed and jiggled in time to the music, sensual and innocent at once. The arms and feet moving in steps and waves emphasised the ample curves of the island women.

They saluted the sinking sun, swept their arms to the east and west; they gathered us up in their arms from afar, like a mother, like a lover. They moved like the waves crashing on the shore. They balanced the earth and sky along their arms. I couldn't look away. When the men joined in, they created a battle out of the same moves. Their arms made a cutlass scything left and right, a choking grip, throwing their opponent down, then cleaning their weapons after the fight.

Dancing in a row near the back, I found myself grinning,

filled with the familiar joy and urgency of dancing. After a month on a ship with limited space for dancing and exercising, it was a delight to stretch my limbs to their fullest in the company of fellow dancers. I was deliberately avoiding anything like my fire dancing techniques until I knew my power was under my control. And yet, not dancing in my own style felt a little unnatural now, as if I was denying myself something vital, like air or water.

In so many ways, I was still a beginner when it came to dancing. I'd spent my whole life herding sheep and goats – what did I know about moving gracefully or enticingly? I still had no idea why Grey and Ebony had practically demanded that I train to become a dancer, after they had seen me jump over a fire at the caravan campsite.

Except ... every time I danced, I felt my soul come alive as my body moved. This new occupation felt more like a vocation, a calling. For all my failure to find a role within my own tribe that would suit me, at least I had found a role in the caravan that I could call genuinely challenging and satisfying.

All I had to do was avoid fire dancing until everyone was satisfied that I'd trained my fire powers and was no longer a danger to anyone else.

When we all got tired and the dance dispersed, everyone began dancing their own preferred styles around the bonfire. Bear led me in the dance he had first taught me months ago: the Grimsall promenade.

As we danced, I enjoyed watching the hula dancers reform into a smaller circle and dance a less patterned form together. They wore grass crowns on their curly, dark hair, and ropes of wooden beads on their ankles, but their wrists remained free, showing off the supple lines of their arm from fingertip to shoulder.

Tau would tell us later that in ancient times, warriors were only selected from the strongest dancers. They had to prove they had the best endurance by climbing the tallest coconut trees, swimming underwater without coming up for breath, and then dancing all night.

At midnight, Chief Lemaota stood and waved Tau over. 'My son!' he said. He clapped him on the shoulder with obvious pride. 'Tau Lemaota. May he kill a thousand enemies and sail a thousand seas before I die.' He waved an arm over the crowd. 'Now my son will tell you a legend of our people.'

Everyone cheered, and Tau smiled. It was clear he liked the attention of an adoring crowd. I just blinked in surprise. I had heard Tau introduce himself earlier, of course, but I hadn't noticed that he had the same family name as the chief.

Tau strolled up to the fireside, the gleam of the flames dancing off his broad chest, illuminating his many tattoos. 'Some time after the first sunrise,' he began, 'thunder eagles soared over the peaks of our islands and made nests on the peaks.'

Near us, Ebony muttered to Dakota, 'Oh, thank the waves, a real story. Usually, our people like to tell genealogies, and it takes hours.'

Tau continued, 'The thunder eagles are so named because they came from the lightning in the sky, making them as hot as the sun. From the sheer heat of their droppings, the mountains began to bake from the inside out. The mountains opened their heads like hungry mouths, spewing forth lava and sulphur and clouds of ash. And the thunder eagles moved their nests to the inside walls of the volcanoes.

'They were beautiful and fierce, hunting the lions of the islands as their prey, and all the men of the villages praised them, because the lions used to eat us. So now the men and women were safe to roam around, knowing there were fewer lions to hunt us, and every night, the thunder eagles lit their tail plumage on fire and flew home to their steamy nests. But one day, there were no more lions left to eat, and the thunder eagles became hungry. One of them spied an older woman walking alone to the sacred spring for some cleansing water to use in the healing rituals. The eagle swooped down, and in his talons, he stole the woman away.'

Tau prowled about the fire, a natural performer. He looked just the part of an eagle, soaring, wheeling, diving to attack. I'd come to appreciate a good performance even more during my first season with the caravan, and even though I didn't want to admire Tau, I found myself noting how well he held us all enthralled. He obviously thrived on the crowd's reactions, much as Bear did when he was performing with his horses.

But that was different – with Bear, he always directed the attention to his horses, to their skills. Even when he performed a trick, like jumping from the back of one horse to another, he always made it seem like the horses were the stars, and they were just letting him share the light. I knew it was real, too – that the horses were Bear's stars, and his friends.

This performance was about Tau and his people's legends.

'What the eagle didn't know,' Tau continued, 'was that the woman was the island chief's dear wife. When he heard what had happened, he was filled with rage.' Tau waved a wooden club in the air. 'He called for war on the eagles, for men from every village on every island to hunt and kill every thunder eagle they found. He offered a bounty of coconut shells for every eagle talon they brought to the chief.'

Tau lowered his voice. 'And they did. The men slaughtered all the thunder eagles they could find. This tragedy angered the volcanoes greatly. They stomped their feet beneath the earth, cracking the sea and the stones apart. Then they spewed their fury – fire and ash and rocks raining into the sky and down over the villages, until the sky was black with ash and the sun went dark.

'For an entire season, it remained dark and cold. Nothing would grow, and the fish wouldn't swim near the islands, and the people nearly starved. They called it "the summer that never came". When the sun finally reappeared and brightened the world, they praised the gods they were free, and tried to forget.'

Tau leaned forward as if telling a secret. 'Only one young boy knew why the sun decided to come back out. He had hidden away one thunder eagle's egg, to keep it safe during the massacre. He kept it warm by sleeping with it in his bed every night, and during the day, he set it in the hot sand on a secluded beach. When it hatched, at last, the sun arose into the sky once more. The boy raised the tiny thunder chick in secret, then bred it with a normal sea hawk. And so, we know thunder eagles still exist, but without the giant size they once had when they were purebred. And every year, to appease the thunder eagles and to reignite the fire in our hearts, we men climb the volcano and light a torch from its lava.'

He smiled expansively. 'We will show our dear visitors tomorrow, if they are willing to climb the sister mountain – to view our volcanoes and our thunder eagles from a safe vantage point.'

I leaned back with a deep sigh. It had been a great tale, and now I was excited to make the climb and see it for myself. I had been sitting forward so eagerly that my ankles and back now ached.

Bear shifted so I was leaning against his chest, and I turned my head to smile up at him. I scrunched the sand between my toes, ready to relax.

A moment later, Tau began looking for a place to sit, and Bear untangled himself from me and waved him over to join us.

Tau strode over with a jaunt in his step, his eyes glimmering like black gold in the firelight. He sat next to Bear. 'How did you enjoy the story?' Tau asked, grinning as always.

'Amazing,' I said despite myself. Even if I found him arrogant, I couldn't deny he had made a wonderful performance.

'Fern's a fire-lover,' Bear said.

Tau tilted his head to me. 'Something we have in common. And what do you do, Fern?'

'Well, normally, I'm a goatherd, but the caravan left our goats on the mainland rather than have them make the sea voyage.'

'A goatherd without any goats,' Tau teased lightly.

I narrowed my eyes. Jamila used to call me 'goat girl', and she'd meant it as a grave insult, not a joke.

'And ye're one of our amazing fire dancers,' Bear added. 'Can't forget that.'

'Oh, you play with fire?' Tau's eyes lit with interest.

'When dancing,' I said, even though that wasn't the whole truth. I kept my words abrupt, trying to cut off that train of conversation.

Bear looked at me, about to tell Tau more than I wanted to tell him right now, but thankfully, Tau had clearly sensed my reticence and spoke first. He asked Bear, 'Now, you, I don't have to ask – I can see you come from the chilly north, where I've heard you have not only volcanoes in the midst of the ice, but also hot springs surrounded by snow! You must tell me, eh, is this true?'

Bear looked surprised but nodded. 'Yes, it's true, we do have all those things. The hot springs are a delight. In summer, we bathe in them, and in winter, many people build huts over and around the spring so they can continue to use them even during the snows.'

'You bathe in hot springs in summer?' Tau laughed.

'Aye, well, it does snow all year round, so even in summer, a hot spring is a nice way to relax.'

'And how is it possible? For something so hot to exist in such a cold place?' Tau asked.

'My people believe that in the earliest days, before the sun's rays could reach the true north, the people called up fire demons to keep themselves from freezing to death. The demons wandered under the ground and the water, creating hot springs wherever they stopped to make camp for the night. But the demons didn't want to leave, so they built volcanoes to live in.' Bear shrugged, as if to say Tau could decide whether or not to believe it.

I could understand Tau's disbelief about things in the north, since I was a little in shock about what we'd seen of the island so far. It was supposed to be spring here, but it had been almost unbearably hot and steamy today until the sun set. 'Is it always so warm here?' I asked him.

'Every day of the year,' he said.

Bear looked over at me, then said to Tau, 'If we wanted to visit one of the volcanoes, how would we arrange that?'

Tau shrugged expressively. 'It depends on who "we" is. You could come, hey. She could only come as far as the base of the mountain.'

My curiosity quickened, along with a hint of irritation at the way he dismissed me so quickly. 'Why?' I asked. 'I noticed you said only the men make pilgrimages to climb the volcanoes?'

He looked like I'd suggested something dirty. 'Of course! Women carry the inner heat of life-bringing. They can't handle a flame, so they can never walk on the volcano. No, only the men make the pilgrimage. Because some of our strongest men, our warriors, are able to wield the fire, you see. When they light their own wielding flames from a powerful source, it strengthens them as warriors.'

The way he said it, I gathered that here in the islands, women were not fire wielders. I sat back again. And yet, here I was, with fire powers. I sucked my bottom lip in with my teeth, thinking. How was I wielding it as an external flame, when the females of this land could not?

Bear shot me a look. 'An inner heat … I wonder if that's why—'

'Why you always complain that I make the bed too warm?' I interrupted, and laughed loudly. I wasn't sure why, but I felt uneasy about letting him finish that sentence and telling Tau about my fire powers. Probably because he was the chief's son … and because he annoyed me. 'Enough of that. It's late, and speaking of bed, why don't we head back to our hut, Bear?' With my eyes, I willed him to understand that I didn't want to talk anymore.

Bear hesitated, clearly not understanding, but he nodded and wrapped an arm around my waist.

'See you tomorrow, eh,' said Tau.

I felt his eyes on us as we stood and walked away. The bonfire fell away, and we followed a line of torches on long poles. The torches lit a small portion of the path, but it was late now, and darkness crowded in over the ground until we could barely see our feet.

I murmured to Bear, 'The chief said he'd talk about it tomorrow, so … tomorrow, all right? I don't want to rush this.'

I didn't feel like I could tell him the real reason I hesitated. It took me only a second of digging into my emotions to see my deepest fear staring up at me: the fear that I would get kicked out on my own again. My own tribe had kicked me out after eighteen years, after all. I didn't think Ayita and Grey could be any more loyal to me than my own people had been. If I made any trouble here, I worried that they might leave me to the sea instead of keeping me on as part of the caravan crew.

Bear looked uncertain, but he said, 'All right,' drawing me close as we walked.

Chapter Four

The combined lulling sound of waves breaking on the shore and the hush of a nearby stream made me sleep deeper than I had in weeks. I still woke early as always, because although I had no goats to feed while we were here on the island, a life's habit is hard to defeat. I wished the sun had stayed down a little longer – I could see its first rays peeking through the leafy eaves of the window hole.

Can I stay in bed a little longer? I wondered, sleepily shifting around under the warm weight of Bear's arm. He made a grumbling noise in his sleep and squeezed me tighter. I smiled and wriggled until I could drop a kiss onto his bare chest. When I eased myself out from under his arm, he groaned and rolled over, still asleep as far as I could tell.

We'd had a late night after returning to our hut, indulging ourselves in each other. I hadn't let us go the whole way, afraid of burning myself again – but the burning pain didn't happen this time, perhaps because I was feeling more relaxed than I had when we were trapped on the ship. And it felt incredible to have a decent-sized bed to ourselves again after the cramped conditions of the ship.

I still couldn't get enough of him, even after being together so many times now. It made me shiver with delight just to remember everything we'd done last night. We'd touched, kissed, sighed, and gasped, and then laughed at how happy we were just spending time alone together again.

The air inside the hut had a pleasant chill as I padded across the wooden slats of the floor to find my nightdress and my long-sleeved shirt. Spring here was steamy and warm, warmer than our summer back home, and it wasn't cool enough for a coat, but at least this way, my bandages would stay covered, hidden.

Outside, I slipped my boots on at the door and wandered a short distance from the hut to relieve myself. Then I walked down the creek to a shallow spot someone had told me about last night. I was glad our hut was situated near the inland creek. It meant I could bathe and get a drink of water without needing to wake anyone from the caravan or the village at this ungodly hour.

I left my boots and my long-sleeved shirt in the reedy grass at the edge of the creek and waded into the water in just my nightdress and bandages. The temperature difference between the air and the water stole my breath away for a moment, and I was surprised. Yesterday, when we had splashed through the shallows getting out of the waterbug canoes, the sea had felt quite warm.

The creek bed beneath my feet was sandy, with very little mud – much nicer than some of the other bathing spots I'd tried while travelling with the caravan. Places like Tallapoosa had mud and algae in most of their streams. The water here looked clean, so I unwrapped the bandages on my arms to take a drink.

After a long, refreshing drink from the creek, I sat back and stared at my hands through the rippling water. My scars blushed up at me, a mix of angry wine and pink. I took the opportunity to wash my skin and the bandages themselves carefully, enjoying the touch of cool water gliding over my ever-hot burns. The familiar ache of shame made my gut tighten as I gazed down at my arms.

On top of feeling ashamed every time I remembered my burns, I felt a little emotionally tired from meeting so many new people upon our arrival yesterday. Everyone's names were so hard to remember here; they had long names, and then most people had their own nickname. I felt certain I was going to offend someone by forgetting their name, or forgetting I'd met them at all. It was going to happen – yesterday was a blur in my mind already.

I heard the splash of a paddle before a canoe slid into sight around the bend. I cursed under my breath and began wrapping my bandages back on in a rush, tucking the ends into each other more loosely than normal.

'Hey there, hello now,' the paddler called to me over the water, not loudly. '*Fa ora.*'

I looked up and smiled. It was Tau. 'Hello.' I was suddenly glad my nightdress was long, modest, and thick. It covered enough of me to be comfortable while talking with a man, especially one I didn't know well.

He brought his canoe to a halt easily, his paddle swaying the canoe up to the bank. '*Witihai,*' he said.

'Huh?'

'It means "sunrise". Like saying "good morning" in Trader's.' He held out a hand to me. 'Feel like a paddle?'

I never thought very clearly in the mornings, until I'd had something to eat and some time to wake up fully. That's the only reason I can think of that, even though last night I'd tried to stop him asking me any personal questions, I now said, 'Oh. Sure.'

I eased into the water up to my knees and clambered into the front of the canoe. It was only designed for one or two people, so there weren't any seats like there had been in the boat he had paddled for us yesterday to the island. I gripped the edges of the canoe, a little unsure why I'd got in at all.

Tau stiffened, his eyes on my arms. My bandages weren't done up properly. I crossed my arms, trying to hide myself, but he had seen. 'What is that?'

'Nothing,' I said quickly.

'On your arms there. I didn't notice those bandages last night; I thought it was just a long shirt you were wearing under your coat. Some of the northerners have strange costumes, so I wasn't sure, but they are bandages, eh?'

I almost laughed at him saying our costumes were strange, when he was sitting there in a pair of linen shorts and nothing else. The Islanders probably thought it strange that we caravan folk wore any clothes at all. I wondered if the shorts were for our benefit. I stared at him, his stupid, perfect body and short hair that made me want to run my hands over his head, admiring his tattoos where I had burn marks.

'They're burns,' I admitted. Just talking about them made the skin on my arms heat. I flinched, trying to suck the warmth back in under my skin.

'So fresh,' he said, curiosity and pity in his eyes. 'Did you touch the bonfire last night?'

'No.' I shrugged, feeling ready to jump out of the canoe. 'They're from a month and a half ago now, but they are not healing well. I keep re-burning them.'

He pulled back, staring at my arms, then back up at my wary face. 'You burned them yourself?'

'Not on purpose,' I snapped, gesturing. Without warning, a flame shot out of my palm. It fizzled out over the water. I sucked in a sharp breath, and lowered the hand to trail in the water, silently praying it didn't leave another burn mark. It seemed my secret was determined to out itself, regardless of how I had held back last night on telling anyone. 'I can't control the fire yet. As you can see.'

I looked up. Tau was gaping like a fish on dry land. His hand was frozen on the paddle, and we were drifting into a still eddy in the centre of the creek. 'Was that … Can you … Fern, can you wield fire?'

I nodded mutely.

'But how? You're *fafine*, a woman. And you don't have any Islander blood in you?'

'I don't know, I don't think so,' I said helplessly. I was starting to feel embarrassed, and irrationally angry at him for pointing out how impossible my situation was. 'The magic only started appearing this winter.'

'Don't you know how to stop the burning?'

'Why do you think I'm here?' I couldn't help but roll my eyes. 'I was going to ask the chief to find someone who could train me. I can't keep burning myself like this. It hurts.'

He was shaking his head in disbelief. 'I'll bet it hurts! Even the youngest boys are trained not to burn themselves …'

I turned my head away. Was he *trying* to insult me?

'It's all about controlling your breath, your emotions, keeping the power contained when it goes in and out, hey.'

'I didn't know that,' I snapped again.

'Of course, of course.' He began paddling again, taking us back towards the village longhut. 'You need healing, first, and then training. Although … to train a woman … It's never been done before, hey. I didn't even think it was possible for a woman to wield an external flame.' He slid the canoe up the bank, and I helped him haul it up into the shade of a palm tree, beyond the tide's reach.

'But *how?*' he asked again, as if talking to himself. 'And so old, eh. You really never knew?'

'Not until a few months ago.' I pulled my wool shirt closer around me, shivering in the breeze.

'And you're definitely *fafine*, and not *treleilehine?* A crossover child?'

'Crossover?'

'Yes, neither male nor female.'

I squinted. 'I assure you, I am definitely female.'

He blinked. 'It's not an insult if you are *treleilehine.*'

I frowned. 'But it's sounding like it's an insult to you if I'm a female fire wielder!'

'Just doesn't make sense. *Fafine* don't make fire.'

I shrugged and tossed my hair. 'I didn't know we couldn't.'

Tau seemed to realise I wasn't responding well to this line of questioning. He softened his expression and gestured to the path. 'I'll take you to see our healer before breakfast, hey?'

I nodded reluctantly. Bear was probably still asleep, and I didn't think I would be gone long. I wished it was someone else taking me to the healer, but it was fine. Clearly there was more to Tau than his overbearing nature, if he had enough compassion to offer to take me to the healer himself. The village began awakening around us, people stirring out of their huts, voices raising, as I followed Tau down the sandy path.

Tau kept talking, occasionally waving to someone we passed. Everyone smiled, happy to see him. *All right, so the chief's son is well-liked,* I mused. *Doesn't mean he's not arrogant.*

'You won't be the first person to discover their fire powers so late in life,' he said, 'but here in the islands, it's usually discovered early, and you would be trained as a young child. Although I've *never* heard of a female having powers … I'll take you to meet our fire trainers later today, and they can assess your situation. For now, you just need Eli, our healer.'

'Eli' turned out to be Elivavan Nopamaua, a water wielder who used his water powers and his skills with herbs to heal all kinds of illness and injury on the island. He was older than me or Tau, about fifty or so, with long, curly hair tied back with a string of coloured wooden beads. He wasn't as fit as Tau, but he also wasn't as padded as some of the other Islanders.

'Can you heal the burns?' I asked, trying not to sound too desperate.

Eli poured a gourd of salt water over my arm as he said, 'Of course! I mean, there's some things I can't heal. Can't heal something if someone's born with it, like a missing foot or weak eyesight; there's *nale*, nothing there you could heal, just something growing different. But this now—' He indicated my arm and chuckled. 'I would heal fifteen burns a day like this when the boy childs are young. They're not like girl childs, not so clever, not so cautious. You get yourself some training and you'll be fine, eh.'

I felt a wave of relief at his words. As the cool of the water stung and soothed along my skin, he began to touch the skin lightly, here and there, gentle prods that somehow eased the bone-aching pain of the burns. Eventually, he ran his whole hand down my arm from fingertip to shoulder and back, in a thorough massage, then sat back and began washing his hands.

When I looked down at last, the scars had been reduced to shiny lines and circles over my arms. My skin was a fawny pink, and perfectly smooth again.

And there was no pain.

After having horrible burns all day for a month, it felt wonderful. I found a lump rising in my throat, overwhelmed by gratitude and relief. 'Thank you,' I said.

As he began packing up his things, I ventured to admit, 'I didn't know there were other types of wielding apart from fire.'

'Fire, water, air, all of these we've seen wielded in the islands. I used to wield the waves themselves,' he said lightly, as if it was nothing. 'But now I stick to the little things. Water is as dangerous as fire, in its way. It is beautiful, but … you can never see the bottom, and it runs through your fingers if you try to hold it. If you fall in unprepared, you can sink and drown.'

I already felt like I was drowning. I was glad to have the burns healed, but mostly I was just wondering how long it would last before I would burn myself again. Wondering whether next time would be worse. I stared down at my bandages and began rolling them into tight little bundles, for whenever I next needed them.

I hesitated, then said quietly, in the hope that no one but us would hear, 'Can you … can you take it away?'

Eli looked at me sharply. 'Take what away?'

I shrugged helplessly. 'Well, I wasn't – I wasn't born with this, the fire. It came on so suddenly, and I don't know why, and I don't need it. I don't want it.'

Eli waved his hands back and forth expansively. '*Nale, nale*. No, that I cannot do. No water can wash away fire powers. It is like the heart of a volcano – it would take an ocean to do it.'

I seized on his words. 'But you said you wielded the waves—'

'*Nale*, this is something you will live with. I cannot change it.' He turned back to his pots of herbs.

'Well, thank you, anyway.' I sighed.

I had survived a lot so far.

I could survive this a little longer.

Chapter Five

efore Tau and I could visit the fire trainers, there were the usual morning activities to do. I told Bear of my plans with Tau, which he only raised an eyebrow to. Then I helped feed his horses some hay and island grass, and then we walked to the longhut to have our own breakfast.

I couldn't believe how hilly everything on the island was, from houses perched along the mountain edge, to roads climbing through gullies and stream-led ravines. I was out of breath long before we reached breakfast.

In the longhut, the village cooks had laid out bowls of coconut rice and huge platters of fruit – whole papaya, pineapple, mango, spiky pink dragon fruit, cherries, and bananas. There were coconuts, cut open at the top so you could drink the juice, and red bean juice for those who were nursing a hangover from the *hava* of the night before. I even scooped a fried egg onto my palm leaf 'plate'.

As we ate, a clear-eyed Ebony instructed a sleepy Dakota and me about random facts she'd decided we needed to know about island culture. Apparently, any non-edible parts of the fruits and vegetables we were eating this morning would be used for building or craft. The crushed red bean shells that didn't make it into the juice were transformed into paint; the coconut fibres became clothing, baskets, and roofing for the huts. The village chickens even ate the shells from their own eggs, to make them and their eggs stronger.

The whole van was getting a tour of the island this morning, before the day grew too hot. We bustled around the island in an unruly, boisterous group. Some of the group were so far ahead – and some so far behind – that they couldn't hear any of Chief Lemaota's pleasant commentary on the sights we were visiting. I pushed Bear to stay with me in the middle, where I could hear and learn.

From the village, we walked inland past the non-volcanic mountain, the one that we would be climbing another day to view Aiatal's volcano. The jungle rose up around us and we were usually in the shade of palm trees and other tall trees. As we ventured further into the jungle, more foliage sprung up to block the sky, and the temperature plummeted. I couldn't help but feel excited. A new place, a new people, and now a type of landscape I had never experienced before …

As we stared up at a beautiful waterfall, watching the water ripple down a moss-covered cliffside, I squeezed Bear's hand. 'Can you believe we're really here?'

'Aye,' Bear murmured and kissed my temple, his arms around my shoulders.

Ebony chuckled behind us, and Dakota elbowed me. 'Go back to your hut, you two! That's what it's for!'

The tour of the island wasn't all magical, of course. There were bugs *everywhere*, from sand flies along the beach shore, stink bugs and mosquitoes in the jungle, to marsh flies and fat, hairy caterpillars as we neared the mountains. Bear and I both got bitten by mosquitoes early into the walk, then spent the rest of the time scratching our arms and legs.

Tau laughed at our discomfort. 'Exotic blood. They don't taste you northerners often.'

'Do people from other places visit here?' I asked. 'Apart from the caravan?'

He shrugged. 'Only the traders, and the slavers.'

'Sex slavers?' I shuddered, thinking of the sex slavers who had tried to steal Dakota and I in Deridai. It wasn't something I would ever forget, and I knew Dakota hadn't been the same since it happened.

Tau's eyes were dark for a moment. 'No, they take all kinds of people as slaves. They come, usually from Chidor, to steal our young people while they are away from the villages, the ones who can't wield fire to defend themselves. They take them as slaves for their Emperor, and our mothers are left grieving. We all grieve it. The loss of any child is unthinkable.'

I grimaced and shifted closer to Bear without thinking. 'What can be done?'

Tau's hand clenched and unclenched with restrained anger. 'They are too fast. Hit and run. We long to fight them properly, but it's difficult to hunt them on the open seas.' He waved a hand towards the ocean. 'We've travelled the whole world, and now we are hunted at home. We won't put up with it any longer. Our children deserve to live free of fear.'

The group moved on, but the conversation stayed with me. I felt deep in my bones that there must be something we could do against such large evil forces, but I wasn't yet sure what. After all, I was only one young woman who couldn't even control her own powers. Who was I to think I could change the world?

When our tour reached the western inlet coastline, we saw something that made Bear – the normally unflappable, unimpressible Bear – stop and gape in shock. Wild brumbies exploded over the sand dunes like thunder, like a squad of warriors breaking onto the field of battle in an ambush. Their coats were a bright sheen of red and brown and black, their hooves unshod, their manes untamed. They looked completely wild and free, muscles flowing over the sand. They slowed at the shoreline and splashed along it in the shallows.

Bear couldn't tear his eyes away from them. I saw how he watched them move, and I could tell he would see nothing but the horses now. He swept his hair back off his face with one hand as if to see the horses better, while his other hand clenched by his side as if he longed to hold a training rope with one of them in the ring.

'Our wild horses,' said Chief Lemaota. 'Are they not magnificent?'

'Magnificent,' said Bear. 'Oh, aye.'

'We have traders who catch and train the young ones, and then sell them at markets here and on the other islands.'

When the horses ran out of sight, like phantoms vanishing again into the jungle, Bear grabbed the chief's arm. 'Chief Lemaota, ye must let me join your traders. As a horse trainer, this is my life's dream. Please.'

I recognised the tone in his voice. It was the same desperate, surprised, hopeful tone I'd held in my voice when I'd begged Bear to take me to the caravan leaders so I could ask to join them.

'Aren't you only here for a few weeks before the caravan moves on to the other islands?' the chief asked.

Bear nodded.

The chief shrugged expressively. 'Oh, well, yes, by all means. I'm sure our traders will enjoy the extra set of hands, hey?' He glanced over at me. 'It will mean some time travelling away from the village to the more remote parts of our island, and maybe even to the other islands as well.'

I could tell Bear was delighted. As they talked over the possibility, I looked away, uncertain. Usually, I'd be excited at exploring new places and trying new things, and I would have insisted on accompanying him. But with the things I was already dealing with … I felt afraid to go out there with him and afraid to stay here on my own with the caravan. I found it hard to imagine either doing more travel or being apart from Bear for a while.

I stared out at the beach stretching to either side and thought hard. If I was being honest, I feared that Bear might still abandon me after I'd committed to connecting my life to his with the hand-fasting ceremony. I wasn't a child anymore, I told myself sternly. I would deal with it, no matter whether it was difficult. I could deal.

As we continued down the beach, I spotted a figure collecting driftwood along the tree line. When we drew closer, I could see that, unlike everyone else here, they wore clothes – an old, ragged shirt and long pants. He turned, and I gasped. The visible parts of his face, hands, and feet were covered in twisted, ugly, burn scars. One side of his face drooped as if his mouth had tried to melt right off, and his left ear was just a shell with ragged edges. He had no eyebrows and only clumps of dark hair on his head. On his left hand, the fingers were fused together into a misshapen lump.

The chief seemed to be trying to draw us away, but I looked around and caught Tau's eye. 'Who is that person?'

The man heard me. I blushed and looked down.

'Old Man Hanini,' said Tau quietly. 'He discovered his powers too late as a teenager, and his powers got out of control. He was burned head to toe, poor wretch.'

My hands clenched and my stomach sank. I wiped sweat from

my upper lip, then my forehead. Everything felt much too hot all of a sudden. My own reaction shocked me. I felt a sudden hopelessness, as if I had tripped into a deep pit.

Tau didn't notice; he continued, 'It's tragic, for sure. Because of his disfigurement, and because he could not control his power, he is unclean, so he cannot join the clan for our ceremonies or our shared meals; he cannot perform any jobs on the island. But that is just one way we keep evil spirits away – if he was allowed to be among the other villagers, we would all suffer like this, not just him.'

'Hmm, a shame that he can't work a job to support himself or the island, though,' said Bear. He went on to ask about the types of jobs that were done across the island – fishing, farming sweet potato and plantains, harvesting coconuts and water chestnuts, carpentry …

I let the discussion move on without me. Dread welled up deep in the pit of my stomach. Outcast like that, with no protection against evil spirits, and unable to trust his own powers … What would I have become if, cast out from my tribe, I hadn't found the caravan? Or if Ayita hadn't been happy for me to join them?

I glanced back at Hanini.

Despite my overwhelming feeling of dread, I knew I had to be determined. Surely it wasn't too late for me. I wouldn't let myself end up like him. I would find a way, with a trainer to help me.

Still feeling much too warm, I stumbled across the sand, falling behind the others. Bear took my hand to steady me, and I clutched to him, afraid.

After a sumptuous lunch of fish, rice, and coconut curry, Tau led me away from the group to the place where the older fire warriors trained the children who showed signs of having the power. It was on the beach, along the shoreline. The sun blazed down, but there was nothing set up for shade. The nearest trees or driftwood were at least fifty yards away. A circle of about twenty young boys clamoured around two wiry, grey-haired men.

'Nothing to burn,' I realised out loud. I was sweating already, and not just from the sun.

'And the sea is right there to cool you and cleanse the burn if someone does backfire,' said Tau. 'Which tends to happen when children are learning to play with fire, eh.'

Backfire, I thought to myself. *So that's what I've been doing.*

As if to prove his point, one of the young boys burst into flames with a shout.

I gasped and froze.

But his classmates just picked him up and threw him in the shallows as if it were nothing. With a hiss of steam, he spluttered for a moment, then stood and laughed. The others called good-natured taunts from the shore. He shook himself off like a dog and jogged back to the group, obviously unharmed.

I realised my hands were trembling. Suddenly, I felt more than just uncertain. These were not my people – how could they accept me? It didn't escape me that, as expected, the circle of instructors and trainees were all male. I lagged behind as Tau called out a greeting to the group.

'Ualesi, *o e manuia?*' he said to the boy who was still dripping.

The boy, Ualesi, shook his head with a wry, self-deprecating laugh, and pushed his wet hair back out of his eyes. *'Manuia.'*

Tau turned to me and said, 'Can you believe this kid? Don't worry, he's fine.' He turned to one of the trainers and gestured with his head, still grinning. 'Sefa, *naniwala ka sa? Papan palusapa?*'

He must have asked for a word in private, because the trainer nodded and walked away from the group a little way, waving for us to join him.

Tau waved at me loosely. 'Sefa, this is Fern Batu-gerel, one of our visitors from the mainland.' He spoke in Trader's Tongue for my benefit.

Sefa smiled at me and nodded.

Tau continued, 'She has come to be trained as a fire wielder.'

Sefa's gaze whipped to Tau's face, then back at me, astonished. 'A wielder?' He looked me up and down without blinking and leaned close to Tau's ear. *'Fafine, nale?* She is a woman, is she not?'

Tau spread his hands. *'Oe, fafine.* Yes, a woman.'

But Sefa was already shaking his head, his grey dreadlocks flying, flicking salt and sand at us with the force. *'Nale, nale.* Not possible.'

'I've seen her flame myself. It's true, hey.'

Sefa shook his head again. 'We've never trained a *fafine* in all our history.'

'I know, eh.' Tau looked confused, looking at me, then back to Sefa. 'But she wields fire, and she's had no training. So she must be trained, for her own safety.'

I could already feel my heart sinking, hopes crushed. I knew they would say they wouldn't train me. *Why can't I ever rely on others to get what I need?* I agonised silently. *I should never have come here.*

I willed myself to speak, in spite of my disappointment. 'Please. Couldn't I learn with the children? I only need to know how to stop burning myself.'

Sefa's broad shoulders gave an expansive shrug. 'No, it's impossible … I am sorry.' He began walking back towards the group.

I stared at the ground rather than watch him go. I felt Tau's presence beside me growing more and more tense. I could hear him breathing hard through his nose, like a bull. 'I'm sorry,' I said, keeping my eyes on the sand. 'I didn't mean to cause trouble.'

He shook his head grimly. 'I had no idea they would just say no. I must speak to the chief about it. Just because we have never done something before does not mean we should never do it.'

We began walking back up the beach.

After a moment, he sighed heavily. 'One day, I will be chief, and this would not be a problem. If we want to collaborate more with all nations, I know change is something we must do. But for now, we must ask the chief.' He pointed at me. 'And you – for now, we must train you in secret.'

'But who …?'

'I will.' He nodded decisively. 'Yes, you and me. I will train you in the *malolo* time in the afternoon, while everyone is sleeping in their hammocks with a full belly.'

Tau's suggestion made me eager and reluctant at the same time. Secrets had not gone well for me in the past, thinking back to my earlier situations with Jamila and Bear. I had come here to be trained, only to be rejected by the people, and yet here was their future leader, offering to train me himself.

I'd thought he was the alpha male type, but maybe he'd just been posturing because he needed to prove himself as a future leader. I knew the islands frequently ran low on resources, causing wars between the island tribes. As a warrior, he would have been in battles over fishing rights, land, smaller islands, perhaps even women. So he needed to be seen as strong by everyone, not just his own people.

Maybe there was more to him than I'd been assuming, if he *was* willing to help me.

Or maybe I was just another accomplishment he could claim later, once he'd been successful in training me, a lowly woman. I kept my guard up.

An irritation was building, stuck in my chest, because Bear had been immediately allowed to join the horse traders, but I couldn't get the training I needed – simply because I was a woman.

Although it was a beautiful morning, with the sun rising through the trees, I was irrationally flooded with rage. I wanted to lash out at these people; they lived what looked like such an easy life here, and yet they couldn't be bothered to help me.

Easy, I told myself. *These people aren't to blame for their culture.*

Unless maybe they *were* to blame … Unless maybe any one of them could have changed things before now, fought against old traditions and prejudices, so that when I arrived in such painful need, they would have jumped to help a female fire wielder instead of looking away.

But how? Who could have possibly changed anything, when they've never even seen a female fire wielder before?

All of this took only a moment or two to process, from sudden rage to simmering acceptance. I knew I would have to convince myself of this many times over, but for now, there was nothing else I could do to change Islander culture, but I could accept Tau's offer. Whatever the reason he was offering to help me, I couldn't refuse, and I didn't want to.

I drew in a deep breath and stuck out my hand to Tau. 'We have a deal. How can I thank you for training me?'

His teeth gleamed white against his dark skin as he shook my hand. 'I'm sure we can think of something.'

Chapter Six

The next day, a hike was planned. We would go through the jungle to a mountain – one of the only non-volcanic ones, the chief's messenger assured us – to see a view of the islands.

The sun woke me early, light bouncing in corrugated curves off the bamboo walls and floorboards of our hut. It was deliciously warm beneath the cotton blanket, against the chill in the morning air. I rolled over, happy to try to sleep in, but the sunlight through the open window was even brighter than its reflections. With a little sigh, I swung my bare feet over the side of the mattress and pushed myself up and out of the low, pallet bed.

Bear made a muffled noise of complaint in the bed behind me. I ignored him. From living together, I now knew that he wasn't like me – he could just roll out of bed and be out the door in minutes. Unlike him, I took time to get myself ready to face the day, with a few simple but vital actions that woke me up. I splashed my face with water from a basin I had filled yesterday, combed my hair, and dressed in lightweight clothing and my boots. Who knew what we might face on the hike, after all? Foreign bugs, steep, rocky cliffs, mud – I didn't know.

Just as I was finishing up, Bear grunted, and came to interrupt me. His eyes were half-lidded with sleep and desire. His mussed hair and bare chest attracted my attention easily.

'One kiss before we go,' he said, and gave me a lingering kiss. He smiled and drew me close. 'Now one more. Just one more.' I started giggling as he continued to kiss me. 'One more. I swear, this one's the last one.'

'Enough, enough.' I wriggled out of his arms with a wide smile. I couldn't be cranky at how he delayed us getting out the door, given how much I enjoyed the ministrations of his lips. But I was hungry, and I was never at my best in the mornings. 'Come on, I'm leaving without you.'

I trotted out the door, water flask in hand to refill from the stream or the well in the village. He caught up with me by the time I reached the stream and bent to refill the flask. He patted me affectionately on my behind, oblivious to the other villagers walking past as they went about their morning chores.

I hurried us to the longhut for breakfast. Someone was already having to guard the food from flies. I made sure to eat enough to keep me going for what was likely to be a long morning of walking.

Full of fruit and fish, we then followed the chief and the rest of the caravan out of the village on a dusty road that turned into a goat track into the jungle. It was hard going – we were slowed by muddy ground woven with a rug of rotting leaves. From above, a nest of teeth in the form of thorny vines caught at our hair and any skin we had left exposed. Bugs large and small made a feast on our flesh. And it was hot – so humid it sometimes felt like we were swimming uphill. Sweat slid down my spine in a slick trail.

The Islanders didn't seem to notice any of these discomforts, but we nomads sure did. All except Ebony, who was from the Golden Islands herself, and Ayita and Grey, who enjoyed a somewhat swampy environment in parts of Tallapoosa.

As we began hiking, my legs began to protest. What had happened to my fitness? I'd spent eighteen years climbing up and down the tallest and rockiest of mountains with herds of sheep and goats, then spent months training and performing as a dancer. How had I let one month of doing light labour on a ship ruin me? I resolved to work out more, starting tomorrow.

The consolations were many, however. The views, scents, and sounds of the jungle were incredible. Green as far as the eye could see – emerald, lime, jade, khaki, and deep forest greens so dark they were almost black. No one tree looked just like the one next to it. Vines wrapped around the trunks of the fattest trees, slowly strangling them. And again, ferns were everywhere, in more shapes and sizes than I had ever imagined. I recognised the ones that spread out like fairy hair, and the thin spiderwebs of leaves that barely rose from their moss-covered logs and rocks, but not the ones that clustered together in giant crowns on palm trunks. The whole place filled my nostrils with the smells of muddy soil, fresh greenery, and rain.

In the far distance, there was a screech like someone was being torn limb from limb. I jumped, looking wildly around.

Tau laughed at me. I stared at him. 'Spider monkey,' he explained, amusement in his voice. 'Oh, you should see your face, hey.'

'Do they always howl in that unearthly way?' I asked.

Tau nodded, still laughing. 'Scaredy cat.'

I frowned at him. 'Am not.'

'Yes, and a small scaredy cat, too. Like a kitten, all puffed up and spitting.'

Eventually, I huffed my way over a ridge to a small clearing. From here, we could see the island's other landmarks – mountains, valleys, sparkling creeks – laid out in all their splendour. Wiping sweat from my lip, I straightened and tried to catch my breath as I gazed out in awe at the view. I couldn't imagine getting much work done if I lived somewhere so beautiful. The temptation would always be to go and lie on the beach, walk through the trees, or climb up to this view just to stop and think.

A flash of gold caught my eye, and I looked up.

Soaring above us in a lazy circle was a bird like nothing I'd ever seen. It looked like a hawk had fallen into a vat of gold dust, its wing feathers sparkling. It flapped once, and then burst into flames.

I gasped. But it kept flying, its wings and tail burning bright against the morning sky.

Another bird joined the first and twirled in a spiral that echoed its mate's. They spun closer together for a moment, then headed for the trees together.

'Doesn't look real,' Bear murmured beside me.

I had to agree with him. Still, their fiery tails called to something within me. Deep in my soul, I felt a connection stir. It wasn't just that they were beautiful, or that their fire was amazing. I felt almost like I had seen a shadow of them before in a dream, and now recognised them by sight in the real world. You could tell they held both a destructive power and a gentle hope at once in their flames.

'Thunder eagles,' said the chief, and I could hear the smile in his booming voice. 'Our visit is being blessed by the gods of the fire mountains.'

All the locals cheered, and some of them even laughed with delight. I smiled, enjoying how they celebrated their native wildlife.

If I remembered Tau's story from the other night, these must be the descendants of the thunder eagles, bred with sea hawks to keep their race alive. Seeing the birds now, their flames sparkling like dew in the early morning sunlight, felt like a gift to me – a moment of true beauty.

After the fiery birds disappeared, the group milled around, admiring the views and enjoying the breeze. I joined Zane, who was asking the chief questions about the thunder eagles' life and diet. I wasn't surprised Zane was interested in the thunder eagles; he was our caravan's hunter and falconer. His skin, dark as coal, made him almost invisible in the jungle, or would have if it wasn't for the bones he wore in his earlobes.

'Oh, they eat almost exclusively fish,' the chief said. 'And they need to roost in the heat of the inside wall of active or dormant volcanoes. It's one of the reasons why the Golden Islands are their only homes in the world that we know of.'

'How do they survive the heat?' Zane asked, playing with the big bones he wore through his earlobes.

'Well, mostly they thrive on it. Helps them build their own flames larger – as you saw. And it's how they incubate their eggs, eh. They nest the egg as close to the volcano's heart as they can stand. And it's really only during nesting that the heat bothers them – sometimes the heat is so much that the parent bird is severely burned by nesting on the egg, and they never fly properly again after the baby bird hatches.'

An incredible sacrifice, I mused to myself. I couldn't imagine why any bird would willingly destroy their life just to have chicks.

Zane seemed equally unconvinced. 'That's crazy!'

Bear had wandered off on his own to explore the mountaintop. The chief nudged my elbow. 'Bit of a loner, is he?'

I nodded, a little embarrassed, feeling like I had to explain or excuse his ways. 'He likes other people fine. He just likes to go off on his own every now and then.'

I strolled into the shade, where more ferns were growing. I would never tire of looking at them – their delicate, frail-looking leaves and thin, whippy branches that spread ever outwards. I liked that they were stronger than they looked, unable to be easily snapped off because they flexed and bent easily. They could easily lose scores of leaves and branches without being irreparably damaged because they grew so enthusiastically.

Thinking of what I'd come through so far – leaving my tribe, training in the new skill of dance, discovering my powers, fleeing from and fighting unexpected attackers in different forms – I decided I'd been right to choose my name. Frail but with a hidden strength that came from adapting to every new thing I encountered. *Maybe I do belong here, far from the cold mountains,* I pondered.

But if these are my people, why wouldn't they train me? I exhaled slowly, looking down at my unbandaged hands and arms, freshly healed by Eli, and examining the pale scars that now decorated my skin. If this were truly my place, I wouldn't be looking at a future like Old Man Hanini. I shuddered. Fear rose again in my gut, twisting like a worm. I felt a trembling beginning in my body, my hands. A weakness in my knees. I couldn't let myself become like him. I just couldn't.

What if it does happen, though? If I couldn't master my powers … I'd been burned before.

What if I was never able to touch Bear again because I couldn't gain enough control to force the flames down when they rose?

What if—

My chest felt tight. My muscles clenched, something deep inside me keening silently. I gasped for breath, panicked by the tightness in my chest.

I exhaled, only able to make a silent scream to anyone or anything that was listening. *Help!*

I staggered and clutched a sapling's trunk. I hunched my shoulders, my body curling over as I tried to suck in another breath.

The ground groaned audibly beneath my feet. I froze.

The rocks and leaf litter shivered once, twice. As if the island itself were awakening. In an instant, the air became even hotter and heavier, until I was slurping in a thick soup with every breath. From across the valley, there was a long, deep rumble from the volcano, like a lion stretching. The thin stream of smoke coming from its mouth grew thicker, darker. The smell of smoke and rotting eggs stung my nostrils and the back of my throat. Sulphur – was the volcano going to erupt?

Now I was panicking for a different reason.

I heard the chief shouting and waving his arms. He was quite close to me, but my head was swimming, his voice coming to me as if from far away. *'Uma tagata!* Everybody get as high up the mountain as you can, now! Go up – to the fresh air. Fire wielders, *sau ii!'*

Everyone started running further up the path, but I couldn't move. My feet were fixed to the trembling earth. With every ripple, my knees tried to buckle. Beneath the rumbling, I swore I could hear – or maybe feel? – a voice simmering. It reminded me of pebbles rubbing against each other and hot springs bubbling and a crackling campfire, all at once.

Dare awaken me? Little flame … What are you?

My own breathing was suddenly loud and harsh in my ears, my throat so tight I almost choked. Pure terror had me in its grip. I could feel the volcano *smile,* and then the ground rolled again beneath me. I lost my balance and tripped.

A hand grabbed my arm, shaking me out of the mountain's spell. Tau shouted in my face, 'The volcano is about to erupt! Fern, what did you do?'

I gaped at him. 'Me? What? Nothing!'

I looked around wildly. Where had Bear gone? Where was Dakota? Almost everyone had disappeared up the trail without me while I was captured by the volcano's voice. The chief, Sefa, and one of the young fire wielders from the beach remained. They were staring at me, a strange expression on their faces. I couldn't tell if they were angry or incredulous. They moved to stand beside the chief, as if to shut me out from secret fire warrior business.

'Stay here, don't move,' Tau ordered me. 'We need to defuse the magma before it erupts. All right? You stand here and *don't* do anything.'

I was shaken as much by the urgency in his voice as by the heat that was now rising in the air. I didn't think *I* was doing anything, but I could still hear that voice sputtering.

Little flame … I see you.

The four fire wielders put their fists down against the sandy earth. I could feel the tension in every sinew of my own body. I wondered what they could do to stop a volcano from erupting – some of them were younger than others.

One of them rose, and the others followed. Together, they stood and began a complex pattern of kicks and punches. Then they began letting loose puffs of fire from their hands, their feet. The chief opened his mouth and breathed out a cloud of flames. Smoke curled from Tau's nostrils. I stared openly, unable to look away.

The shaking of the rocks stilled almost immediately.

Slowly, the air changed again, the heat dissipating. The stink of sulphur remained.

I could feel the moment the volcano surrendered, like a belligerent ram kneeling under a shepherd's crook. Coiled strength, momentarily laid down. As one, the fire warriors exhaled. The younger warrior, younger than me, gave a nervous laugh.

Then the chief turned to stare at me. The weight of his stare held me fixed to the spot, terrified as much by the anger in his eyes and the tension of his giant muscles as I was terrified of what had just happened.

I had no doubt my face was pale as death. I couldn't believe what had just happened, that they had forced a volcano to turn the tide of its fury. Did I have that kind of power?

Tau barely glanced at me, checking I was all right, then put himself between me and his father and rounded on the others. 'Now do you believe she needs training?' He let loose a stream of Aiatalei, then snapped, 'Raising the volcano. Could have killed us all.'

The chief flicked a hand angrily. 'Go down to the village, hey, check everyone is all right.'

The younger warrior gave me a wary glance and headed back down the mountain track the way we'd come.

The chief continued giving orders. 'We'll go up and check on the rest of our hiking party in a moment, but first, Sefa, Tau, we need to talk – and you, girl.'

My mouth went dry with nerves.

'Her name is Fern,' said Tau, his tone bordering on the biting side of polite. I was surprised to hear him speak up for me.

Sefa walked over to me, his grey dreads swaying, flecked with sweat. 'Eh, girl. That was really something!'

'Yes,' said the chief. 'We've never had a *fafine* with fire powers before, though. To train an outsider in our magic, and worse, to train a *fafine* in fire … Surely this would violate the spiritual law. Sefa, what do you think?'

Sefa sucked in a sharp breath. 'Well, chief, you're certainly right, there's no way a *fafine* should be able to have fire magic. And our laws prohibit *fafine* from touching the volcano or our other sources of fire power. But as for training … I mean, maybe we're better off training a *fafine* to at least control her fire than risking her hurting us?'

Why wouldn't they stop calling me *fafine?* I had a name, as Tau had reminded them!

The chief rubbed his hair, a mass of greying stubble. 'Hmmm. Our elders are usually more inclined to banish someone if they're a risk to us, rather than keep them hanging around.'

'Oh, please,' I said in spite of myself. They all stared at me, and I found myself shrinking back, but I had to defend myself. I couldn't let myself get kicked out again, like I had with my tribe. 'Please don't banish me. I came here to ask for your help, to ask for you to train me, so that I stop hurting myself and so that I can't hurt anybody else. There's nobody else I can ask.'

The chief's eyes locked on mine and I couldn't look away, even though I was terrified of the power he held over my future. I quaked inwardly and bit my cheek to keep myself steady.

He must have seen something that convinced him, because he said, 'All right, then. Since there is no one else who can train you. We don't need any more Haninis running around destroying themselves and everyone around them. As long as everyone who trains you does extra rituals for spiritual purification after each session, it should be fine.' He threw a rough look at Tau. 'Let no one say I can't adapt the traditional ways to meet new challenges.'

Sefa nodded to the chief with easy deference, then said to me, 'In that case, you come back to the beach tomorrow. Tau and I can teach you in the mornings with the other students, and Tau can keep an eye on you between times.' His eyes pierced mine. 'And watch it, eh?'

I coughed to clear my throat, filled with confused embarrassment and relief. 'All right.'

He walked away, muttering. '*Fafine*, eh. Who woulda thought it …'

Then Sefa and the chief began walking up the mountain to meet the others. I waited until they were gone, so embarrassed that I wished I were invisible. I had no doubt my face was blazing red like a tomato.

Tau grabbed my arm again and tugged for me to follow him down the mountain. 'Do you even know what just happened?' he asked me as we trailed behind the others.

'No,' I said.

'The volcano awakened. In response to *you*. For years, it's laid there quietly, and now some tiny *fafine* comes along and wakes it up.' His eyes were wide, as if he didn't quite believe it himself.

'How can you tell?' I asked, trying to stop my legs from trembling.

'You were sending out a heat signal for miles.'

I stared at him. 'But I didn't know I was.'

He clenched his jaw, clearly unnerved. 'Which is exactly why we are going to train you.'

'What you all did to make it stop – will you teach me that?' I asked him, trying to watch my step. I didn't usually have trouble with uneven ground, but my legs were still shaking.

'Yes, Fern. I think we *have* to.'

Chapter Seven

'So, they're going to train you now,' said Dakota. 'That's good!' She and Jamila and I were walking down the hard sand near the water, heading towards the fire training grounds. I couldn't help practising dance moves on the way, revelling in how different it felt to dance on this type of sand – nothing like the fine, dirty sand of the deserts. This sand gave a satisfying crunch under my feet with each step, squeaking when I shuffled the ball of my foot, shushing if I dragged the blade of my heel along the grains of sand.

'I hope it's good,' I said. 'I can't imagine being trained by a group of men and boys who don't even want me there.'

'Who cares if they want you there or not?' said Jamila, adjusting her veil over her henna-red locks. Her kohl-lined eyes narrowed at me. 'You know what you can do.'

I blinked at her, surprised. She had been so different towards me since I'd saved her life in the desert, fighting off our attackers and carrying her to safety. She still gave me the cold shoulder most of the time, but the fact that she spoke to me like this now, frankly but not unkindly – and even the fact that she was walking with Dakota and I along the beach at all – gave me hope for our future.

I wondered if she realised how funny it sounded to hear her lecture me about not caring what other people thought, when it was her who had tried to drive me out of the caravan troupe just over a month ago.

I tried a few cartwheels, able to enjoy the sensation of the sand against the palms of my hands for once, because my skin wasn't painful anymore after Eli's healing. The burn scars were still there, making my skin tight in places, but it sure felt great to be free of pain for the first time in weeks.

Pulling my mind away from that train of thought for a moment, I focused on my forward momentum and threw myself into a forward flip. I stiffed the landing, both legs straight and strong. My heels stung with the impact on the hard sand, but I laughed with glee.

Dakota cheered and clapped.

'First time!' I cried. 'I've never managed to do that right before.'

'Well done! You star.' She clapped my shoulder and pulled me in for a quick hug, never one to miss an opportunity for physical affection.

Even Jamila smiled.

Dakota stopped for a moment and squatted to re-tie the strapping on her bad ankle. It must have been paining her to walk on the shifting sand; she hadn't had to strap it for a while since it had healed after her dance injury. 'I have to admit, I'd be nervous,' she said. 'All those men. And a bunch of boys and teenagers. Awkward.'

Not for the first time, I considered how she was really doing, after everything that we'd gone through in Deridai. I wasn't sure how to ask the question, so I didn't. Instead, I said, 'I think Bear feels the same way.'

'How's that?' asked Dakota.

'He was …' *Disappointed?* It had been hard to tell, but I thought that might be it. 'He might have been a little jealous, that I'll be spending time every day with a male that's not him.' I shrugged, trying not to dwell on it.

'Well, you haven't been engaged long,' Jamila murmured.

I nodded.

Some women from the village walked past, a beautiful array of multi-strand necklaces set off against their tan skin and grass skirts. One of them waved at us with one hand, her other arm holding the hand of a young child. They both had hair that was a springy mass of curls.

'That's Peri,' said Dakota, waving back with a wide smile.

Peri beamed at us. She spoke to her child, and they waddled over together, matching curls bouncing with every step. The boy grinned up at me and then hid behind his mother's pillar-wide legs. Peri was a large woman, with buttresses for a bosom, but she didn't look fat, just strong, as if most of her weight was muscle.

'Perenike Savaliga of Aiatal,' she said. She pressed her hands together and then stepped right up to me. I froze, but she just pressed her nose against mine and then bounced back. She waved an arm back and rustled the boy's curly hair. 'My boy, Roa.'

I breathed out and smiled, laughing at my own surprise. I'd seen Islanders doing this greeting with other caravan members, but I hadn't done it myself yet. 'Well met, Perenike and Roa,' I said. 'I am Fern Batu-gerel, from Bat-Erdene.'

'Ferrrr?' Roa copied me eagerly, not quite managing the end of my name.

I smiled. 'Yes, Fern. That's right.'

Satisfied with this, he bounced away a few steps and started shovelling sand over his toes.

'Peri runs the weekly market in the big village,' said Dakota.

I was amazed. 'I thought women here couldn't be in charge of things? Someone told me women here cannot even own property, let alone run a business …'

Peri winked. 'There are *ways* of being in charge of things, eh. Enough years of working around the men, and they finally realised it was easier to just let me run the market for them.'

Dakota shook her head with a little laugh. 'I think Peri may be an exception to everything we've heard about the islands.'

'Crab! Crab!' Roa shouted, and sprang straight up. He ran across the beach as if his toes were on fire, skipping like a gazelle.

Peri just smiled and started walking towards Roa. 'I'll see you both at lunch, hey? Me and the ladies are harvesting the cassava plantation today, so we can sell them at the market tomorrow.'

'Oh, I'll come with you,' Dakota said immediately.

I relaxed at that. It would be good for her to be among the other women. I knew she was unhappy spending any time alone at the moment, especially in this new and unfamiliar territory. With Ebony meeting with the leaders of the hula dance troupe today and me going to fire training, Dakota might not have had anyone else to spend time with this morning.

'Who watches the children while you work?' I asked Peri.

Peri waved an arm, indicating a herd of children, ranging in age from two to twelve, who were wandering down the beach behind us. When Roa saw who she was waving at, he laughed and ran over to join the group, his fat legs pumping to get through the sand.

'The children all just play with each other,' Peri said. 'And usually there will be a grandmother or two around to keep an eye on them.'

'So, children here are raised by many people in the village, not just their parents?'

'Oh yes. And you know, even during the wars, if a parent dies, their siblings would raise the abandoned child as their own.'

We chatted for another minute and then I wished them luck with the harvesting and waved goodbye. Dakota and Peri walked away to join the other women. I couldn't help wondering how children could defend themselves from slavers with only other children and grandparents around, but I didn't live here; I didn't know how it was. I couldn't talk, anyway. I'd spent my whole childhood wandering isolated mountains, almost completely alone, tending a herd of sheep or goats by myself or with another child for company.

My heart, cheered by being included in interesting conversation, began to sink as I remembered where I was walking to. I continued on my way to my first fire lesson, under the growing weight of many things on my mind.

Tau was already there with Sefa when I arrived at the edge of the beach. I was glad I wouldn't be on my own as the only non-teaching adult. When I got close enough, I could smell Tau's particular mix of coconut oil, the ocean, and sweat, his scent sweet and salty at once.

Like everything else, the classes operated on island time. The other fire students, mostly teens and younger boys, were sauntering a few at a time out of the jungle and onto the beach, but it took more than half an hour for everyone to arrive. I watched with some apprehension as they walked and ran down the beach towards us, straggling like seagulls across the sand.

Sefa hadn't mentioned I would be training with six-year-olds, but I supposed it made sense, if the boys here always discovered their powers much younger than I had. I tried smiling at a few of them as they arrived, and several of them gave me curious looks, but all of them avoided my gaze, clearly as shocked to see a woman here as their elders had been.

'What's she doing here, elder?' one of the boys asked Sefa loudly.

Another one said, 'Won't she contaminate our fires? *Fafine?*'

The rest of them spoke in Aiatalei, but it seemed everyone had a question to ask about me. I stood there silently, no longer trying to smile, just doing my best to wait out this embarrassment. Sefa answered everyone in Aiatalei, not bothering to translate it into Trader's Talk for me. Tau didn't translate, either, and instead just stared sternly at each of the boys in turn until they finally stopped asking questions.

When everyone had arrived, we sat in a circle in the sand. Sand had already itched its way into every particle of my skin and every crevice in the days we'd been on the island, but I was used to it. The sand had gotten into everything when we were in the desert in Deridai, too. At least it was something physical to keep my mind off how embarrassed I felt.

'Let's check what you remember, hey,' said Sefa. 'Fire lore from last week. Who can tell me who made the first fire?'

Several of the boys raised their voices.

'Tuatahi!'

'The first man!'

'Tau!'

Everyone laughed. Beside me, Tau threw his head back and laughed the loudest. I smiled uncertainly.

'*E ia* Tau?' Sefa said. 'Really? You think Tau was alive when the gods walked? Well, I'll tell you the quick version again, hey? Since you think Tau brought the fire and all.' He launched into a stream of Aiatalei, clearly in story-telling mode.

Beside me, Tau translated as quickly as he could. Long ago, before the first sunrise, the islands were without fire, and it was very cold. So the people and the animals all gathered, as was their habit when something important had to be decided.

Someone would need to go to the fire god, they said to themselves, and bring back a flame to warm up the islands. They knew that fire was somewhere up where the gods lived, because from down in the islands, the people and animals could sometimes smell the smoke.

First, the wild boar tried. It ran up the side of the volcano to the fire god's lair, but the heat of the volcano singed its snout, and it had to snuffle its nose against a tree to stop the burning. That is why the wild boar has a flat, black snout.

Next, the seal tried. It got a little further than the wild boar, but its ears caught fire, and it got covered in ash. So it had to retreat to the ocean. That is why the seal has such small ear holes and grey fur.

Finally, Tuatahi, the first man, snuck up the volcano and hid in a cave while he worked out how to get closer to the flames inside the volcano. That's when he saw a thunder bird coming back to its nest. He followed it and stole one of its flaming tail feathers. Then he brought it down to the islands and started the first fire.

'Does that sound right?' Sefa asked his students, and everyone agreed that this was where fire came from.

I was just starting to think I might like Sefa's manner as a teacher, jovial and relaxed, when he said, 'Right, let's begin warming up. We have a new … student.' I could see the effort it took him not to call me 'new boy'. 'So to start, we'll all practise our spark.'

I flushed. 'What's that?'

The others tittered. One of the younger boys laughed out loud. I stared at my feet for a moment to regather my composure before looking Sefa in the eye. I didn't regret asking the question. I needed to learn, even if I was embarrassed.

'Eh, well, new girl, you come with me, and I'll show you how to make a spark.' He said to the others, 'The rest of you, groups of three, eh, and everybody get sparking. You can test each other however you like.'

I ducked my head in a nod. He seemed surprised by my reaction. *Are students normally more rambunctious here?* I was very used to the Bat-Erdene way, where unnamed children under eighteen, although they were well-loved and cared for, were expected to be quiet in the presence of elders or teachers.

Tau seemed to see my reticence. 'I'll be your third,' he said to Sefa.

I shot him a surprised look, then gave a grateful half-smile.

The way Sefa described it, sparking was supposed to feel like breathing and seeing within yourself. 'Fire is breath. The first spark that quickens the fire needs a breath of air and the heat of your own emotion, or it can't light anything. Maybe it looks like a dry nest of kindling ready to flame, or a single candle flame, or a pool of molten liquid, or a pile of burning embers. You focus on that and use your breathing and a powerful emotion—' He made a tapping gesture. '—to tap into it. Maybe happiness, sure. Usually anger, if you're about to use your fire to fight. Maybe you're just plain hungry. Then you—' He exhaled and threw a punch at nothing, and I flinched. When he opened his punching hand, a single flame hovered just about his palm. 'For beginners, this shows your power is alive and ready. As you train, you'll learn to spark immediately, ready for a fight.' He nodded his chin at me and lowered his hands. 'All right, now you try.'

I had no idea how he'd just done what he'd done, but at least tapping into an emotion sounded familiar. That was how I'd created fire every other time before – wonder and awe when I used it while fire dancing, fear for the safety of others, even anger when the caravan was attacked. And surely I knew how to breathe!

I thought of my fear that I might never be able to use my fire without hurting myself, and curled that emotion into my fist. I took a deep breath, then threw a punch at the ocean. I opened my palm …

Nothing. My palm stayed empty, wavering in the air between us.

I looked at Tau and Sefa and frowned in confusion. They frowned back.

'Again,' said Sefa. 'With a stronger emotion, maybe.'

I aimed for anger, thinking back to how Dakota and I had been hassled by men in the markets in the desert months ago. I sucked in another breath, punched, and opened my palm.

Nothing.

'Try a different emotion,' Sefa suggested.

I nodded silently, suddenly not trusting my voice. I tried to think of something happy, but I could barely think. Frustrated confusion was quickly being replaced by a wave of fear washing over me. In order to use my fire safely, this was the first step. I *needed* to know this.

What if I can't get this? I'll end up like Old Man Hanini, a shrivelled-up, burnt-out husk. They'll kick me out of the caravan. I'll have nowhere to go.

Around us, the other students were doing whatever it was that helped them to find their spark – different stretching poses, fighting stances, and the like. But I wasn't brave enough yet to try anything beyond Sefa's simple one-punch method.

I threw another punch.

Flames sizzled all the way up my arms from my fingertips to my neck. I cried out in pain, and hunched my shoulders.

No, no, no, not again. I shook my arms, trying to suck the flames back in.

Tau and Sefa both hissed. Sefa said what I could only assume was an Islander curse word, and he hurried to pick up some sand and began pouring it over my bare arms. The flames died almost instantly, as if scared away just by the thought of being extinguished. I groaned in relief, and sat in the sand, my heart pounding. My skin felt like I'd cut it with glass where Sefa had poured the sand over the burn. It had been an effective way to extinguish the flames, for sure, but painful.

'*Manuia, manuia,* you're all right,' Tau said awkwardly, squatting next to me. He reached out towards my arm, then thought better of it and rubbed the back of his neck instead. 'Well!'

'You can't let your emotions get out of control like that,' said Sefa, standing over us. 'If you let your emotions run over you, they will run right over your body, too, and you'll be helpless. You won't be able to fight or protect yourself, because your own body will fight you. And you could harm others.'

'I wasn't trying to lose control,' I got out. I pulled my bandages out of my pants pocket and began wrapping my arms, wincing. It incensed me that after Eli had just healed me, I had burned myself again.

Sefa rubbed his face as if weary of me already. 'I mean, usually we spot the boys' fire powers so young, we teach them how to use the fire before they've had much opportunity to lose control … Only when they're fighting hard, sometimes they might lose it …'

I tried not to start crying again, but my emotions were still so close to the surface that I'm sure it must have shown in my face. The two men seemed taken aback. Sefa just lifted his hands as if to say, *This is beyond me.*

Tau said, 'Well, eh, why don't we try some of those relaxation exercises first, sort of ease into the breathing side of things?'

Sefa looked sceptical, but nodded.

Tau explained, 'There's a few things we can try when emotions are difficult but you know you need to stay in control. For example, meditation to control your breath. Looking inwards for that fire, that spark, but not actively trying to start the fire, not trying to activate any emotion. We just sit, and we breathe deep, and we look and listen to see what is inside.'

'I'll try anything,' I said.

The trouble was, it was seriously hard. I was actually in a lot of pain already, from burning my arms again. And there were constant distractions – other people talking, laughing, the sounds of their fires crackling to life. The sun was heating the sand. Sweat was trickling down the small of my back. A sand midge buzzed near me.

I could barely focus on my own breath, let alone access some inner piece of me I'd never heard of before. I sighed and took a few deep breaths.

I tried, honestly tried. I tried to quiet my thoughts, but that only made me feel more pressured. The inside of my head was only full of racing emotions and thoughts and fears about all the problems I'd been pushing aside or trying to avoid.

And Sefa still seemed bothered by the idea that women could be fire wielders. He kept offering suggestions, his frustration growing audibly. 'Can't do that, eh? Um, try this, then. Eh? Don't know? All right, what else could we try, then? I don't know, I don't know, *fafine* and fire, man, what's that about …'

In frustration, I peeped an eye open. Sefa had stood up and was walking over to where some of the advanced students were now experimenting with new skills, splashing each other with seawater and turning the drops into steam. Tau still sat cross-legged across from me, perfectly at ease, breathing deeply. His left hand was resting on one knee, palm up, a long, thin flame hovering above it.

I scowled at him. 'How do you make this look so easy?'

He broke into laughter. He opened his eyes and pushed my arm lightly, his flame winking in a wisp of shimmering air. 'Come on, kitten!'

'I'm sorry, but this is not easy!' I muttered.

'Well, how about we try something a little different?' He rubbed his palms together. 'We could try music … A guided meditation …'

What does it matter? I won't be able to do it anyway.

I can't believe I can't do this. I can't even do this first thing – and it's just breathing and looking within!

How am I ever going to get control over my powers if I can't do this first, tiny step?

My awareness of everything around me faded as I sank into my spiralling thoughts, fading down and down into a dark pit.

'Take a moment to listen to your body,' Tau's voice interrupted my thoughts. 'Adjust any small parts of your body that feel uncomfortable.'

I took a shaky breath and tried to focus on my body again. My left foot ached, so I shifted it in the sand.

'Now turn your mind to your breath. Inhale slowly, aware of the breath as it fills your lungs and your belly. Exhale slowly, letting your belly fall. Let your breath flow effortlessly.'

I focused on slowing down my anxious breathing. At first, it made me feel sick in my stomach to be breathing slower, and I nearly opened my eyes again to tell him I'd given up. But I kept breathing, slower and slower, and eventually the nauseous feeling passed.

'Notice how warm your skin is. Allow the sensation of warmth to rise from your legs up into your belly, then your chest, then your shoulders. Your arms feel warm … actually, let's ignore your arms for now, eh, sorry about that.'

I almost laughed.

'Soften your face, let the warmth rise up to the crown of your head.'

As I consciously relaxed my face, my mind began to feel a little calmer.

'Now look inwards. Still breathing deeply in … breathing out … As your mind calms, impulses and thoughts rise up more and more slowly. Any tension left is gradually releasing out through your fingertips and your toes. And then there is just you, and the distracting thoughts will fall away.'

I heard the ocean waves *shushing* on the sand. I felt the wind across my skin. There was still pain, but I was also noticing that less, feeling more focused.

'You will begin to feel alert again, but at peace. As you feel relaxed but aware of your breathing again, notice your power. Your body has its own natural ability to shift and change. There is a small, dry source that you use to spark your fire. The strong emotions you focus on to make big fires are just fuel that you use to build the fire in your desired style. Your technique and training are what will help you use that fuel in the right way, so you can grow a fire to full strength.'

I gathered myself together, opened my eyes, and tried again. I exhaled sharply as I threw a punch, then opened my fist.

There was nothing there.

And again.

Nothing.

Can't do it, can't do it, can't do it, why can't I do this when everyone else can?

Is this because I'm a woman? That doesn't seem right. First woman wielder they've ever heard of, and I can't even do this …

Am I being punished for something?

A hand tapped my knee, and I jumped.

'Hey.' Tau's voice was firm, but not harsh. 'You look like you're going to throw up. Just relax.'

I held back a groan. 'Relax?'

Well. Maybe he was right. I knew I was stressed. Who wouldn't be, after all I'd gone through in the past few months?

Tears began leaking out of the corners of my eyes. My throat grew tight. I felt so embarrassed, trying not to cry in public where everyone could see.

Tau didn't look away, just let me feel that he was still there, with me.

I swallowed, blinked the tears away, cleared my throat. I stared down at the sand.

Oh, what a failure.

Don't cry, don't cry, don't cry.

Come on, Fern, pull yourself together.

God, help me.

I shut my eyes and tried to pretend I was on my own. I tried again to search within myself for that inner pool of fire and strength.

Still nothing.

After a while, I sighed and stopped trying to fight the thoughts that danced and whirled through me. I rolled my shoulders and began shaking my hands, then my whole arms, shaking the feelings of frustration out of my limbs. I let my mind run wild for a while, and gradually, like dew dripping down a leaf, I felt a natural silence seeping in between the thoughts.

My heartbeat slowed. Each beat felt like the clicking of flint against stone.

My breathing deepened. Each inrush of air began to remind me of my mother's old tent stove, opening its tiny door to add more wood, the *whoosh* as air entered the stove and fueled the fire.

I felt a tiny glimmer of hope light up within me, the first emotion I'd felt in days that wasn't fear or embarrassment. It was beautiful. I gripped onto it desperately.

My palms began to itch. I opened my eyes to see that a small flame was hovering just over each upheld palm.

'I did it!' I whispered. I met Tau's eyes, stunned and relieved that it had worked. I gave a hoarse laugh.

'Well done,' he said, and grinned. 'Now extinguish it and do it again.'

My smile disappeared. 'What?' I whined.

He waved a hand impatiently. 'Go on, go on, eh. Again. Until we know you can do this whenever you need to.'

I sighed but obeyed. I inhaled and sucked the flames back inside my hands, just as I had done after the riot, when the whole tent ground was burning. Only this time, the flames I'd made didn't burn my skin on the way back in. This time, I felt more in control.

Then I exhaled in a big rush, closed my eyes, and once more began looking inward to find that peaceful place where my mind was quiet and my breath could fuel or extinguish a flame.

That was all I accomplished for that first day's lesson, but it was everything I needed.

Chapter Eight

After my first fire training lesson, I was so tired that I went back to our hut without even going to the longhut for lunch. I slept like a log and didn't remember anything after laying my head on the pillow.

I woke late in the afternoon, as the sun had already begun to fall towards the sea. Groggy and disoriented, I went for a walk along the beach and listened to Bear talk about how he would be accompanying the horse trainers for a couple of days on a hunt.

I didn't feel quite all there, and later I couldn't remember what day he'd said he would leave. All I could remember was a horrible, sick, sinking feeling in my stomach from hearing that he was leaving me at all.

'Don't spend all your time with the chief's son while I'm gone,' he said.

I hoped he was teasing. 'I won't. You know we're around others while we're training.'

'I know, all those boys and my Fern.' He kissed me and said wistfully, 'I wish I wasn't leaving you.'

I tried to laugh it off, saying, 'So don't go.'

But he left anyway. He squeezed my hand twice on his way out the door. *Love. You.*

He might as well have gutted me like a fish, for how it tore me up inside.

The next morning at the fire training class, it took me a while to remember how to relax enough to successfully light and extinguish a small 'spark'. But once I had done it seven times in a row without incident, Tau had me perform one of the first fire wielding moves: use my powers to safely light a small campfire. First, we gathered dry seaweed to use as tinder, because it would spark easily and burn quickly. Along the shoreline, we gathered twigs and sticks to use as kindling, which made the first layer of a fire.

'Normally, eh, you'd cut some logs for the fuel layer, so the fire burns as long as you want it to,' Tau said. 'But right now, we just care about whether or not you can start a fire and get it going, without using flint or another firestarter.'

We sat cross-legged and he began arranging the twigs and seaweed into a teepee. I remembered sitting across from a wounded Bear in a tent through a long desert winter night, lighting a campfire in sheer desperation to keep him warm. If emotion was fuel, I'd used a lot of fear to build that fire.

Tau looked up at me, and for some inexplicable reason, I felt myself blushing. I didn't know whether I was blushing because his attention made me nervous, or because of the intimate memory of that night with Bear. I stared away at the sea for a moment, pretending something had distracted me. The ocean was just as bright today – aquamarine and beryl blue, colours that sparkled like gems over the sand. Then I turned my attention back to the little pile of sticks.

Lighting a fire this time was easy. I'd found my spark. I used the emotions I was already feeling – embarrassment, nervousness, excitement – and the seaweed puffed into smoke and flames immediately.

It felt good. It felt so, so good.

Never again would I be weak, I told myself.

Never again would I be vulnerable.

Never again would I let my own body fail me.

And with that done, the real work of my training could begin.

On Aiatalei, fire wielders were trained in both dancing and fighting – their power was never used for only one or the other, art or war, but for both. When Tau pronounced my spark was steady enough, I was allowed to try the first dancing and fighting techniques. The island fighting methods – all kicks and punches and swinging clubs – recalled to me one of the first dance types I'd learned with Ebony. It was swift and brutal, deceptively stiff and simple-looking. Each move was calculated to strike courage into the heart of the warrior and fear into the heart of their opponent.

The first fighting move I was to learn, however, was not offensive, but defensive. A heat shield could be used to protect myself or others, Sefa explained, by burning incoming attackers and their weapons to a crisp.

Everyone around us was trying out what they were currently learning. The attacker did a side-facing kick and flame shot out from their heel, while the defender used a defensive heel sweep to dissipate their opponent's flame mid-air. Some of the boys were practising the moves as part of the ritual art and dancing patterns they were required to learn. But most of the older teenage boys were clearly more interested in using the moves to fight, whether against warring tribes or just each other. Tau told me they were close to their coming-of-age trial, so they must have felt the pressure of soon becoming real warriors for their island.

All the boys dove right into practising their latest moves, but by now, I was feeling much too timid to try anything at all. My small amount of success at lighting a fire still felt like nothing against the hour it had taken to find my inner 'spark'. I also knew if I were to try this technique, I would probably have to unbandage my hands again, and I didn't want to. After re-bandaging my hands when I burned myself yesterday at training, I hadn't had time yet to visit Eli to ask if he could heal me again. If I took the bandages off again, everyone would get a good look at my hands and my fore-arms. The scars there.

Tau saw me stepping back, wringing my hands behind me. 'What are you doing?'

'Hiding,' I said tersely.

He looked at my hands and his eyes widened in comprehension. 'Why? Ashamed of your battle scars?'

I shrugged, nodded.

He pointed to a jagged scar along his ribs. 'This is from my first time fighting against a serrated blade. Do I look ashamed of it to you? Am I covering up any of my scars?'

'It's different for you,' I said. 'You're a man.'

He shook his head. 'It's nothing to do with that. Become who you were made to be. You'll never learn until you accept that this is who you are.'

I stared at him. Of course, he was right. *How'd he get so wise when he looks like he's not much older than me?*

I was stunned and a little embarrassed to realise what I was feeling for him now was not the simple admiration of student for teacher, or traveller for local. It was more heated, the confused longing of attraction, exciting and terrifying at once. I could feel butterflies in the pit of my stomach every time he looked at me. I was painfully aware yet again of his bare chest and arms and legs, and the tattoos that covered his big muscles.

It wasn't just his body or the way he handled his fire powers. He seemed to rebel against the traditional ways of his tribe – his laidback calm juxtaposed against a restless edginess, an urgent desire for change. It reminded me of … me.

Why him? And why now, when I was in a loving relationship with Bear?

I felt even more embarrassed as the feeling grew. Was I blushing *again*? Unbelievable. Could he see what I was thinking in my eyes?

I'd thought I was safe from feeling attraction to others, and from others being attracted to me. I'd thought I was protected by the bracelets Bear and I wore as a sign of our commitment to each other. But I was wrong.

I swallowed. Surely these types of feelings would go away when Bear and I were properly married. Right now, during this period of handfasting engagement, we'd acknowledged that things could still change. Although we were committed, and it was hard to imagine feeling anything other than the overwhelming love I felt for him, some handfasted couples didn't get married at the end of their handfasting year.

Once we were married, I wouldn't feel attracted to other people anymore, surely. Not like now, captivated by Tau's eyes.

'Hey, Tau!' Sefa called.

I blinked and refocused, looking at the sand, the sea, at Sefa – anywhere but Tau's gaze.

'Yeah?' Tau said, but I could feel his eyes still on me.

'You gon' help us with the sparring for the warrior trials?'

Tau's gaze finally broke away from me and he nodded. 'You

know it. Ruffle some feathers with these young Kamahimaihi parrots, eh.'

'What happens at the trials?' I asked, curious.

Sefa explained, 'Every second year, the islands hold the trials on Aiatal to see which young men will become warriors or dancers. Mostly, there's a lot of sparring, obstacle courses, public demonstrations of strength and skill … and a private trial on the volcano. If a young man passes his trial, he can choose to become either a warrior or dancer for his island. Of course, these days, most of them want to be a warrior because the best warriors among us earn more food, maybe earn their own hut by their bravery.'

I felt my competitive spirit rise up, but that was ridiculous. I'd only just learned about sparking, and now I thought I should be included in a competition? But I couldn't help myself. 'Can anyone do a trial, if they are the right age?'

Sefa's eyebrows rose. I almost laughed out loud imagining what he was thinking. *First week here, can barely spark, and she wants to challenge in the trials!*

But Tau tipped back his head and looked at me seriously. 'You want in?'

'Well, maybe,' I said.

Sefa laughed out loud. 'You got guts, sis.' He walked away, still chuckling.

Tau shrugged. 'In a few weeks, you could try entering the kids' practice trials, I guess. It'd be good experience for you. Bit of fun. It's just training for the kids, but they still take it seriously. You know, people sometimes get hurt, though.'

Behind him, some of the other boys were starting to look over and give me dark looks and sneers. I could tell they were not only laughing at me for being ridiculous, but they were also angry and offended that I would think I could lay claim to something that was theirs. 'Not one of us' was written all over those looks. I felt my stomach drop, and my shoulders sagged, but I tried to shrug as if I didn't care.

Tau raised an eyebrow, making it quite clear he knew that *I* knew I was nowhere near ready to compete.

I dropped my eyes submissively, like I would have in my tribe back home.

He didn't let me break eye contact though; he craned his head down like a parrot, so he was still looking me in the eye.

I couldn't help it – I giggled. It bubbled up out of me, delightful and easy. When I stopped, I clapped my hand over my mouth, shocked. I hadn't laughed in weeks.

He clapped his hands, satisfied. 'Well! First things first, hey. Get those bandages off and we'll get started.'

I hurried to unwrap my hands, hoping to get it over and done with. I did feel eyes on me, but I kept going. Thankfully, nobody but Tau was close enough for me to see his reaction. He stared at my burned hands, and I swallowed, feeling a new shame at the angry red and pink patches and lines. But I put that feeling aside and focused on breathing deeply and accessing the emotions that would help me make fire.

Facing out towards the water, I trained to create not a flame as such, but a wall of heat in front of me. At first, I created a flat wall of heat, then a cone or a shield that curved around me. It was only a weak, small shield – a pathetic thing.

Tau seemed to find no small amount of satisfaction in telling me that the first fire punch or fireball that was thrown at me would have disintegrated my shield. 'More, more,' he kept saying.

But even with only that weak wall in front of me, I could feel the heat radiating from it. My gut tightened. My hands shook.

Sweat formed on my upper lip. I began to feel the heat getting closer to me, and I began to panic.

It's burning me!

I pulled back, made the heat shield smaller, weaker. But that just brought the heat closer to my hands.

I dropped my hands and sucked the power back. It stung on the way in, like touching the beach sand at midday with bare toes. I flinched, and shied away a few steps, hunching my shoulders.

'Hey.' Tau put a hand on my shoulder, forcing me to look up at him. 'You stopped hiding there for a second, don't go back in your shell now.'

'I don't want to burn myself again,' I whispered, ashamed of myself for saying it aloud.

His eyes were steady on mine. 'You didn't. And you won't. Even if I wasn't here, you've got more control than that now. If you feel the heat, you rein it in. You can do it.'

I was standing straighter already. *How does he do that?* It wasn't even because he was telling me these things – it was his tone of voice, as much as anything, that was reminding me of the strength within me. I felt ready to try again.

When I made my next shield, it was much bigger, and it didn't burn me as I held it out before me.

Chapter Nine

I was back in the desert.

Inside the tent, a group had surrounded Jamila and the others. Dakota and Kazim were swinging their knives around, trying to clear the space so they could get the performers out, but their attackers kept pushing them closer and closer together. Around them, the tent was falling down, torn to bits by the crowd as they tried to escape.

Heart pounding, I grabbed Bear's arm. 'Get our people out of here.'

'I'm not leaving ye!' His eyes flashed in the lamplight. He drew his daggers, one in each hand.

One of the men noticed us, and Bear moved to fend him off, using both daggers and the brute strength that made him such a force to be reckoned with. But he'd been injured, I remembered that; he needed to be careful or he would hurt his ribs again.

I didn't have time to hesitate, but I was shaking with fear and anger. I stepped out of the way and rubbed my hands together, trying to get my powers to work.

But it wasn't working.

I moved my hands together in a circle, as if I were carrying my fire staves or another prop. I tried to imagine flames whipping around me, coming out of my hands. But nothing came. My breath started coming in panicked gasps. I couldn't get any air to breathe.

This wasn't how it happened, I thought.

'Get out of here!' I shouted to the performers as I got closer. 'Go with Bear!'

They just stared at me, not moving. Around the performers, their attackers began to close in, ignoring me. I squeezed my eyes shut to try and get my powers going.

Remember what Tau said, I told myself. *Remember how to spark …*

But how could I remember what Tau said? I hadn't had any training when I was in the desert, facing the witch doctor and the mob he'd gathered.

I couldn't do anything.

I couldn't breathe …

I opened my eyes with a full-body jerk. My thin sheet was soaked. Sweat was dripping all the way from my hairline to my ankles. I felt like I was going to throw up. I threw off the sheet instead and shifted my legs off the edge of the mattress so I could sit up, gasping.

Small, yellow flames rippled up my fingers in the dark, tickling the hair on the backs of my hands. I looked down and froze in horror. Instead of my fingernails, my fingers ended in embers and flames. Little flames licked up from red stumps in the dark, as if each of my fingers was a coal in a campfire.

Breathe. Just breathe.

I shook my hands and clenched, then unclenched them, trying to relax. I sucked in using the new mental and physical muscles in my chest and gut, and the flames fizzled out. They hissed against my skin on their way in, like accidentally touching something hot for only a moment. The heat faded, and as my fingers turned from red coals into light brown fingers with normal fingernails again, I dropped them to my sides in relief.

The sheet on the bed sizzled and I jumped. Smoke rose, just a tiny wisp of it, as if I'd blown out a candle.

I swore, softly but keenly. All of that progress, only to be back where I'd started, still burning myself any time something upset me. I knew from experience that even that light sting would be followed by hours of aching pain.

At least Bear wasn't next to me, to see me losing my mind.

I sat there for I don't know how long, pulling my sweat-soaked hair away from my face and willing my stomach to settle, willing my hands to stop aching. Every hair touching my hands and face felt like the slice of a thorn. I stared out of the window of the hut to see that the sky was a deep grey rather than a midnight blue, so the sun must be coming up. I could hear the waves through the window, thrashing the shoreline in the dark. I held back a groan, realising it was too early to be awake, but probably too late for my body to let me get back to sleep.

But I could make my time productive.

I pushed myself off the mattress and stumbled into my clothes. I had started wearing sandals instead of my normal boots, and I didn't bother lacing them up; I just pulled them on so I wouldn't step on a sharp rock in the dark, then stepped outside.

I walked down the long, winding path to the beach. It was fairly quiet at this time of day, as if even the waves were hushing themselves so people could sleep. The air was crisp as it filtered into my lungs, and I could feel the dream sinking out of my body with every exhaled breath. I washed my hands in the salt water, and I had to let the immediate sting hit me until I was nearly crying, because I knew it would cleanse my hands to prevent the burns festering. I could soothe the skin later with one of my growing collection of creams and lotions, or I could visit Eli again.

After drying my hands gently on my shirt, I found myself a patch of hard sand mixed with grass. It felt solid enough for moving around on, so I began practising the latest dance routine Ebony had taught me on the ship over here. As my body moved, its stiffness eased, and the nausea sank out of my belly. Another day had begun.

Training my fire wielding skills was every bit as intense as training to become a fire dancer. But I already knew how to deal with the inevitable burns I got as I practised new techniques, and they no longer happened every time I made fire. In fact, my spark held almost as often as it failed now. Whenever I was distracted, though, the familiar backfire stung my fingertips or my forearms. And I found plenty to be distracted by, whether it was my fellow students sparring and playing with each other, or the verbal sparring with Sefa and Tau, or the nightmares that haunted me.

So my days began to fall into a familiar routine. In the mornings, I learned fire lore and wielding on the beach with 'the boys', as I was beginning to think of them. The more time I spent meditating with them and practising with them, the more they seemed to relax around me.

Most of them.

I still got a very distinct feeling that many of the boys thought I shouldn't be training with them. But I wasn't sure whether they would confront me about it. There seemed to be a lot in their culture that emphasised looking to their elders for guidance, so since Sefa and Tau had clearly accepted that I was there for now, the boys might leave me be.

About a week into meditating each day, I suppose I was already expecting to be a calmer, more in control version of myself – but I wasn't. Slowly, however, I felt I was developing more patience and tolerance for my own shortcomings. I was coming to accept that I was learning and growing, and it wouldn't be done overnight.

In the afternoons, everyone always had a *malolo*, or post-lunch nap. After that, I would eat some fruit to get my energy back up. I liked to join Ebony and Dakota to watch them practise fire dancing with Jamila and Kazim, our other desert-born dancer. He and his wife were our best musicians.

Of course, I wasn't supposed to do any fire dancing myself until Ayita and Ebony were satisfied that I wouldn't suddenly burn everything – and when would that be, I questioned? Secretly, I wondered whether they ever would be satisfied.

But I was allowed to practise the routines 'dry', without flames or props. Annoyed at being hampered by other people's concerns, I thought about trying to integrate my fire dancing into my regular dancing – but I wasn't brave enough. Dancing was where I had first discovered I had these powers, when my fire fans lit themselves without me touching them to any flame. It felt like it would be easy to slip up.

I didn't feel the same guilt when fire dancing as I did when I practised fire wielding. I didn't have flashbacks to the people I'd injured in the fighting over winter. I'd never hurt anyone by dancing, after all.

And in the evening, there was Bear – when he was on the same island, anyway. We were only together a couple nights a week now, with him travelling. When he was around, we went for walks along the beach, moonlit swims in the ocean or the creek, which were both only a short hike from our hut. We made love in our hut until we were both too tired to continue. I no longer stopped us from enjoying each other fully, now that I was less afraid of bursting into flames any time I felt any kind of emotion. We talked about everything we were seeing and doing during the day, to the point where I felt like I'd been present at many of his conversations as well.

It was the closest I'd ever felt to him … but only when he was there. We were spending most of our nights – and most of our waking hours – apart. Every second day, he'd leave to visit a different island to see what type of wild horses were there.

It felt strange. We'd spent every day together, or at least in the same general vicinity when we weren't spending time together, since I met him a month and a half ago. I hadn't wanted to be apart from him, but it seemed like being apart from me didn't affect him. But I could tell that he loved me; it was clear in everything he did every day when we were together.

One twilight, I knew Bear was on the island, but I couldn't find him around the dinner campfire. I ate with Dakota and Ebony, then set off to look for him. I was fairly certain he had either gone for a wander on the sand for some peace and quiet, or he was with the horses. I checked the stables and training ring quickly, and stopped to listen to the horses whickering softly as they fell asleep with the sunset. It was a longer walk to make my way down to the beach from there, but the breeze was cooling the air quickly now that the sun had set. The sand held a touch of the day's heat still.

I found him stretched out on the sand under a palm tree, his hands beneath his head. He was facing away from the dying sun, staring up at the vivid colours splashed across the sky. His fair skin was a nice shade of pink, mirroring some of the sky's colours. He smiled up at me lazily.

'Aren't the sunsets beautiful here?' I said.

He made a face and grumbled, 'But hot. Too hot on these islands, all the time.'

I smiled and knelt in front of him. I leaned forward and put my palms on his thighs. 'Is that so? Didn't we survive the desert?'

'Aye, so we did.'

I brushed his face with the palm of my hand. 'Caught a bit of sun, didn't you? That'll hurt in the morning.'

'Aye, it's the worst. And on top of the heat, there's too many bugs here.' He sat up, bringing his face close to mine. 'And not enough time with you.'

He was close enough to kiss, so I kissed him, lingering. 'If you don't go with the horse traders, we could have more time together.'

'Hmm.' He let his hair brush my face. I laughed as it tickled. Then he kissed the hollow of my throat, and I caught my breath.

I leaned into his kiss and wriggled my way up between his legs.

'You could come with me,' he said.

'We only just *got* here,' I said, surprised. 'I need to be here for my training.'

'There's a lot to learn from each of the islands,' he told me. 'Ye'd be surprised.'

'Oh?'

'Chief Lemaota here rules over the two biggest of the islands, but … There are worlds worth of sea between some of these islands. And with each island having its own chief, and each island always fighting each other for the same resources, it's interesting to see who has come out on top in each island. On some of the places I've visited, it's like here, where the warriors have had their noisy uprising and they're now in charge under a tribal chief or a war leader. On other islands, the merchants have taken over, but it's a quieter, subtler type of undertaking.'

I stiffened. 'All of this is starting to sound dangerous. I'm not at all interested in visiting other islands now. Are you sure you should be travelling at all?'

'I was just talking. What, ye dinnae want me t' go now?' I could tell he was annoyed by the way his accent thickened.

'No, it's fine. I'm probably worrying for nothing, I know.' I wrapped my hand around the back of his head, tugged on a lock. 'But come back as soon as you can? I'll miss you.' I was struck once again by how quickly I'd come to love this strange northerner.

'And I'll miss you,' he growled, and kissed me. But somehow, I felt I'd be missing him more than he was missing me. 'Let's go. Back to our hut. Somewhere I can take ye how I want to, without people seeing.'

I shivered with delight and followed him back up the beach.

Chapter Ten

Bear left the next morning before dawn to visit Lateilei Island with the horse traders. I felt him kiss my cheek in the dark, and I drifted towards consciousness but fell back asleep. When dawn came, I woke with the sweetest memories of last night, and the bitterest knowledge that Bear had gone and I wouldn't have another night like that with him for several days. My stomach sank. I wished I'd fought harder against him going, and then immediately felt guilty. I rolled over, not wanting to get out of bed, which wasn't normal for me.

When I got up, the fire training sands were already abuzz with those practising the first fights and dances scheduled for the trials next week. Every few minutes, a scuffle would break out between the students, as the children and adults alike all ached to compete.

Tau kept me away from them. 'Pay attention. I'll get you training to do that when you're ready, maybe after the trials.'

'Why can't I compete?' I grumbled.

'Not until I say you're ready, no matter what anyone else says about you and the trials, eh.'

'Right,' I griped, but I knew he was right.

That morning, the boys were focusing on a defensive, fire-countering move where someone shot fire at them and they breathed it in, neutralising it. It reminded me of how Kazim swallowed fire in some of his nightly performances with the caravan.

I was almost getting my grounding and heat shield perfectly formed now. After I let a particularly good shielding fade gently into shimmering smoke, Tau smacked me on the back. 'That was passable! Good.'

That got a smile out of me.

'Don't get cocky, kitten!' he warned.

I laughed. 'Jerk.'

'Next, I'll teach you how to use fireballs.' He waved a hand. 'You said you made them a few times out in the desert. So we'll work on doing that again, but more, and better. With more precision.'

The words alone made my hands start to tremble. I didn't like the idea of repeating what I'd done in the desert. I could still hear the screaming when I closed my eyes. I didn't know who I'd killed or maimed, apart from the witch doctor I had incinerated. Sometimes I didn't even remember that I'd been acting in self-defence, and all I could remember was that I'd hurt other people.

I stood still and gathered my spark again, then tried to show him how I had shot fireballs from my hands. I tried to recall how it had felt to make a fireball – terrified, mad, alive with adrenaline – but it made me feel a little crazy. When masses of flames finally gathered around my hands, I was so relieved and jittery that I almost forgot what I wanted to do with the fire.

To Tau's credit, he didn't step back or even look nervous.

I rubbed my palms together and shot the flames out over the sand and shallows in an uneven, rushing stream.

The flames sputtered and died, and I sucked in my breath, expecting an afterburn. But it appeared I had held my spark well – there was no singe, no sting. My flame was under my control. I felt giddy with relief.

'Very good,' he said. 'Now let's see if you can make them more controlled, more focused, so they're more like cannonballs and less like a bushfire. Right now, you're waving it all around, destroying everything in your path. You don't want to hurt anyone who's on your side, hey.'

I nodded.

'So, form a ball again, and hold it just here, in front of you. Don't release it yet.'

I wrapped my hands around an imaginary circle in front of me, and concentrated. I sparked, and let the ball begin to form. It felt almost too easy. I could feel it pushing at the boundaries I had set, and it felt good, that power hissing and spitting under my skin without hurting me – so I began to experiment. I let the ball of flames grow a little, and I tried seeing how hot I could make it.

Red.

Orange.

Yellow.

White.

I still couldn't make a blue flame like Tau and Sefa could – the hottest flame I'd seen.

But in just moments, I was pushing the limits of how hot I could keep it under control, and I began to feel afraid that I would lose it. I could all too easily be consumed by the fire. My gut tightened. My hands shook. Sweat trickled down my brow.

I tried to cool it a little, but the ball just kept growing, getting bigger and bigger until I was holding something the size of the bowls of food at the breakfast hall. It began to feel heavier than I could hold, and my arms drooped a little.

'Rein it in a little, Fern,' Tau warned. 'Once you've got it to a nice size, you can point it out to sea again.'

I shot him a panicked glance, then started trying to suck the fire in like he'd shown me, to reduce the size of the fireball.

The fire kept roaring under my gaze.

It was like when I'd first tried to spark – there was no response when I tried to bring my emotions under my control. I pulled and pulled frantically, but the fire stayed, still growing.

Soon there was something almost as tall as Tau in front of me. My hands were not so much holding it in place as clutching desperately to its tail.

I could feel the heat of it on my face. It was going to swallow me whole.

Oh, shepherd of all, save me. It was less of a prayer than a desperate arrow shot to the heavens.

'Rein it in,' Tau barked. 'Your will is stronger, remember.'

'I'm not sure it is,' I said.

He must have heard my voice shake, because he grabbed my upper arm and said, 'Just keep your eyes on me.'

I held the fireball away from him and looked into his eyes, sweating. He looked alert but I could see that he wasn't panicking, and that was enough to calm me down a tiny bit. He held my gaze with such intensity that I couldn't have looked away even if I wanted to. Without my attention feeding it, the flames died down a little in intensity.

'That's the way,' he said firmly. 'I'm not doing anything. I'm just here with you. You're going to control this, because you *can*. Say you can.'

'I can.' I breathed shakily.

He nodded. 'Now you're going to take a breath in and close the fireball back into the shape you wanted, nice and small and manageable.'

I took a deep breath and mentally reached into those flames. Connected to the heart of the fire again, I sucked away at it, pulling at its core and rounding its edges in, starving it of the air it needed to grow.

It began to shrink.

'Great, great, that'll do.'

It still seemed pretty giant to me, and the second I looked at the ball, it started to grow again.

That's when I lost it. I hauled with all my might to extinguish the flame, and because I was so panicked about it, the flames caught me on the way back in. Released within me, they started a new kind of torture, burning me from the inside out.

I cried out in shock. 'Tau, it's burning me!'

I'd never felt an afterburn like this before. My skin stung all over, as if poisonous ants were biting every inch of my arms, their poison spreading into my shoulders, my neck ...

He took both of my arms now, his big hands wrapping around my muscles. He brought his face right up against mine, forehead to forehead, and breathed in deep, nostrils flaring. I froze, surprised to find I couldn't move. I could feel the depth of his breath reaching into my power and pulling, as if he was tugging on my waist to make me move somewhere. When he breathed out, his breath washed over my whole body in a wave, and the heat and pain faded silently.

He opened his eyes again, and I looked at him aghast, terrified and relieved at once. I trembled, panting from the pain that was already nearly gone. My stomach rolled again and again, reacting to the pain and panic I'd felt, and I bent over with a hand against my mouth to keep from vomiting.

'It can be intense,' he said. 'I know.'

'That's certainly one word for it,' I said breathily. I was struck by equally overwhelming feelings of awe and amazement at how he had stopped the burning and how he had gotten completely into my personal space to do it. I didn't know if I could look him in the eye yet.

'I know,' he repeated. 'Just take your time, and then we'll try again.'

'Again?' I whined, and then immediately regretted opening my mouth. I panted until I no longer felt like vomiting, then straightened.

By the end of the morning's two-hour session, I still couldn't tie the end off on a glowing fireball without it either dissipating into a whiff of smoke or exploding in size and roaring away from me over the ocean.

The training finished earlier than usual, for the boys and the few adults who were there to practise sparring. We made a loose ring, and two of them would face off against each other. They sparred with a mix of kicks and punches, but no one got badly hit – everyone was too fast. When the Aiatalei fought, it was scary – lots of shouting and fist-waving and stomping of feet. I watched, jealous and attracted to the excitement of it, but knowing I wasn't ready to face someone else with my basic skills and lack of knowledge.

As the match wrapped up, Tau turned to me. 'I'm beginning to think that your situation isn't just about sparking.'

'Oh?' I asked.

'Yes, most of the time, when the fireball is getting out of control, I can see that your spark is still there, and it's mostly under your control still. So I was thinking.' He gestured to the ring that the boys were jumping in and out of excitedly. 'There's this thing some of the boys have instinctively, and all the adult warriors learn it. It's this layer of gentle, warm breath that hovers around their skin when they're shooting flames out of their hands or feet. You're missing that steady flow of warmth, I think – so the flames go back in as hot as they come out.'

'Great,' I muttered. 'Another way I'm failing at all this.'

He gave me a long look, unwrapping the sparring wraps he'd worn for his own exercises earlier that morning. He seemed to be asking me a silent question with his eyes, but I couldn't read it. Aloud, he said, 'Well, we'll try working on that tomorrow. Hot today, eh? I'm going for a swim in the waterfall pool.' He indicated into the jungle with his head. 'You want to join me?'

'Oh. Just us?' I felt a twinge of desire, but I tried to squash it down.

'Sure, yeah. Unless you … can't swim?'

'I can swim,' I retorted. 'Ebony taught me on the voyage here.'

'So, then …?'

I felt embarrassed about saying aloud what I was thinking, but I got it out. 'It's just, if there's no one else there, Bear might not like it. He got annoyed when I paddled alone with you that one time.'

'So?' He shrugged, his eyes piercing.

Unsure what to say, I looked down, only to watch as his bare feet stepped closer to mine in the sand. The sun was quickly warming the sand and air. It would soon be time to move off the beach into the shade, one way or another. I met Tau's eyes warily, still not certain that Tau was implying what I thought he was. We had a language barrier and cultural differences between us, after all, and I'd been mistaken about people's intentions before. After all, when I first met Bear, I hadn't initially realised when he started flirting with me; I hadn't known what it meant.

I tried again to explain. 'I just think Bear might take it the wrong way. He might think I wasn't being faithful to him.'

Tau smiled. 'You really care what he *might* think? It's just a swim. It's a hot day, and he'd know that if he was here … which he's not.'

I opted for a casual, polite smile. 'Another time, perhaps. For now, the ocean is right here.'

I could feel his eyes on me as I walked down into the shallows, near where the other students and wielders were eagerly splashing their way in. As I waded in up to my waist, the water splashed higher and higher, cooling me off all over. It was a pleasant contrast to the heat that was flushing through me.

I glanced over my shoulder to see him still watching.

'All right, all right already,' Tau called, and he followed us in.

Chapter Eleven

The caravan had been on Aiatal long enough without giving a performance – now it was time to earn the free suppers we'd been enjoying. The next day, the caravan troupe all gathered to practise for that night's show.

It felt odd to be watching Bear train in the ring with his horses again – to see him from a distance instead of up close. He'd brought three of his best horses with us, and I was glad for him and for them, because it was clear they'd all missed playing with each other. It reignited my passion for him, to see his muscles moving and working, to see his talent and his strength. We'd spent the past month just working on the ship, and such a long break without performing or even having the space to practise had felt unnatural for all of us.

Ebony gathered us together to practise our dances again – the five of us including Dakota, Kazim, and Jamila. We found a nice smooth, grassy patch and started stretching and limbering up. Even though I hadn't been granted permission to perform with them yet, I felt invigorated by warming up with the others, who were alive with energy, anticipating getting to perform, not just practising for the sake of practising.

I thought maybe, if today's rehearsal went well, I might ask Ebony if I could fire dance with them again. I would tell her how Tau said my control was improving, how I wasn't burning myself – well, not constantly, anyway. I hadn't forgotten how my fireball training had gone yesterday. But after how Tau had shown me that I had the strength to shrink such a large fireball, and how easily he had calmed the flames when the afterburn got stuck inside me, I had so much less fear.

While the other four of us were stretching, Dakota hung back. She watched for a long moment, playing with her hair, fussing with her dress as she walked back and forth nervously. Then she turned on her heel and started to walk away.

'Dakota?' I asked.

She turned and made an odd kind of shrug. 'I'm sorry, everyone.'

'Oh hey, come on now, *lou alofa*,' said Ebony, and walked over to her. 'I thought we talked about this.'

Dakota shook her head mutely, looking as if she might cry.

I ran up to her. 'What's wrong?'

'I can't dance with you tonight,' she got out, her voice tinny with tension. 'It was different when we were just practising together, but I can't perform with you. I can't do it. I'm sorry.'

'But why?' asked Jamila bluntly.

'I just feel like … it put me in danger in the desert. I don't want to be … I don't want to feel like that again. And I don't need to.' She waved her hands in a way that seemed angry and anxious at once. 'I have my basket weaving, I have my crafts I can sell; I don't need to dance to earn my keep, Ayita said so.'

I was so surprised I didn't know how to react. 'Oh.'

Ebony gave a big sigh. 'Oh, *lou alofa*, I know, and if you don't want to, that's your decision. You know I want you to dance with us. Truly. But it's up to you.'

And that was that. Dakota nodded and walked away.

Kazim and Jamila raised their voices almost at the same time, confused, demanding answers from Ebony. They both came from a desert culture where even friendly conversations sounded aggressive, so I knew Ebony wouldn't take it personally.

I just held my tongue, hoping I could talk to Dakota later and try to understand better what she was going through. She seemed so upset, and I didn't want her to be unhappy. I'd only ever seen dancing make her joyful – and she was the one who had helped me to open up in my dancing and be liberated to dance joyfully for just me, not just for other people. I couldn't imagine her going from that freedom to feeling like she didn't even want to dance anymore ... But then, she'd had an injury and the attack by the slavers last season, so I supposed I could understand wanting – and needing – to take a break.

The others moved on to arguing about what dances we could do now that we didn't have a fifth member of our little troupe. I didn't think there was anything I could add to the conversation, because after all, I was so new that I still only knew a few of the dances they performed regularly, so I stayed silent.

Eventually, they settled on performing two particular dances that night for the chief and the Islanders, and I let Ebony direct me as to where I needed to be at each point of the dances. The four of us weren't exactly the perfect team – Jamila and I still clashed, and often, without Dakota there to buffer us – and it just wasn't the same. But at least we were working together more smoothly than we had when I first joined the caravan.

I didn't expect to feel any urge to use my fire powers while practising. But with every wave of my arms, every step I took, I could feel the power calling to me.

Use me.

Fire up.

You can do it.

It'll feel great.

Call on me.

I resisted.

I could feel it there the whole time, like an itch I was refusing to scratch. It was starting to drive me a little mad, but there was no point indulging it. I didn't fully trust that I could fire up my tools without getting burned again; I was still in training, after all. But I could feel the pressure rising, like a dam that might burst.

At the end of our training session, Ebony said to me, 'Look, you seem like you're … feeling well, and Tau says your training is going smoothly … Do you want to dance in the performance tonight?'

Before practise, I had been so ready to ask for this, but now, with the temptation to use my fire power still singing its way through my veins, I had to stop to think about it for a moment. If I wanted to dance, this was a risk I was going to have to take eventually. And she was right that Tau had said I'd been doing so much better in my fire training. So, I nodded.

But it might have been a mistake, because that night in the show, I accidentally let loose.

I was doing a leaping move while Ebony supported me from behind, lifting me up, when I felt my *poi* balls swing a little harder. The dam burst before I had time to think about holding it in. A rush of power slid out of me, and the *poi* balls burst into a stronger, brighter flame.

I nearly dropped the *poi* in shock, but I kept going. I heard Ebony gasp under my shoulders. For a second, I wished I'd held my power in, like a sneeze. I did my swings, she let me land in centre stage, and I met her dark eyes for a blink. I tried to put an apology in my eyes, make it clear it had been an accident, but we had to keep dancing.

It certainly got a reaction from the crowd, though, and that was enough to buoy my spirits until we could get offstage. I felt a tiny thrill of pride for having managed it – and without burning myself, as well. Shaking it off, we finished our routine as best as we could.

Backstage, in the sand behind the curtain, I could feel that I'd started trembling, but I couldn't tell if it was from the sheer bliss of fire dancing or the terror of realising I'd just used my powers in public.

Ebony grabbed my arm, hard. 'What in the waves was that?' Her voice was angry, but she kept it quiet, so as to not interrupt the other performers.

I shrugged helplessly. 'I'm sorry – I didn't mean to.'

'I trusted you!' she said. 'This was your chance to prove you're ready to perform with us again.' She spun away and stalked to the other side entrance of the tent, to wait for her next cue in the dance with Kazim and Jamila. I could imagine she might need a moment to herself, too, to recover her sense of stability after what I'd done. I know I needed a moment.

I began to feel dread in the pit of my stomach. I'd promised Ayita and Ebony that I wouldn't do any fire dancing performances until my fire was under control. And here I'd gone and blown it on my first try.

I turned. Dakota was in the shadows, staring at me. 'I'm sorry,' I whispered again.

She wrapped her arms around herself. 'No, don't be silly, don't worry. But … you know you just can't do stuff like that, Fern. Not again. It's just … we've all got enough to worry about when the caravan does shows. Now's not the right time to be practising the other things you can do.'

She'd *never* talked to me like that before. In shock, all I could say again was, 'I'm sorry.'

'Yeah, sure, don't worry. You're spending so much time with those boys; they're probably just rubbing off on you.'

'I'm only spending time with them because I'm training to *control* my power. I didn't mean to let it slip.'

'Sure, but you know how young boys are, always wanting to draw attention to themselves. You just can't do that when you're part of the caravan.'

Her words were like salt water on broken skin, raw and stinging. I couldn't even think of what to say, so I shut my gaping mouth and walked away. Into the darkness, into the crowd. I didn't even care where I went – just away. She was the first person in the caravan I'd trusted, and until now, I would've said she was my best friend. I needed a moment to exhale, to process what she'd just said and figure out why she'd said it, whether I'd done the wrong thing or whether she was just projecting her fear onto me.

I found a gap in the audience and sat there, hoping no one could see me in the dim lighting. In that moment, sitting there shaking on my own, waiting for it to all be over, all I knew was I couldn't bear to be rejected again.

Chapter Twelve

I slept poorly, tossing and turning all night long, without Bear next to me to soothe my anxieties. By the time the sun rose, I still hadn't decided what to do or say around Dakota. I skipped breakfast and went straight to the fire training beach, and just waited for the others to show up. My plan had been to ask Tau for advice about what had happened last night, but he didn't arrive until the morning session had already started, so I couldn't.

The next move I learned how to do, while still practising my heat shield and fireballs at each session, was a net or web of flames. I was grateful a lot of the younger boys were also learning this move for the first time, so Sefa wasn't just explaining it to me. I knew he got impatient with me more often than with the male students.

'You can use this as a web to trap your enemy, or a net to ambush them,' he explained. 'Or you can throw this like a shield around yourself or around someone else, to stop your enemy from touching them.'

It was a beautiful move when done correctly, like a lace wall of flames. It was a move I could have easily integrated into a fire dancing pattern, but since nobody wanted me using my powers in performances ... I tried to convince myself it was still a helpful exercise to learn to control my powers in this more intricate way.

I felt odd practising on my own without Tau; he'd been by my side throughout my whole training journey so far. Today, though, because he'd arrived late, one of the older boys had asked him to spar with them in preparation for their warrior trials. With Tau not standing beside me, I didn't have the same level of confidence in the abilities I'd learned so far. But I told myself to do it anyway.

I'm strong. Not just when he's there. I'm strong on my own.

I sparked and lit several lines of heat in front of me, then wove them together before they could fade. But after last night's disastrous performance, I wasn't about to experiment or try anything fancy.

Instead, I focused on seeing how many lines I could make, how complex I could make the lines of the web, rather than how hot or powerful I could make them. I was still feeling the thrill, addicted to the feeling of power hissing and spitting under my skin, but I wasn't giving in to the urge to make my net any bigger or hotter.

Eventually, I had a full-size net built, and I was pushing the limits of how many lines I could keep under control at once. And I was a little worried that I could feel something tugging on me through the net. It wasn't like Sefa had described it; I didn't feel like the net was separate to me — it felt more like it was attached to me.

I began to tie off the net, about to extinguish it.

'Don't pull back!' I heard Tau shout.

I turned.

His sparring match with one of the older boys had ended, and he was now watching me.

I shook my head silently, but he didn't seem to understand. He probably hadn't seen what had happened, I reasoned.

'No, go hotter, Fern, bigger!' he insisted, approaching.

'No!' I countered.

I extinguished the net with a hard wave of my hand. Smoke puffed, a short and sharp scent, and was then blown away on the breeze.

Tau stared at me.

I stared back. Was I crazy? What could I say? Only last night, I'd let my fire get away from me again, let it take over, and no one had been too happy about it.

After a stretch of silence, Tau leaned his weight over to one side, muscles shifting impatiently. 'You seem frustrated, Fern.'

I blushed. 'Well, yes! Everyone else just seems to *get* it right away, and I'm still getting it wrong or burning myself or freaking out every time I show up for a lesson.'

He laughed, and I nearly smacked him for it. He saw it in my eyes and sobered quickly. 'Well, all right, look. These boys have been training since they were five years old, or younger, some of them. Of course they get these techniques faster than you do, hey.' He gestured at the others further down the beach and lowered his voice. 'And I'm not exaggerating when I say most of them have a drop of power compared to you – you're sitting on buckets and buckets. The more power you have, the harder you'll have to work to control it.'

I paused, confused. My frustration was still there, especially hearing that I might need more time to learn control, when the caravan was here for a limited amount of time. But ... I had *power*? A *lot* of power? 'Truly?'

'Yes, buckets.' He looked satisfied that I was hearing him. 'I have an idea. You'll probably say no again, but ... What if we went out in the ocean? We could swim, or we could borrow a canoe. You can burn anything you like out there, and if anything goes wrong, there's no risk. Plenty of water to put out a fire. Maybe then you won't worry so much about testing your limits.'

I didn't have to consider it for long. 'Yes, good idea.' I could tell I'd surprised him, but this was an easy decision. It wasn't like I was doing this because I was constantly tempted to spend more and more time with him; I was doing this for training. And if I did get burned, the salt water would be good for healing. Cook had told me that tip when we'd first reached the mainland's coastline and got on a boat to come here. 'And if the whole boat burns?' I asked.

Tau shrugged, his pecs and abs rippling. 'We swim home, I guess.'

I laughed, wondering. Was he that unworried about it because he was the chief's son? Because it was the Islander way? Or because trees were plentiful here, so it was easy to carve out a new boat?

I walked down the beach with him a short way. A line of boats made a wandering curve along the tree line, mostly dugout canoes and the waterbug canoes that had balance poles on either side of their hull. Tau picked one of the waterbug canoes, so it would stay steady when we stopped in the water to train.

'Is this one yours?' I asked.

'Close enough,' he said. 'It's my brother's.'

I chuckled a bit at that. I'd heard enough chatter in Trader's Talk among the other fire wielding students to know that 'brother' was just the preferred Islander word for any man living on the island. I'd even heard the chief, Tau's own father, calling Tau 'brother' once.

'Well, I hope your "brother" who owns this boat won't mind its disappearance for a few hours,' I said. I didn't imagine they would – things seemed easy-going here.

'Most belongings are shared here,' said Tau. 'No fixed owner, not like on the mainland. A family might have a cooking pot for a few months, and then the next week, their neighbours can have it. And the largest things, anything we build using lots of people's efforts, are owned by everyone. Like the longhut where we eat our meals together.'

It reminded me of the tribe I'd grown up in, but only because it was so completely the opposite. In the mountains, the tribe was the tribe, but someone's hut was their domain. Everything in it was theirs to keep and theirs to carry when we moved around the mountains and valleys. It meant everything we owned was special, because we only made or bought as many things as we knew our family could carry during the warmer nomadic seasons.

If everything had been shared, would we have had more things, I questioned? If my parents hadn't been solely responsible for me, would I have had more care or less? As it was, I'd spent half my childhood wandering the mountains with my herd of goats. It hadn't occurred to me until now, seeing children roaming the island in packs, that my childhood might have been a lonely way to grow up. I hadn't felt lonely often. My family had been everything to me in the time I'd had them. And I hadn't related much to the other children in our tribe, anyway.

Tau put himself at the rear of the boat and grabbed the oars, then lifted the back. The balance beams on either side of the boat lifted with it. 'Lift the front there a little,' he instructed, so I grabbed the prow and lifted. It was lighter than it looked. We slid the hull down the sand into the shallows, until only the back third of the boat was still on the sand. 'You go *kene*.' He waved a hand as he arranged the oars, but I didn't catch the direction of his gesture.

'Huh?'

He pointed to the bow, laughing. 'The *kene*, the front of the boat, kitten. The *pase* – the back – this is where I steer from in a boat like this.'

I stepped into the front carefully, wobbling with every movement of the boat. I sat myself down on a thin bench and gripped the sides of the boat with white-knuckled hands. Tau lifted one side of his mouth in a smirk and pushed the boat out a little way into the water.

I'm not too proud to say I tensed up as the canoe rocked. My heart was racing already.

'If someone ever told me I'd end up on so many boats …' I shook my head.

I hadn't known I didn't like boats until we made our voyage to the islands, and the memory of being seasick still made me shudder. But there was no way I could have known until now. I had grown up countless miles inland, far from any water except trickling mountain streams and dew-covered moss. The most water I'd ever seen before I travelled was rain. And we always stayed on high ground when it rained, because if the valleys caught too much water, they could flood with only an hour's warning.

And to think that last night I'd been imagining I belonged here in the islands with all these water-babies …

Tau got into the stern – the *pase*, I remembered – in a single flash of golden skin. He paddled us swiftly and easily out past the breakers. At first, I began to panic as the water crashed around us, drenching me from chin to toes. But I caught glimpses through the spray of Tau's powerful arm and leg muscles bulging with each stroke of the oar blades. I found it reassuring – he had done this every day of his life, and he was strong enough to keep us safe.

As we entered the calmer swells, and the ocean stopped trying to drown me, I was able to start looking around again without fear. The balance beams on either side kept us steady as the sandy seabed dropped away to a deeper blue.

Further out, I could see a mass of green and silver shimmering just beneath the water. 'What's that? Out there.'

'The reef. We won't go there today, but maybe another time. It's beautiful, with all kinds of fish and coral and the manta ray. But you need the right tide, or you can easily get your boat crushed on the coral by the waves.' Tau pointed to a calm stretch of water. 'There, that's our spot for now.' In the slower water, he hooked the oars to the sides of the hull, then lifted them out of the water and propped them on the balance beams. 'Now, down to business. Let's try your fire punch again.'

'At what?' I looked around.

'The ocean, the sky, whatever. Just not the shoreline or the boat, or me!' He winked.

I laughed. With two deep breaths, I sparked my power and felt it wash through me. I was amazed at how quickly I could do it now, compared to when I'd first started training. Then I let loose a double punch, 'one, two' out across the ocean. Fire gushed out in two balls, leaving tails behind them. The boat rocked a little from side to side.

I hissed. The tails of the fireballs had burned my knuckles on their way out.

'All right, what happened there?' Tau asked. 'You sparked correctly … Were you angry?'

I leaned over the side of the boat and plunged both hands into the water. Cool wrapped around them immediately, soothing all the way from my fingertips to my armpits, and deep enough to touch my bones. After giving myself a moment to think before replying to his question, just enjoying the healing touch, I sighed and looked out over the boat, where I could see the fire dissipating before it reached the horizon.

'Nervous, if anything,' I said. Then I thought about Bear ditching me that morning – again – on an island where I knew almost no one – and added, 'Maybe a little angry.'

'All right, we can work with that. Let's talk about something else, get your mind clear, and try again.'

'Good idea.' I cast around for a topic, and my eyes settled on the whorls and spikes that covered his right shoulder and upper chest in ink. Intricate lines covered his chest and arms, and even his calves. I tried not to think about whether his short pants hid any extra tattoos. Or what it might feel like to explore those tattoos with my hands. Or what it might feel like to have his hands explore my body … 'What do all your tattoos mean? Do they mean something?'

He looked surprised by the question, and I nearly smiled, amazed that I could do anything to surprise him, this strong, constantly self-assured person. 'Most are tribal,' he said. 'Male tattoos are *peya tatau*; females' are *fafin tatau*. Kids get their first *tatau* here when they turn nine and begin participating in our ceremonies and hunting and things.' He pointed to a dolphin on one bicep. 'It's our island's totem animal. Then there is one you get at sixteen, when you are eligible to marry. Then if you marry, that *tatau* gets completed at the ceremony.'

'Do you have a marriage tattoo?' I asked, then blushed as I realised what I had asked.

Tau grinned. 'No, I'm not married.' He gestured to the ocean. 'And I think that's enough time relaxing. So, try it again?'

I did, and a perfect fireball soared over the water without touching my skin.

'Excellent,' he said, gracing me with his blinding smile again.

It lit me up inside.

'I want one,' I blurted out, still thinking about the tattoos. I'd been thinking it since I arrived on the island but hadn't had the guts until now to admit it.

'One what?'

I waved my hands over my arms. 'A tattoo. To remind me of my own strength when I feel weak.'

He nodded slowly. 'Of course. I'll help you get one. Of a giant tortoise.'

I laughed, a little too loud. 'What, why?'

'Strong, sure, but slow as anything.'

'Hey!'

'Kind of heavy, too.'

I leaned over the edge of the boat and splashed water up at him.

We laughed and practised, and we trained just as hard as we laughed. By the time Tau declared I had practised enough for one day, I had a massive headache building behind my eyes from concentrating so hard for so long. The sun bouncing off the water hadn't helped. Tau stood and stretched his legs, then threw his arms over the side of the boat. He dived into the water in one smooth motion.

I laughed in surprise, flinching as water splashed me all over. The drops were cold in contrast to how overheated my skin felt from the constant sun.

He came to my side of the boat and rested his arms on the side. 'Feel like a swim?'

I tilted my head from side to side, considering. 'Water's a bit cold.' *He's only being a friend,* I reminded myself. *A mentor. Besides, it's hot! He's hot. I mean – ugh!* But I would have done almost anything to see his smile again. And after an hour floating on a boat in the middle of the beating sun, I deserved a swim in the cool water. 'Well, maybe,' I said.

'Great.' He grinned.

It was my only warning before he reached up, wrapped his arms around my waist, and hauled me out of the boat. The water hit me like a wall of daggers crashing into me, and I nearly inhaled the sea in shock.

I surfaced and wiped the water from my eyes. 'You – you!' I spluttered.

He laughed.

I splashed a wave of water at him in a vicious rush. Water went in his mouth and nose, and he coughed, then laughed some more.

After the initial shock wore off, the water felt beautiful. I could feel my headache melting away. I tried to stay close to the boat, just in case my swimming lessons from Ebony weren't enough, but the water seemed friendly today. It played around my body like a happy puppy. I felt myself relaxing as new muscles unwound in the water.

Tau swam around and under the boat and me the whole time. He was like a fish in the water, or a seal, maybe. His skin shone like bronze under the surface, his tattoos making him look like a striped fish or a turtle with a particularly interesting shell.

Eventually, we decided to bring the boat back towards the shore by pulling the balance beams behind us while we swam. Having the beam so close made me nervous, like it might push me under, although I knew Tau was going slower to keep up with my beginner's pace. Relief filled me as the beam stayed behind me with every stroke we made towards the shore, air rushing in and out of me with the effort. I shook my wet hair off my face and gave a good cough to make sure there was no water left in me from Tau's dunking.

When I looked above the swell of the boat on the water, I could see Tau watching me, checking I was still swimming safely, but he just smiled and kept going. His mouth was made for laughing, for humour – and yet he was so calm in commanding his tribe and the fire students.

When we neared the breakers, Tau helped me clamber back into the boat and then took his place at the oars again, so he could scull us through the foam safely. The waves lifted us with every breath and *crunched* back down. He ran the boat onto the sand and lifted me out of the boat.

Before I could protest, I was in the shallows with him, the water crashing around our knees. His hands on my waist, I smiled up at him. Without thinking about it, my eyes drifted to that ever-present half-smile on his lips. I tugged at the hem of my shirt, trying to get my wet clothing to stop clinging to me. His gaze travelled up my form in appraisal, and I could tell he liked what he saw.

'I've never seen you with your hair down,' he murmured.

'What?' My hand flew to the back of my head, and I realised the ribbon tying my braid must have come undone in the water. My hair fanned out around me like a scarf of wet silk. 'Oh. Yes, it's such a nuisance when it's unbound. Gets in my face, makes it hard to work, or dance, or anything, really. That's why I usually keep it braided.' *I'm babbling, need to stop talking.*

But he said, 'It's beautiful.'

I smiled without thinking about it.

His eyes lit with a playful kind of hunger. I recognised that look only because I knew I was probably looking exactly the same way at him.

I realised my body had begun to lean into him with yearning. I jolted and stepped back nervously, accidentally splashing droplets of cool water all over us both. 'Thanks for the lesson, and the swim,' I managed.

Then I lifted my heels and ran out of the water as fast as I could.

Chapter Thirteen

I saw Dakota at lunch and mustered up the courage to gesture to the spot next to her on the palm-woven mats. 'May I sit with you?' I asked.

She nodded with a small smile, and I sat carefully, holding my lunch on my knees, a bowl of fish, rice, and fried yams.

'Hi there,' she said.

'I'm sorry for what happened last night; it won't happen again,' I blurted out. I'd debated within myself last night about saying to her, *Well, you refused to dance at all, so how was there a risk to you if I used my fire once while dancing?* But I valued her friendship more than I valued my pride. I didn't have many friends – I couldn't afford to lose her.

'It's fine, it's fine,' she said. 'Do you want to join me this afternoon? I'll be selling some things at the market.'

I breathed a sigh of relief. My gut unclenched a little, enough to eat lunch together. I wished she had said more, even just to offer the excuse that she'd been afraid.

That afternoon, I helped Dakota carry some of her weaving

and knives to the market to sell and trade. The market was a riot of colour, with people selling everything that grew on the island – wood, stone, vegetable fibres, shell, and bone – all brightly painted in its various forms. The smell of meat and onions cooking was a constant delight wafting past my nostrils, and I told myself I'd buy something tasty for myself.

When we were practising dances together, I often forgot that this was Dakota's primary way of making a living. Just like I tended the goats, she spent time each day weaving baskets, fans, mats, and other things to sell. As she pointed out, this would be more important for her now if she refused to dance in the caravan anymore.

'Until I … unless I go back to dancing, I need to start selling more to support myself,' she confided. 'Can't think too far ahead. Just have to sell the next one. When the caravan moves on to the next island, which I think will be next week, Ebony and I may go with them and see what I can sell there. Kamahimaihi Island, I think that's the one. We'd been thinking we would spend more time here, but maybe it would be better to make the money while we can.'

Once I'd helped Dakota set up her wares under the shade of a tree, I had a wander, looking for some fish and vegetables I knew how to cook. I was thinking of cooking a special dinner for Bear and me to enjoy, as he was finally going to be here tonight. I wanted to see if we couldn't make our relationship more comfortable again, and to assuage some of the guilt I was feeling over being attracted to Tau.

Being here gave me a sense of how large the island was, because the market had about twenty people running it and more than a hundred people browsing at any one time. It was near the port, and plenty of sailors were there among the other Islanders. For a moment, I wondered how it looked to the Islanders, seeing all of us foreigners walking around their island, looking so different to them. I wondered if they didn't even see those differences anymore, because so many visitors came to these islands so often. Or maybe the differences only seemed starker to them over time – perhaps they would feel only other Islanders could possibly be kin.

On the edge of the market, under some far-reaching fig trees, a couple of grandparents were running what looked like a school. All the children were sharing leaves and bits of wood and were practising writing on them.

'They're great mentors, our elders,' Peri said behind me. She was carrying a basket full of clothing made of plant fibres and feathers.

'Hello.' I smiled, glad to see her, and to have the chance to see her in action as market leader.

I followed her over to where she was manning a stall. Brightly coloured beads threw the light in patterns everywhere. Silk and flax garments lined her tables in vivacious colours and rich threading.

When I looked over at the school again, I saw that her son, Roa, was there with the other children. 'Do they do this every day?'

Peri shrugged. 'Most days. Not on feast days, though – our spiritual holidays.'

I nodded, thinking it was a very Islander answer. Nothing happened here to a rigid kind of schedule, I was learning. 'What do they learn?'

'Oh, everything. Reading and writing in our language and in Trader's Talk. The lore and stories. Sex education.' She laughed at the expression of surprise I must have let slip.

'Nothing is that open in our tribe,' I said. 'People are always moving, with the herds, so I was always either on my own or with just one person, like cooking with Mother, or out herding with another child, or hunting with Father.'

She reached out and touched my arm. 'It sounds like you were very close.'

'I suppose.' *Were. Not anymore.* I bit my lip. Maybe when Peri found out the truth about me, about what I'd done, that I was a monster, she would reject me. But for now, I would try to enjoy this moment, when she thought I was a friend. When she thought I was worthy.

Roa ran up to us from the school then. 'Mama, come see! Aunty said there is a new type of yoghurt drink at the market tonight.'

Peri smiled indulgently and waved at the stall people on either side of her, indicating she was taking a walk, then she left her stall, walking with Roa and me. When he got his yoghurt, he drank it so quickly it dripped down his chin and over everything. Then he ran at us, trying to hug each of us in turn as we giggled and tried to escape the mess of his yoghurt-covered embrace.

After buying some food for Bear and myself for that night, I wandered around the markets for a little longer, talking with people. As the sun set, the market turned into a twinkling, beaming mass of colourful lanterns and oil-lit torches held upright on wooden poles.

While we were in the islands, the caravan members were paid with basalt chips we could use as currency within the islands, and we also had the opportunity to trade our goods at the markets for precious island things we could then trade when we returned to the mainland. I was planning on picking up some pearl shell and bone items to take back with me – and maybe some of the red feathers this island was famous for.

But unlike the others, I didn't plan on buying or trading for any of the island weapons. I was spending enough time becoming a weapon myself.

Reciprocity was a key part of the markets here – the trade had to be equal in value. If someone gave another person something, they owed them something equivalent. If the chief said something was needed by the community, it didn't matter whom it came from – it would be redistributed. It reminded me in a strange way of Deridai, in the desert, where the people had been so rich in possessions personally – here, the opposite was true, but it didn't seem to matter. These people were rich with family.

I kept wondering what I could possibly do to repay Tau teaching me to wield my powers. If the law of reciprocity applied, saving me from my own destructive powers – especially when Sefa had first refused to teach me, and then walked away when I couldn't get a spark going right away – left me in a pretty big debt to him.

Maybe a debt like that couldn't ever be repaid.

Training immediately improved for me after my successful practising on the boat. I had a new confidence, which remained unbroken as I quickly mastered additional skills in the days that followed. When the competitive training for the trials began heating up, Tau and Sefa agreed to let me *try* training with the fire dancers' next session.

It felt good to be planning for my future again, instead of feeling stuck in the nightmare of just trying to stop hurting myself.

And true to his word, Tau introduced me to Savan, Aiatalei's senior *tatau* artist. She was an older lady, over seventy, with short hair curled in almost impossibly tight ringlets against her scalp, but still spry and keen of eye. And I could tell within minutes of meeting her that she was still keen of wit, too.

She beckoned me to her open hut, where her tools were all laid out: bone chisels and needles of different sizes to carve in the shape, and vats of different-coloured inks. My nose wrinkled as I walked up the steps to her hut – the ink was made from a mix of ash and fat. I stared at one of the instruments on the mat. It was a series of short, thin bone needles attached to a hammer on a wooden pole. My stomach sank. I didn't think many people would enjoy willingly subjecting themselves to pain, and I was no exception.

Suddenly intensely aware of what I was getting myself into, I turned to Tau and asked, 'Will you stay with me?' I didn't even care if I sounded desperate – I was.

He winked. 'I wouldn't pass up the opportunity to see you get that tortoise.'

I reminded myself of why I was doing this. To claim my power as my own, so that I wouldn't shrink from it anymore. To remind myself of my own strength, in the many moments I felt weak. And to express myself in a beautiful way, because I'd so often admired the tattoos on all the Islanders I'd met.

We sat on a mat made of rushes, and Savan – with Tau translating when necessary – told me how Islander tattooing was done. Young artists-in-training would spend hours, days, tapping designs into tree bark, or sand, before etching on themselves for the first time. Only once their designs were assessed as perfect by their mentor would they be allowed to mark the skin of another.

Savan began asking me what were clearly questions in the Islander tongue, waving her hand over the pots of pigment. She had a line of twenty pots of different colours, ranging from what looked like charcoal to crushed beetle red and deep, berry blues.

'These are the colours,' said Tau. 'Savan can do dots, lines, anything. What would you like?'

Savan nodded, and tried some Trader's Talk of her own. 'What you want *tatau*? On what … style … colour?'

I asked for the image I'd been picturing over and over in my mind, outlining with my fingers where it would cover my hand and arm.

'Are you certain?' Savan asked me through Tau. Fingers had very little flesh to cushion the needles against the bone, she explained, so the marks could be extremely painful. And the elbow was another tricky area, often ticklish and bony.

'Most people … first time … small,' Savan said in halting Trader's Talk, her eyes keen.

But I was sure. For me, this felt like the next logical step. I was trying to embrace all the parts of my new 'self'. And I hoped it would be a talking point when I went back, instead of my scars being something that isolated me from people, made them avoid me.

The first incision was a shock, quickly irritated by the rubbing in of the black pigment. I felt like a small but angry bee had stung me. I gasped, gritted my teeth, and blew out slowly. Savan gave me a sideways look, and must have been satisfied, because she immediately continued.

While Savan began her work on my forearm, Tau and I chatted. He shared with me that his father was the one who tutored him in fire wielding as a child.

'I didn't know at the time, but now I can see how many of his "real" responsibilities he must have entrusted to his second-in-command. He spent hours training me in every aspect of fire wielding and fire dancing.' Tau looked solemn for once. 'I wouldn't be the man I am today without him.'

'What a good father,' I said, and winced as another needle jabbed me. I was glad of the distraction of our conversation; the small bee had turned into an army of wasps that was taking turns at jabbing my arm. It felt like my skin was on fire. Perhaps fitting, I thought, given what was being inscribed upon me as we spoke. 'It must feel like a lot to live up to.'

He smiled. 'Learning to be chief is a lot like any other apprenticeship. Sometimes I feel my father expects too much of me – other times I feel like he trusts me with nothing but the most basic of tasks. It is all helpful and all of it is difficult. Like dealing with the council of elders, it's all training to be first among equals.'

'Hmm.' It sounded interesting to me, to hear that the chief wasn't just an unquestionable leader.

'Of course, the closer you are related to the first fire wielder – you remember, Tuatahi?'

I nodded.

'The closer you are related to the first fire, the more power you have – usually. The chief has been descended directly from that line for as many generations as we have recorded. So he's powerful, but we still acknowledge that fire wielding is only one type of power. The council of elders has our most wise, most knowledge-able of the tribe.'

One of the needles stung, and I hissed through my teeth before I caught myself. 'Will you get a special tattoo when you become chief?'

'Yes, but hopefully I won't have that for a while yet. That would only be if my father decided to secede to me, or if – flames forbid it – he was killed in battle. But if you look at my father's tattoo—' Tau ringed his throat with both hands. 'It goes here. Most of the time it's visible, but for all the big meetings, it's partly hidden by his ceremonial wear. For now, I just have the symbol of the gods' blessing.' There were three dots at the base of his throat. He pointed to each dot in turn. 'The flame of the gods, a drop from the oceans, and the breath of the cyclone wind. Each one will guide me as I learn and prepare to take on the role with real authority one day.'

I felt a familiar tingling, just as I had felt when Bolormaa allowed God to speak through her to me. The night I had chosen my name and begun my first steps towards leaving the tribe, she had warned me that danger lay ahead and said she saw me in the sand, wreathed in flames. Something about hearing Tau talk about becoming chief one day filled me with that same sensation – as if I had seen something unexpected coming but didn't know quite what it was. I shivered, unnerved and awe-struck at once by the sensation.

'That's beautiful,' I whispered.

Tau just laughed and gave Savan a wry look. 'Well, they were a surprise to me. Part of my manhood *tatau*, when I successfully hunted my first boar with the men.'

'He is chief in good deeds,' Savan said, slow and deliberate to find the right words. I knew she probably hadn't caught much of Tau's words, which had been in Trader's Talk, but she had caught the context of Tau explaining his blessing tattoo.

Tau laughed and slapped his knee. 'Savan!' He rattled off some Aiatalei, and the older woman laughed and pointed her needle at him with a sly look before returning to work on my arm. 'She just says that because I built her hut after her partner passed. Anyway, don't be shocked if Savan adds a little something extra to *your* tattoo, Fern – she always does, for someone special.'

'Oh, so you think I'm special?' I teased, wiggling my toes as the needling intensified in one spot.

He just nodded.

My brow wrinkled in confusion. I certainly didn't think I was as important as a chief's son. I was in line for no throne, after all.

Tau looked at me like I was being deliberately slow. 'Fern, no woman has ever wielded fire here before. And *nobody* – man, child, whatever – has picked it up as quickly as I've seen you do it, these past few weeks, with as much power.'

I was stunned into silence. My chest swelled with pride. I took in a few breaths, looking down at my feet on the mat, barely even feeling the pricks of the needle or the smear of the ink. I'd noticed it looked different when the young boys wielded their fire, about how their flames were smaller than mine and they sometimes took as long as I did or longer to grasp a certain move we were all learning, although they had known about their powers for longer than me, had been training for longer than me.

I'd seen all of that, but I'd still thought I wasn't doing as well as them in the training.

It struck me truly then, that I hadn't been seeing myself clearly for a while now.

When I met Tau's eyes again, the strength of his gaze made me catch my breath all over again. He looked like he was trying to read my thoughts. I just breathed for a moment, catching his scent all around me, of salt and coconut oil and sunshine.

'And what about your family, Fern?' he asked. 'You've heard about my father — who was yours?'

My eyes watered almost immediately, shocking me. Even after how I'd reacted when Peri said something earlier at the market, I was surprised to find my feelings of abandonment from my family were still riding close to the surface. 'Umm ...' I cleared my throat. 'I had a great childhood. Lots of responsibility from a young age, being a goatherd. Some days I would just walk my pony among the herds, up and down the mountains, from sun-up till sun-down. My parents were loving enough. They definitely had their ideas about what would have been best for me, but they let me make my own decisions. They were good parents to have.'

He paused. 'Oh ... You say they "were"?'

'I've been away from them for a while now.' I stopped, unsure what to say. How could I say what I'd avoided thinking about for so long? Would it change how he saw me? Although, what did it matter? He'd already seen how pathetic I was in our fire wielding lessons; he'd already witnessed me cooling my burned arms in the streams here. 'I was kicked out of my tribe when I turned eighteen.'

He sounded like he couldn't believe it, as if he was genuinely shocked. 'Kicked out? Did you commit some crime?'

'The crime of not fitting in,' I said simply, and shut my eyes for a moment. 'My tribe kicked me out because I couldn't choose an occupation or a mate within the tribe. There was nothing my family could do.'

Even as I said the words, I wondered if it was true. *Surely. Surely they could have done something, negotiated something.* But no. They were both tribes people through and through. Our traditions – their traditions – were law.

Tau looked like he was thinking something similar. 'I would have expected a family to fight to keep you,' he said simply.

'Maybe,' I said. 'I would've expected that, too.'

Savan worked intently, barely looking up, lost in her art.

Hours passed.

When she at last sat up and stretched her back, I wasn't surprised to see how she had added to my vision and made it grander.

The outlines of flames, both big and small, wrapped around one arm from the tips of my fingers up past my elbow, like a falconer's glove. It would cover the scars on one arm, reminding me that although I'd been badly burned, I'd also learned a new strength I never had before.

I also didn't miss the pattern of fern leaves that curled around my thumb where the flames ended. I smiled softly. I liked that it was carved into my flesh, etched permanently.

Then I saw that Savan had added a firebird rising from the flames above my elbow joint, spreading its wings across my lower bicep. Tears stung my eyes. Somehow, as much as I'd been missing the 'home' of travelling with the caravan, the firebird spoke a new truth to me. I was at home in the flames, wherever I flew.

'Thank you.' I bowed deeply to her, palms on my knees in a gesture of respect and gratitude.

I looked Savan in the eyes and trusted Tau to translate. 'How do I repay you? Do you take silver, or copper? Can I do some task for you?'

Savan was shaking her head as Tau spoke, her eyes locked on mine. He shrugged as she looked away and began cleaning her instruments. Then she began to speak, with a powerful tone in her voice that shook me.

Tau translated, 'She says to tell everyone you meet that Savan of Aiatal was the one to ink the first woman fire wielder. And come back to her if you ever want more ink.' He then said to me as an aside, 'But just so you know, she is partial to honey melons.' He winked.

Bear was in our hut when I walked home after supper, already fast asleep. I wondered if he had eaten or come straight from the boat. I hoped he hadn't been waiting for me. I was willing to bet he hadn't eaten yet. I slid into bed beside him, still marvelling that we could do this. Sleep in the same bed, curled up together. It felt cozy and safe in his muscled arms, his chest against my back. I loved it.

When he woke, I kissed him and showed him my tattoo. I was surprised to find I was trembling, nervous he wouldn't like it, or he'd disapprove of the whole concept of getting a tattoo at all.

'Amazing,' he murmured, and kissed above the firebird on my clean skin. 'Does it hurt?'

I exhaled, unspeakably relieved. 'No. Well, a little. Well, yes.'

I eased onto his chest for a cuddle. 'But I can't get it wet for a day, and after that it needs salt water to help it heal. Will you help me wash it in the sea, after we spend some time together?' I teased, tracing a finger over his chest hairs.

He tilted his head to kiss my brow. 'Ye know I would … I'd love to, Fern. But …'

I stiffened. 'You're leaving again?' *Why? So soon?* I felt betrayed, but a tiny part of me held out hope. Surely, he wouldn't leave me straight away again, with everything I had going on.

His eyes lit up. 'We found a grove of wild brumbies on Lelena Island. Fern, they were so beautiful, I tell ye, it was like looking at a lake of water after a month in the desert.'

With every word out of his mouth, I felt my heart sink further and further into my stomach. I sat up and shut my eyes for a moment.

He sat up next to me and nudged my shoulder with his. 'Hey, hey. I'll only be gone for three days this time.'

I looked at him silently, not sure what to say. I was angry, and I didn't want to speak my anger aloud. I was afraid if I let that anger out, it would only grow.

He took my silence as acceptance. 'And in the meantime …' He waggled an eyebrow.

I surrendered my misgivings and disappointment, and tilted my face to meet his kiss.

Chapter Fourteen

One morning, I realised I'd run out of the herbs I took faithfully every morning to prevent pregnancy, whether or not I planned to spend the night with Bear in amorous activities. As the sun rose while we began our fire training session for the day, I was distracted. Where would I get more? I hadn't seen any growing near the paths I'd taken so far on the island.

Would Cook have some? And if not, she was from the Golden Islands, so she'd know where to find some; besides, she was a woman, which from my point of view was a huge point in favour of asking her. I had very little interest in trying to describe the type of herbs I needed to a man, so I was glad the caravan hadn't yet left for Kamahimaihi, because it meant I could still ask Cook instead of having to ask Eli. It shouldn't have been a big deal, talking to a male healer about my health needs, but on top of everything else that was happening right now, I just wanted this to be easy.

I was so distracted by thinking about all of this that I didn't even see the fireball that hit me.

I'd been in a drill session with one of the boys, Monu, and we were standing in the shallow water, dodging fireballs. It was hard work, and we were taking turns to practise throwing and dodging. His curly locks kept flinging around, flicking sand and salt water at me, like a secondary form of attack.

Dodging fireballs wasn't a skill I envisioned needing to use any time soon. In fact, I hoped not to *have* to use it at all. But it was still good to learn. It was making me feel more confident.

Unfortunately, that confidence was being shaken by the fact I was facing off against Monu. I was used to training with Tau or some of the younger boys; Monu was older, and angrier, and I could tell he was one of the boys who didn't think I should be allowed to train with them. He was one of the teens training for the warrior trials, and he had an attitude about everything.

And Tau was busy doing chief-related work that morning, so I was on my own.

His fireball caught me on the side of my ribs, knocking me backwards. I flew five yards, landing on my back in the ocean, out past the shallows. Water bubbled up and over me. It was in my eyes, my ears, my nose. I coughed in shock and choked water into my lungs. I thrashed about, breaking into the air for a second. I spluttered, seeing sky above me and water all around my flailing limbs.

Then a wave crashed over me, and I was crushed back under the surface. I tumbled sideways and then head over heels. I shut my eyes to keep out the barrage of salt and sand, but then I had to open them to figure out which way was up. The salt stung my eyes, and I struck out with arms and legs. I grasped sand with my fingers. Where was the sky? It felt like a minute passed while I panicked.

Stupid! Was I going to drown as punishment for going for a swim with one man while I was engaged to another? This was insane. A mountain girl shouldn't die in the water! I kicked my legs and moved through the water, but I didn't know if it was the right direction.

It wasn't, but my knees hit the sand, and I realised which way was up. I hauled my body around sideways and pushed off against the sand with my feet, rising up and out of the tumbling water. The air hit my face in a cool rush, and I rose, coughing and spluttering.

Then Sefa was there, hauling me upright by the underarms. We were in water past my chest. I coughed and coughed, unable even to thank him for a moment, my nose running like a stream.

He held me steady as another punishing wave hit from behind. I clutched his arm, unsteady and bewildered, and then it was past us.

We wandered through the water up to the beach. My limbs felt like dead weight. Someone wrapped me in a towel.

'You all right, girl?' Sefa yelled in my ear.

I felt half-deaf and half-drowned, but I nodded. 'Thank you,' I said, and my voice croaked. 'Sorry.'

Monu actually looked mortified. He rubbed the back of his neck and apologised glumly, but I shook my head politely.

'It's nothing,' I said. As the salt water dripping from my hair made a pool on the dry sand, my eyes blinked away the blurriness and saw everyone looking nervous. If I'd been a boy, they'd have laughed it off, I knew, but for me …

'You must go see Eli!' Sefa said.

'*Nale*, no,' I protested. 'I'm fine.' But he was insistent, so I conceded, 'I'll go and come back. It's fine, really – *manuia*.' I'd been enjoying picking up a few words of Aiatalei here and there, and despite the situation, I was proud of myself for remembering to use them. 'I'll be back in a few minutes and keep training.' I had no intention of visiting Eli, but I told myself I'd see Cook and ask her for the herbs, and that would be the same as seeing the Islander healer.

Sefa gave me a grudging nod. 'It's up to you, hey, but just so you know … There's no violence within the island's tribe. As the victim here, you'd be allowed to deal out the punishment you think is fair.'

I didn't know how to respond to that, being an outsider. Did he mean that? In the tribe I'd grown up in, we didn't respond to violence; we practised non-aggression in everything. Another kid hit you? You kept your mouth shut and let them feel the shame. Someone spilled your bowl of food at the supper fire? You got another bowl of food, or went hungry. Out there, in the most unforgiving of mountains, you couldn't afford to hold a grudge. The tribe wasn't big enough that you could afford to punish people any time they did something you didn't like.

I'd sure found that out the hard way, when they kicked me out because I wasn't enough like them.

'Well,' I said. 'It was an accident, it's fine.'

Finally, Sefa turned away reluctantly. 'Everybody, back to your drills!'

Seawater still dripping out of my ears, I walked back up the beach past Monu, towards the treeline in the direction of the longhut where Cook was often to be found hanging out with the island's cooks. As I passed Monu, I wondered if I imagined the proud look that now flashed in his eyes.

I trotted over to Cook's hut, determined to get some herbs and 'forget' to mention my embarrassing moment of falling into the sea. After all, I hadn't even been that scared by it – not that much.

Cook was helping to prepare a pit roast with one of the island cooks for the caravan's supper. In a hole dug into the ground, they were placing fish and chicken wrapped in palm leaves, as well as a bunch of root vegetables such as sweet potato and pumpkin.

She smiled when she saw me approaching. She sat back on her heels for a moment, looking totally at home, even though she came from a different part of the Golden Islands. 'You been for a swim, eh, Fern?'

'Sort of,' I said.

'How do you "sort of" go for a swim?' Cook asked.

I sighed – there was just no keeping things from Cook; she was too inquisitive, an Islander trait. I kept my explanation as brief as I could. 'Wasn't paying enough attention in training, and I got knocked into the water.'

Cook burst at laughing. 'Girl, you fell in the ocean? You feeling a little green in the gills?' She crowed at her own joke, and the lady who was working with her laughed uproariously.

I chuckled. I didn't mind if they laughed at me – it was all good-natured fun, not bullying jibes like Jamila used to make at me. 'Yes, it's pretty funny.' I crouched down beside her in the dirt. 'There's something I need to ask you, though – I need a certain herb and I'm hoping you have it, or you know where I can find it? I've been looking.'

'What you looking for?' Cook wiped a hand over the sweat on her forehead. The heat from the coals in the pit was intense. 'I've got damn near everything.'

I looked down and rushed the words out, blushing. 'Herbs to prevent babies?'

She laughed again and clapped me on the shoulder. 'Oh, child! No problem, no problem. Oh, but actually, there is a problem with that. I'm out of that one right now.' She shrugged apologetically. 'My herbs for that went mouldy on the ship, they didn't put my cases up high enough in the cargo hold, the festering puss-pots. But you find Eli, you tell him Cook sent you. He's got bunches of the stuff.'

I sighed.

She didn't seem to notice, and continued, 'Stoneseed root, they call it here. Don't let him give you wild carrot herbs instead – they use that here sometimes instead, but it's a different herb. Stoneseed prevents the baby starting, but wild carrot lets the baby start and makes the womb harden against it, so the baby can't hang on. You don't want that. Too much grief, eh? You need directions, you know where to find him, eh?'

'No, thanks. I know where to find him.'

I'd pretty much dried off by the time I reached Eli's hut, except for my hair.

He gave me a pound of the herbs without comment or question, but he did ask, 'I hear you joined the fire kids on the beach, eh?'

'Yes.' I was still embarrassed.

'Why you looking for training?' he asked.

I shrugged helplessly. 'I don't know what I'm doing!'

He looked at me thoughtfully. 'I didn't have no training in using my water powers. Nobody like me here on Aiatal, or any of the other islands nearabout.'

'I guess I'm scared,' I admitted.

'Don't get very far in life if we let fear hold us back, eh.' He waved at me and went back into his hut. 'Good luck, eh.'

*

When I finally made it back to the beach, the lesson and drills were over. Everyone was now watching as one pair at a time sparred in the training ring, a rope circle our instructors had laid out to give us a contained space in which to fight. The boys were all cheering and joking and laughing in turns as the pair in the ring practised what they'd learned.

When Sefa grudgingly said I could have a turn, he asked, 'Who will face off against the girl?'

I tried not to scowl, but I was a woman, not a girl child. And I had a name, chosen with great care.

'I will.'

My gut sank as Monu stepped forward to face me again. The cold, angry look he gave me sent a shiver down my spine. I definitely hadn't imagined the look he'd given me as I'd left the beach earlier. Clearly, he was intent on crushing me and proving that he was good enough to compete in the trials. He was old enough for it, at fifteen, and seemed more than ready to me.

I didn't care who won, but I didn't want to embarrass myself or make Tau feel like he had wasted his time mentoring me. Even if Tau wasn't here to see it.

We squared off against each other, and I realised I had no idea what I was going to do. I hadn't trained much for sparring, apart from the few defensive and offensive moves I'd learned with the younger boys. I'd trained for dancing, and that didn't usually involve fighting anyone! And with Bear away again, my anxiety was already spiralling, until I was barely in control. I took a nervous step sideways, wondering if I could back out of this.

Monu immediately lunged, sensing weakness. He threw several fireball punches, his flames green, like pale leaves.

I dodged, pulse racing. My feet tripped over each other. I felt the heat pass by my arm on one side and my head on the other. *He's aiming at my head!* This was a bit more serious than I'd thought I was getting myself in for.

'Give it a rest, eh?' he sniped. 'Make it a quick match so I can get into the trials and take the rest of the afternoon off.'

'You – no!' I spluttered. I reacted, getting angry and hitting back. I let out a side kick, and a knife edge of yellow flame hit him in the ribs.

He sagged, and for a second, my stomach dropped. A little squeak of fear came out of me without me thinking about it. *Did I injure him?*

Then he slapped the flame off his bare skin, and swept a leg at mine. I jumped it easily, but he followed up with quick punches of green flame, then a leaping-turning kick. I had to move as quickly as I could to stay out of his way.

I couldn't understand how he was fighting so intensely but still clearly keeping a calm head, when I knew he wanted to make the trials so badly. With my feet in the sand, I felt grounded in a bad way, unable to think ahead, just reacting to each move he made.

'I don't want to hit a girl,' Monu growled. 'Sit down and save us both the embarrassment.'

There was nothing I could say to that, so I just ignored him and struck out with a back kick. I could have said what I was thinking – *woman hater!* – but I felt like I shouldn't say that out loud.

My lack of reaction seemed to irritate Monu. He gave a blood-curdling roar, like a jaguar. I felt a chill run down my spine. He increased his power and I found myself being forced to the edge of the ring. I pulled up my best fire shield, but I still took blows, more than I could count. The heat and pressure were incredible.

My fire shield began to shake, and I teetered on the edge of falling out of the ring. But I couldn't lose. I didn't want to let Tau down. I didn't want to embarrass myself.

How am I losing so badly? It was hard to understand. I was pretty sure, from training, that I was stronger than fifteen-year-old Monu. But right now, I was sweating from head to toe with the effort of not letting myself be burned to a crisp.

Could the instructors not see what was happening? Would they actually let him burn me up? Let him kill me? Was this their sick form of justice against me for daring to exist as a female fire wielder?

Hunched beneath my shield, I looked deep inside, checking what power I had left. There was a good well of gold light left, so I relaxed for a second and took a chance on a move I had tried only once before in training. It hadn't gone well then, but this sparring match wasn't going well for me anyway, so I had nothing to lose. I jumped up, half-spinning into a kick as I did. It threw my balance off, just as it had in training, and I staggered backwards, almost out of the ring.

Well, that had been a mistake.

Monu blocked it easily and began another series of punches that saw me duck below a fire shield again. I needed more power. I looked within, to see that almost all my gold light had dimmed. I needed to rest and recover. Maybe I should forfeit.

But there – a vast, bubbling pool of magma. That would be stronger! I dipped into the pool of raging lava. It thrilled me and terrified me at once. But I could feel it getting out of control from the moment I touched it. It forced its way out of the shield, and I blasted Monu back with a double-handed fan of black-edged flames.

He fell on his backside, stunned. He swatted out the flames that lapped at his skin. When he rose to his knees, he was out of breath. He growled.

I laughed. It suddenly seemed absurd that I had been afraid of him a few seconds ago. I lifted the river of heat flooding me and unleashed it as a whip. It was beautiful, flowing like art instead of a mere weapon. It was a line of red, black-tipped flames that smoked with each flick of the whip. I delivered a front kick, then double turning kicks.

Monu collapsed, knocked out.

'Put that out right now!' one of the elders yelled, eyes wide.

I blinked at him, freezing. The flames shivered on my fingertips as I came back to myself … and noticed everybody else watching me. Horrified, I hauled the whip of flames back, and it swayed by my side. But it wanted to be free so much, more than anything, and it almost had me convinced that it would be better to let it out, let it free.

Let it burn everything.

I inhaled deeply. It took everything I had to reel the power in. Then I swayed on the balls of my feet, light-headed.

I lifted a hand to my collarbone to find it stinging with a fresh burn in two lines, as if the whip of flames had licked over me one last time on the way in.

Everyone was staring at me. A wave of shame washed over me, as if all the flames had fled to my cheeks, leaving tears in my eyes and a raging headache pounding inside my skull. I flicked from face to face, then stared down at Monu, who was coming to. He looked up at me, dazed.

'What—' he began. Then he looked around, saw everyone staring, and scrambled to his feet.

'What you thinking, girl?' the elder shouted, advancing on me. I recognised him as one of the former instructors who sometimes filled in. 'Didn't you see the black? Don't you know not to play with the dark side?'

'I – I didn't know,' I whispered. Heart in my throat, I said to Monu, 'I'm sorry!'

'Eh, girl,' Sefa started to say, but without another word, I fled. I pushed past everyone without seeing them, running away over the sand.

I could hear their voices arguing on the beach behind me and I choked back a sob. I ran down the beach away from the village, away from where anyone might see me. But I couldn't outrun the deep well of shame I could feel myself sinking into, deeper with every breath.

Barely able to think, I found the rocky beach caves where the high tide visited each day at sunset. With Bear away, I didn't know whom I could talk to, or whom I would want to talk to. I could have asked Dakota, but she wasn't a fire wielder, so she wouldn't know any better than me what had happened, or why. I should've waited to hear Sefa explain what had happened, and waited to apologise properly to everyone.

Maybe the elder who chastised me didn't know how new I was to all of this. But he must have known I was the new one; he'd called me 'girl', after all. And I seemed to get in trouble more often than the boys; they'd all made it clear enough that none of them thought there should be female wielders at all … except Tau. He hadn't made me feel like that.

I sat on the cliff and watched the sun set over the water. The colours were stunningly beautiful, but I couldn't appreciate them. They were all vibrant reds and oranges and yellows tonight – the colour of flames. They weren't soothing colours for me tonight. Instead, the reflections of the dying sun's rays on the waves half-blinded me, and I shut my eyes and tried to pretend today hadn't happened. Surely tomorrow, this would all be easier, be better, be over.

But how could it? I couldn't go back. I couldn't bear to face the other trainees now, or the instructors, after such a public dressing-down. And I definitely didn't want to face the elders again. Or Sefa. Or Tau. I grimaced. What if I'd lost Tau as a friend? He'd stood up for me initially, but he wouldn't want anything to do with me now.

I wouldn't have a friend left on the island now.

Chapter Fifteen

I stayed in my hut for the rest of the morning, skipping lunch. After waking up slowly from the Islanders' favourite thing – a *malolo*, afternoon nap – I went for a walk to one of the jetties near the main port. Staring across the water as if I could see the mainland from here, I didn't hear them come up behind me.

'You could've hurt him, *fafine*.'

They cornered me, blocking the path, so I couldn't just walk off the jetty past them. Monu stood at the back of the group of five young men, looking smug.

'We don't want you training near us,' one of them said.

'You've contaminated our leaders. We know Tau and Sefa must purify themselves every time they teach you, any time they've been near you. They hate it.'

I tried to defend myself. 'What? He hasn't complained about it to me.'

'He's too proud to say anything. You're wasting his time, training you when you won't amount to anything anyway, hey, and then he has to waste more time going and purifying himself every time.'

'And more than that, eh, what if the island spirits decide they won't allow it, for our leader to be near a *fafine* wielder? It's unnatural. You're risking the whole future of the island by being here, purifications or not!'

They were crowding all around me, not giving me space, as they spat their accusations.

One of them pushed me; I didn't see who.

'Do us all a favour and stay away.'

I couldn't think of anything to say in my defence, and it didn't look like they were going to leave me alone. So I lifted my hands in surrender. It was their island, not mine.

They must have thought I was lifting my hands to fight, or to wield fire at them, because they suddenly looked wary of me. One of them took a step back, leaving just enough space.

I squeezed through as quickly as I could, and walked away, trying not to run, trying not to show fear.

'Yeah, you better go!' one of them called after me.

Once again, tears welled up and streamed down my cheeks.

The next morning, I rose before breakfast and walked to the cliffs. I felt as if watching the sun rise – far away from any of the others – might help restore my restless soul, after another sleepless night.

As the sun turned the sky from black to deepest indigo, and then blue-green, I heard someone approaching. Tau clambered over the rocks to reach me, making it look effortless as he leaped from rock to rock.

'Up before the sun, eh?' he said, clearly in a jolly mood.

Ugh. Morning people. I managed a polite nod.

He sat next to me on the rocks, sprawled with his legs in front of him. 'I thought I sensed you out here.'

'You sensed it?' I was waking up fast with the thrill of having him so close, but the idea sounded fantastical. I squinted at him as golden rays began to sparkle towards us from the edge of the horizon.

'Somehow, I always know when you're around,' he said. 'It's like your inner flame burns so bright, I can feel it from a mile away. It has its own signature, its own stamp.'

I didn't know what to say to that. To pre-empt his next question, I said, 'I'm not going to training today.'

He made a face. 'Sefa told me what happened. I should've warned you about that. But I can teach you about it this morning if you come along.'

I shook my head firmly. 'Yes, you should've warned me. And I'm not going. You weren't there, you don't know what it was like.'

'Come on, eh, Fern, it can't have been all that bad,' he said. 'You know you can do better than that. Ready to train some more today?'

'No, I think that's it for me,' I said, my voice flat. I kept my eyes on the ocean. I was barely holding back tears of frustration and self-pity, mixed with relief that he hadn't outright rejected me.

'What? No ... You don't mean that.' He bumped my shoulder. 'You've been holding back, but yesterday you finally tried something. That was good.'

I stared at him. 'But it didn't work. I hurt Monu, and it could've been so much worse. And I got hurt, as well.' I showed him the roll of bandages I held. I hadn't found a way to bandage the new burns across my collarbone, so I was just twisting the fabric back and forth between my fingers.

'So we'll train some more.' He reached over and plucked the bandage from my hands.

'Hey! That's mine.' My heart sped up at the brush of his hands on my fingers, but I felt more frustrated than ever.

'So take it from me,' he teased. 'It's all things you'll learn, if you train harder with me. Come on, Fern, eh?'

'No,' I snapped. 'Enough.'

He looked surprised.

I continued, 'If you're going to be my training mentor, or my friend, or whatever this is, you need to know that I *have* to make my own decisions. It's why I left home in the first place. I needed to choose my life for myself. Even when I became a dancer, it bothered me that it was something people pushed me into, and I wasn't comfortable with it until I learned to choose to enjoy dancing for myself.'

Tau's brows drew together, whether in annoyance or because he was really listening to me. 'Well, if we're going to be friends, *you* need to know that I'm always going to try to push people towards their full potential. That's what will make me chief one day.'

'But it doesn't make you a great friend right now,' I muttered. Maybe we weren't truly friends. Maybe he was too important to be friends with.

He ran a hand over his close-cropped hair, then squatted in front of me. 'Look. Look. You could really be something. I don't just mean as a fire wielder. I mean you could be a force to be reckoned with, in our fight against the slavers. You could help us, work with us. If only you would push past your fear.'

'Help you?' I scoffed. 'The boys don't even want me training anywhere near them, and you want me to fight in your war? You've all made it more than clear that I can't do anything right.'

'I'm sorry they've been hard on you.' To his credit, he did look disappointed. 'But even if you don't want to help us, if you *don't* learn to control your fear, with that level of power ... it will destroy you.'

I wanted to shout, and push him, and say I didn't want any more control. I could feel all my thoughts crowding in on me, too much to deal with at once. It felt like all I did was walk away, so I stayed where I was. 'I need a moment to think.'

He seemed to accept that. 'You know where to find me when you're ready.' He stood, walked around me, and leapt from rock to rock back to the beach.

I stayed where I was, pulling my knees into my chest and hugging my arms tight around them, holding myself together while I thought.

So my first real sparring session had been a bit of a disaster. And there was still so much more for me to learn. All right, I could deal with that. But knowing that nobody wanted me there ... It hurt too much to think about staying there.

I could feel panic rising within me, just like I'd felt when my tribe had kicked me out, when I had nowhere to go. And sure, I had somewhere to go now – I was still a part of the caravan – but maybe they wouldn't want me now, half-trained and miserable.

My stomach rumbled, reminding me that it was breakfast time and that I hadn't eaten many meals over the past two days. I stomped my way back into the village, and then I ate towards the back of the crowd in the longhut. Tau might have been there, too, but I didn't pay attention. I thought it would be better if I didn't talk to him until I'd calmed down.

I decided I needed some time with my friends, to blow off steam and have some relaxed fun before I tried to decide what to do about my training, so I looked for Dakota and Ebony. They were sitting in the shade with a group of women who were making baskets and bedrolls out of palm leaves. Each layer was woven by hand, and the women sang songs as they worked.

I wasn't at all surprised that Dakota was making more friends – she always surrounded herself with people wherever we went. And I knew from experience that it energised her to be around people; she hated to be alone. I didn't feel threatened anymore by her always meeting new strangers, now that I knew this. I had witnessed a few times how she kept me as a friend even when she made new friends.

I sat with them and the woman next to me handed me a few strands of palm leaves so that I could join them if I wanted to. I marvelled at how different this experience was to everywhere we'd been with the caravan so far … The Islander people were so welcoming and whole-hearted. In Tallapoosa, we'd been quietly greeted but never invited to the tribe activities as we passed through. In Deridai, we'd been harassed and then chased off. In Gabon, we'd nearly been killed. And here in the islands so far, I hadn't been allowed to train until I nearly woke up the whole volcano. Only in Tokseng had I felt truly welcomed by the locals, and that was because I'd been travelling with my fellow tribesman Nugai, and he knew the merchants there. Everywhere else I'd travelled with the caravan; it was only the members of the caravan troupe themselves who made me feel at home in their midst.

I looked up as Peri approached. I smiled in greeting, thinking how much I admired how she was strong and kind at once, and she gave a brilliant smile in return. She reminded me a little of Dakota, actually, because even though they looked nothing alike, Dakota also had a smile as bright as the noonday sun. Peri's boy, Roa, wasn't with her right now.

'Do you ladies want to join us for the night hunt?' she asked, squatting down next to Ebony. 'It is a tradition for us women to go looking for fireflies at this time of year. We consider them a sacred secret to purifying our inner heat with firelight. Like the visit to the volcano is a pilgrimage for the men.'

It sounded interesting to me, and I wanted to take the offer of friendship as it came. Not only was I feeling out of sorts from my fire training failures, but I was genuinely lonely from Bear leaving every few days for one island or another.

'Is it allowed?' I asked. 'Since we aren't members of any of the island tribes?' I cringed inwardly as I said it; it felt like I was constantly asking permission everywhere I went now. *Peri just invited us, so why do I still feel like I need to check it's all right? I wondered. What would it feel like to just know who I was, where my boundaries lay, and just live in that freedom?*

'Of course!' said Peri. 'Tonight is for us women, and you are women! All the women and *treleilehine* on the island will be out tonight, honouring the fire spirits, playing through the night.'

I smiled at the word *treleilehine*, which referred to Islanders who identified as neither male nor female, or a mix of both. It made me happy to know that everyone on the island was able to join in one sacred ritual or another, even if they didn't fit into the category of 'men' or 'women'.

We followed Peri and a group of women through the jungle, with more and more women joining us as we went. None of the women had brought any of their male children, only their female children. The men we passed steadfastly kept their eyes averted, honouring the tradition of the women's fire night.

'They better look away,' Peri said when I commented on it. 'It's secret women's business; it's a deeply spiritual experience. It would make the men unclean to even look at us.'

I thought back to the boys saying I had made Tau unclean, and I felt saddened all over again. Had he truly had to purify himself after every time he spent with me? It seemed crazy, even though I remembered the chief saying that would be required for the people who trained me. I knew so little of this culture, when it came down to it.

The sun was setting, making our footing treacherous on the path. Out of nowhere, a series of caves opened up into the jungle floor, and we all entered the largest cave together and sank into darkness. For once, I didn't feel trapped being in an enclosed space with so many other people I didn't know. As the sun set behind us, glow-worms began to shine along the walls: iridescent greens and yellows.

Peri explained quietly, 'We wait here, in the light of the glow-worms, until the sun has fully set, and then we'll all exit the cave and find another type of light.'

'Another type of light?' I asked, curious.

'Yes, look.' She waved a hand.

Little lights began to appear outside, pinpricks in the darkness. One by one, a swarm of fireflies lit their tails in a long, rustling sequence. They began their beautiful dance among the trees, like moving stars in the night sky. All of us left the cave and flowed among them, captivated by their light.

The women giggled like young girls and ran among the twinkling lights as if it was the first time they had seen the fireflies dance, not the hundredth. A few had brought glass or ceramic jars, and we shared them among us, trying – and failing – to capture a firefly in its dance.

We laughed for the sheer joy of it, and Dakota, Ebony, and I all began hopping and skipping and leaping about among the fireflies, not watching our feet in the jungle, reckless for our own safety in the under-foliage.

Peri laughed at us. 'You and the hula dancers! It's true – dancers dance everywhere they go.' She waved her arms around her, watching the fireflies float around her. 'Thank the flame my child is a boy. This time with the fireflies is such a rare break – and I need it!'

The other mothers nearby laughed in empathy with her.

I smiled but didn't say anything – I didn't know anything about motherhood. I studied the fireflies instead. From a distance, they were no more than a will o' the wisp, a bobbing light in the dark. But up close, they were funny-looking things, fat and alien with their long butts that flashed at the tip, filmy wings, and short antennae. Six flashes about a second apart each. They were actually a beetle, so they had a hard outer shell over their wings, and red and yellow markings. They thrived in damp, low-lying areas where they could see each other's light easily. It was fairly dark before they started flashing.

As I watched and chased them, I felt a sense of some great, feminine power spreading inwards from the periphery of my senses in the dark, changing from a tingling in my scalp to a pleasing warmth in the front of my face and chest. Each flashing light seemed like a heartbeat. I felt a kinship to these tiny bugs, flashing to each other and to me across the dark. It was a wave of joy against the melancholy of the world.

And then, in sudden and heart-aching contrast, I felt so alone. All these bugs had their tribe. All the Islanders had each other. Whom did I have? The caravan – a strange mishmash of people who changed season by season, except for the stalwarts. Now Bear wasn't even with me most days, in spite of his promises, in spite of everything. And even Dakota didn't seem to get the same joy as before out of performing or being part of the caravan. What if she and Ebony decided to stay here in the islands for good when the caravan left to return to the mainland?

I would be alone again.

Maybe I was always alone, destined to be that way. *Oh, why did I ever leave home?*

The sound of my name interrupted my grim thoughts. Dakota was talking to Peri about me.

'Oh, are you with Bear?' Peri asked me, her tone surprised.

I nodded mutely, still processing my wash of feelings.

'I didn't realise,' she said. 'I've never seen you two together, I guess.'

I winced. That hurt far more than I would have expected it to. Even now that I had chosen a mate – success, according to my old tribe's standards – I was still alone. Peri viewed me as single, unattached, unloved. I gave a deep sigh and said simply, 'He got into the horse trading.'

'Never mind him,' said Dakota, linking her arm with mine. 'He'll be back, and until then you have us.'

My heart filled.

Peri gave me a conspiratorial look. 'Anyway, you've got more exciting things to think about – training your fire powers!' She tilted her head. 'I have to ask, how is it possible?'

'What do you mean?'

'I mean, how do you even have powers like they do?'

'I don't know.' I stopped. I hadn't often wondered about the 'why' behind my powers – I'd been so focused on trying to use them, then restrain them, and now explore what I could do with them. Why *did* I get these powers? Why me? Why a woman? If these powers were for men, why did I have them? I was beginning to feel more and more like nothing in my life was in my control at all. Maybe it never had been.

I would regain control, I told myself. *I can. I will.*

No wonder I couldn't persuade Bear to stay with me, I thought bitterly, *when I can't even persuade myself to stay in control of my own thoughts or actions.*

I wished I could do as Dakota did, and just revel in the sheer fun of the fireflies and the energy of the other women. There she was, twirling, grinning … but then suddenly she sat down on a log, put her face in her hands, and burst into tears.

'Dakota!' I gasped. I couldn't remember ever having seen her cry before, even when she hurt her ankle recently and couldn't dance for a while. 'Are you all right?'

She shook her head without looking up at me. I lowered myself to my knees before her, but I couldn't see any physical injury, so I wasn't sure what to do. Anxiety slid a knife into my gut, and I gulped, but no more words came out. Why couldn't I support her now, when she'd supported me so well during my transition into the caravan and training as a dancer? I looked around for Ebony but couldn't spot her.

Peri acted faster than I could think – she sank to the ground and wrapped both her big arms around Dakota in a fierce hug. Her embrace softened as Dakota's sobs slowed. It was several moments before Dakota shook her head, unable to say anything; she just waved a hand helplessly and kept sobbing. Feeling wretched, I reached out to rub her back. Still hugging Dakota, Peri gave me a sympathetic smile.

After an age, Dakota stopped crying and blew her nose on her scarf.

Peri said simply, 'Hey.'

Dakota choked out a nervous, helpless laugh, and said, 'Hey.' She bit back another sob.

'What's been happening?' Peri asked.

Sniffing and gulping her way through, Dakota explained, 'About a month and a half ago, in the desert, Fern and I were attacked by sex slavers. We got away, but I realised everything I could have lost by being careless in a city full of men. Being careless around people in general. Everyone says all I do is chase fun. And now, being here in the islands, hearing about your people being stolen as slaves, I feel afraid all the time, waking and sleeping.'

Peri looked angry. 'That's awful! If I could find the slavers, I'd kill them all!'

Dakota sighed.

Peri said, 'Dakota, truly, that is awful. I wish I could make it better. I hope in time, it won't be so scary for you. You know not all people are like that. I too fear the slavers, but my anger is stronger. And my peace can be found everywhere when I remember that not all people are slavers.'

Listening, I felt so much healing happening inside my heart and mind that I could only imagine – and hope – Dakota was feeling the same. All three of us sat together in empathy for what felt like forever, but might only have been an hour.

'The thing is …' Dakota started, her voice barely above a whisper. 'It's happened before. A man – when I was young, he tried to force me to be with him. I said yes to a kiss, but he took it further, and he tried to—' She choked on another sob.

Peri and I gasped in shock and outrage. Peri made an angry yet soothing murmur against Dakota's head, cradling her.

When Dakota continued, she said, 'Afterwards, when I confronted him about it, he said – he said I was asking for it. He said it was my fault, said I wanted it.'

I gasped again, then swore. 'Oh, Dee.' I couldn't believe that had happened to someone I knew. My whole body trembled with an impotent, raging urge to go and find the man who did this to my friend, rip his gonads off, and shove them down his throat. I clenched my fists.

Peri nodded solemnly. 'He hurt your spirit. But you were stronger. And he can't get you now. You are safe with us, and you are safe within yourself.' She then said fiercely but quietly, 'Don't let the bastard win. He's been keeping you in the pit even after the stone has been rolled away from the opening. A pit of fear.'

'I don't want to be afraid anymore,' Dakota whispered.

'Be free, fair one,' said Peri, with a squeeze of Dakota's hand.

I breathed out as Dakota did, shakily. Just like that, the raging heat along my arms and throat fled to my belly, where it belonged. There, the heat could help me build a fire strong enough to burn the world, to keep Dakota safe.

Ebony reached us then, her eyes showing pain at seeing Dakota distressed. She gathered Dakota into her arms and murmured against her hair, and Dakota threw her arms around her lover's neck and sobbed all over again. I waited until their grip on each other loosened, then I gave Dakota a watery smile and rubbed her arm in solidarity.

We all walked back into the village, arms linked, feeling closer to each other than we ever had before.

Chapter Sixteen

Screaming near my hut shattered the thin air of morning. It was a sound of a child's sheer terror, very different to the sounds of everyday play – you couldn't have heard it and not run towards it. I had been lazing in bed, starting my day slowly. But as soon as I heard the noise, I pulled on my sandals and ran out to the beach, where I was among the first to arrive.

A boy, not one of our fire wielders, was being dragged down the beach by two big men. I tried to make sense of the situation in an instant, the last wisps of sleep cleared by adrenaline.

The men didn't look like Islanders. They had wide shoulders but wiry frames, not like the Islanders' big bones. Their hair was unkempt, their teeth snarling and yellow.

The boy thrashed, very clearly not wanting to go with them.

In the water, beyond the breakers, a shortboat was escaping out to where a ship waited.

A ship with red and black sails. *Slavers.*

They'd struck before breakfast, while the parents were all preparing breakfast and the children were playing together on the beach. Maybe they'd already taken some of our younglings, I didn't know.

But not this one.

A wave of desperation crashed me into action. I ran to the shore and threw a long whip of fire behind the men's legs, so that they burned themselves and fell, taking the boy with them.

He wriggled free and ran past me, sobbing.

The two big men roared in displeasure and advanced on me. I quailed. This wasn't a fight I could win on my own, I knew, not without using my powers. And I didn't feel ready to rely on my powers to fight in a dangerous situation like this. So I followed the best piece of self-defence I had ever learned with the fire warriors on the beach: I ran.

'Fire warriors, to me!' I shouted in Trader's Talk, then yelled the same words again in Aiatalei language, some of the few Islander words I'd learned so far, '*Sau ii, afi toa, sau ii!*'

I heard the two men chasing after me, and I knew they were faster than me. My heart pounded, racing so hard I thought I might die of fright before they even reached me. I looked back, checking only to see that they were indeed following me, not the boy they'd attacked. I headed for the longhut, still shouting. My voice was getting hoarser as my lungs tried to use every available scrap of air for pumping energy through my limbs.

'*Afi toa! Sau ii! Afi toa!*'

I was nearly at the longhut when some of my fellow fire warrior students appeared out of the trees. I waved my arms at them, then at the men chasing me. The men slowed, seeing the ambush I'd drawn them to. But then they grinned, seeing more children, none of the boys yet men – more easy prey.

For a second my gut dropped. Had I made a grave error? Was I leading my fellow students into an ambush?

Then Monu let out a war cry, and began running down the beach, calling the other two boys after him. I turned, grinning suddenly, as I realised they were going to help me fight off these slavers. We were a team, and we would win.

The two men blanched as the three boys met me and we all dropped into identical fighting stances.

'Fireballs!' Monu shouted, and we let loose.

The men turned and ran.

'After them!' Monu cried. 'Fireballs as we run!'

We chased them, shooting fireballs in front of us that, while not so well-aimed, were enough to scare the men into fleeing. They thrashed into the sea and somehow made it to their shortboat before we could burn it. How they were so fast, I didn't know, but then we were all younger, with shorter legs than the grown men.

The boys and I yelled and screamed curses at the men as they rowed away as fast as they could.

When the men were far enough away that I knew they couldn't simply turn around and harass us anymore, I sagged with relief. The boys began high-fiving each other, and before I knew it, they were high-fiving me, too, including me in their celebrations.

Things moved quickly from there, until I could hardly follow what was happening. The adult warriors arrived on the beach and waded into the water or boarded canoes to fight back before the slavers could escape in their ship. *Of course*, I realised. Of course they'd have to get close enough to attack where they could steal back any of our children who might already be on the ship, without hurting them.

Apparently, the slavers didn't care much about their own, because the ship with red and black sails lifted their sails and began moving, leaving the two men in their shortboat to our mercy – or lack thereof.

The fire warriors captured the men and dragged them back to the beach. To kill them or torture information out of them, I didn't know. They took them up the beach into the jungle, past my fellow students, who jeered and shouted at the men. I was glad they took them away. I didn't want to see what would happen to anyone who tried to hurt the Islanders' younglings, but privately, I hoped it hurt them as much as they'd tried to hurt our defenceless ones.

Everyone from the village was gathering now, whether warriors or not. All the parents were checking they had their children. Fear and rage permeated every stirring of the breeze.

The caravan members clustered together at the edge of the beach, clearly sensing the tension in the air. I joined them, thinking that perhaps this wasn't a safe time to be seen. The Islanders might see other foreigners like us and take their rage out on us. Ayita waved her hands, motioning us back to our huts, and we began to move.

Then wails shattered the thin air of everyone talking on the beach. It was a sound thick with grief, and when I turned to look, I saw a woman trying to plunge into the water, and a man holding her back.

'*Maya!*' the woman screamed. 'Baby!'

That's when I realised – the ship must have already taken her girl.

A wave of desperation crashed through me. I wanted to run to the shore and throw fireballs until I had nothing left, but I knew the real warriors would handle it better than I could. I wanted to hug the bereft mother, but the other Islander women had her.

I felt ashamed that I hadn't been able to save her daughter, and perhaps had even put the other boys, my fellow fire students, in danger by encouraging them to fight the men with me. What if something worse had happened? What if the men hadn't run? What if another parent had lost their boy – because of me? I felt a surge of bile in my stomach from the sheer horror of the thought, and I wiped my face with my shirt sleeve, trying not to vomit.

The woman ran to the chief's side, crying to him in the Islander language. The chief began calling up and down the beach, for every available warrior to gather to work out a plan to defend the children and go after the slavers.

Dakota touched my arm, and I turned to go, following the other caravan members back to our huts. This wasn't something we could help with; it was island business. It felt heartless to leave while a mother was grieving, and my heart ached for her, but there was nothing I could do. I couldn't even imagine the horror she must be feeling.

When everyone gathered later for lunch, the chief issued several more decrees. From now on, no one under the age of sixteen would go anywhere alone on the island. The slavers always targeted young children who were reaching the age where they often wandered away from their parents or from the group of other children. The chief explained that they were being targeted because they were easy to catch and because they could be sold in the marketplace for a higher price, where the slavers would say, 'This one is so young, they will give you forty years of service, at least!'

The chief then cancelled the public fire wielding trials, saying it would be better for each island's warriors to remain on their own island, to protect their own young ones from the slavers. The trials could be completed on each island instead of all together on Aiatal. The teenagers appeared disappointed – both the young men, who I knew had been looking forward to showing off their skills and strength, and the young men and women who I guessed had probably been looking forward to watching the fights.

But in the next moment, everyone was excited again, because instead of the trials, the warriors and older students would patrol the beaches surrounding the entire island at intervals throughout the day and night, prepared to attack any invaders.

'Meanwhile, some of our warriors will go hunting,' declared the chief, 'to find our children who have been stolen, and to stop these slavers coming back to our shores ever again. My warriors, my students, choose which you can help with, either patrolling or hunting.'

When the chief asked for volunteers to patrol the island, all the fire warriors and students stepped forward – a wave of people. My heart thudded with fear and the sudden conviction that I should join them.

One more time. I could try one more time, to be worthy.

Despite my hesitation, despite how badly I felt training had been going, I stepped forward alongside the warriors and my fellow fire training students. For once, the boys made space for me to stand beside them. One even looked up at me and met my eyes, his gaze stern but accepting.

When I looked up, pride swelling in my chest, Tau caught my eye. He nodded at me, his approval clear in his eyes. At least he didn't seem to think I would be risking anyone's safety by joining the patrols. I found that reassuring.

And then, on the edge of the crowd, I spotted Bear.

My heart leapt when I saw him, and his smile filled my whole world for a moment. He looked rougher than I remembered, his hair longer, his beard growing from more than mere stubble. It held a golden tone to it. I wanted to rush at him and jump him right then and there, and simultaneously wanted to back up, keep my distance. It had hurt me so much that he'd been gone for so long this time, and so much had happened while he was away.

'Good to see ye again, darling.' He met me in two big steps and caught me up in his arms, enveloping me.

His usual scent of woodsmoke and tea tree oil was overpowered by a cloud of sweat, dusty dirt, and the musk of horses. I leaned into his embrace but wrinkled my nose. Couldn't he have bathed after returning? I thought unbidden of how Tau always smelled sweet, even the scent of his sweat mingling with salt and sand. He called to mind the smell of skin lit by the island sun.

I muttered, my words muffled against Bear's shirt, 'It's good to have you back. It's been such a rough day.'

'Oh. Aye, well, I'm back now.'

I knew he was trying to be reassuring, but it just made me mad. As if him being back made everything all right. As if him being back was the only thing that mattered.

He brushed my face with his hands, then brought his palms down to my cup my rear. I felt a now-familiar thrill swimming through me, but I also felt an odd sense of frustration. As he kissed my mouth, then my neck, my collarbone, I felt again an urge to pull away. But I knew that would hurt him. Although, maybe I should let him be hurt – after all, he was the one who'd hurt me first, by leaving me here on my own.

I flinched, conflicted.

He stopped and pulled his head back, his eyes seeking mine.

I looked him in the eye reluctantly.

'What's wrong?'

'Um …' I struggled to think. What could I possibly say? 'Can we just eat lunch for now? Or go for a walk? I'd like to … talk.'

'*Talk?*' He sounded incredulous. 'After a week apart?'

I nodded.

He rolled his shoulders back, let his hands fall to his sides. 'Aye, then, if ye must.'

*

After lunch, he took my hand as we wandered through the village to our hut. In his free hand, he carried with him a bag that held piles of horsehair. I guessed he was probably planning to make it into intricate braids for a bridle or halter, as he always did.

I felt utterly exhausted. People gave us a few funny glances. I could only imagine what we looked like, so tense and rigid. By the time we reached our hut, I could barely stand it. My heart was in my throat. My gut felt weighed down with lead. My legs were sluggish, unwilling to keep trudging.

The spark between us had dimmed. Surely he felt it, too?

I didn't tell him what I was thinking, everything I wanted to tell him, to catch him up on what had been happening in my life while he was away. About how I kept hurting myself, and the elder had reprimanded me for getting out of control, and I'd somehow touched 'the dark side' of my powers without even knowing what that was, but I had still managed to earn the acceptance of the other fire wielders this morning by defending their children.

He didn't seem to notice that I was unusually quiet. He didn't ask why it had been a hard day for me. He just wanted to tell me all about the wild horses he'd seen on the island he'd visited.

By the time he was running out of new stories to tell me, I had decided to try to lighten the mood by pretending everything was all right. I lifted my arms and kissed him, and he responded back readily. For the first time in a long time, our kiss felt tentative, and the angle seemed a little off. I didn't know what to do with the uncomfortable tension that somehow remained between us.

He said he was looking forward to spending the summer somewhere in the north. 'Just anywhere cooler than this. It's too hot for loving, even.'

I laughed, knowing he'd been getting cranky during the daytimes on the islands, when the heat and humidity was at its peak. I knew he must be loving the cool air of night now. And I thought to myself that he didn't belong in heat like this. A niggling doubt said that maybe I was too much heat for him, but I let that thought slide by like a wave.

'Oh, I forgot to show you,' he said, rummaging in his pant pockets with his free hand. 'I got ye a little something.' He pulled out a necklace with a small, ceramic pendant on a line of leather. When he placed it in my hand, I saw that it was a horse, or a pony.

I gave him a confused look. 'It's … um, beautiful.'

He looked a little offended. 'You don't like it?'

'Um, I do, but … why a horse? I mean, horses are your passion, not mine …'

'I thought because you talked about how when you became a teenager in the mountains, they gave you your own pony to ride when you were herding the sheep … If you don't like it, I'll take it back.'

'No, no, I like it.' And I did, sort of. But it wasn't my kind of gift. I didn't normally wear any kind of jewellery, apart from my handfasting bracelet, and we'd been to enough markets with the caravan that I could have bought myself some jewellery if it was something I wanted.

Well, I told myself, *at least he tried.*

But it was hard to imagine how he could think now was the right time for gift-giving, with everything that was going on. We spent a tense night, lying near each other but barely touching.

Chapter Seventeen

I returned to the beach the next morning, knowing I would need more training if I was going to help patrol and fight the slavers. I can't describe how embarrassed I felt as I walked up to the other students and saw Sefa notice me. I thought my whole face would burst into flames. I could feel my body trying to shrink in on itself, but I forced myself to pretend that nothing was wrong, that nothing bad had happened the last time I was here.

As I approached the training circle, most of the boys seemed like they were willing to play along, pretend I hadn't done anything wrong. They basically ignored me as usual, except for Monu, who gave me a quick glance before looking away. My stomach sank, but I was determined to stay, to stick it out, and to prove myself. After all, Monu hadn't been innocent either – he'd come close to killing me until I'd fought back. And he'd fought the slavers alongside me yesterday, so he couldn't think I was all bad, surely.

Sefa didn't seem inclined to ignore me or pretend it hadn't happened, however. 'So you all saw what happens when a student is tempted by the dark side of the flame and doesn't know well enough to avoid it. To make sure this doesn't happen again, we will be going over all of this again today.'

Everyone tensed up, and several of the boys looked at me. I noticed Sefa didn't mention Monu's actions at all, even though that had been the very thing that had spurred me to look for more than my usual amount of power.

'Flame has two sides, and while one is creative – the one that warms us, that lights our path, that cooks our food, that melts and shapes our tools – the other side is darker, destructive. Looking from the outside, you can sometimes tell the difference from the colour of the smoke, which is why we'll talk about smoke next. But usually when looking from the outside, you can only tell the difference from the effect of the fire, whether it destroys or creates. It's when you're looking with your internal eye, as the elder did yesterday, that you can see a dark flame building in power before it acts.' He explained that for the person using fire power, you could feel a difference in how the power felt to your touch, and how it changed your emotions, before you used it.

I thought back, and remembered how the dark flame had felt raw, tempting, rather than the powerful feel of the gold flames I normally produced.

Thankfully, Sefa moved on to talking about different smoke types before long. I kept listening carefully, but I began to relax at last. No one had outright rejected me. I would learn what I needed to, and move on. I would join the patrolling squads, and make myself useful.

'When you come upon fire,' Sefa said, 'ask yourself about the smoke, "how much, how fast is it moving, how thick, what colour?" Then you'll have an idea what you're dealing with. You can sometimes tell what's fuelling a fire from the colour of the smoke alone. If it's a wildfire in the jungle, you can tell how far along it is by the colour.

'First, the moisture evaporating is a white smoke. Next, the kindling – that's your light wood and leaf litter – creates a light-coloured tan smoke, and then later the colour of the smoke will grow darker brown as the fire gets into the thicker wood of the trees themselves. A black smoke usually means the fire is now full of ash, and the fire itself is getting out of control, destroying everything in its path and even burning the rocks.'

Sefa glanced at me, and I met his eyes as steadily as I could.

He continued, 'You can also use colour to tell how close you are to the fire. The darker the smoke, the closer you are to the flames. And also, the darker the smoke, the hotter the smoke itself is, which is very dangerous because the smoke can flashover and burn you as much as the fire itself would. If you ever find yourself near black smoke, you'll want to vent and cool it however you can. There are a few ways to do that, and we can teach you.'

After the training session, Tau met me on the beach. The sweat on my skin was cooling now that I'd stopped throwing fire and running around. I wiped my upper lip with my shirt collar as he spoke.

'If you wish to join the patrols, I need something to prove to the elders that you've got enough control to not burn us all to the ground,' he said.

I raised both eyebrows, not sure what to say or how to act around him, after everything we'd both said about pushing each other.

'We've already seen you've got the power, Fern. You woke the volcano!' He clapped his hands together. 'So, as a test, I'll take you back to the mountains near the volcano again. It's perfect.'

'I'm not sure that's a great idea, Tau.'

'Come on, it'll be fine. You're doing so much better.'

I could tell Tau needed something to do, so I nodded. He'd been in the councils of war all morning, but the talking was over for the moment, and I could see that he was still filled with a restless energy. I guessed he needed to feel like he was doing something to protect the islands, and if that meant testing that I was ready to join the patrols, I didn't mind. I wanted to do something to help, too.

It was cooler this time as we climbed the mountain next to the volcano, but it was no less muggy. The sweat from the climb pooled on the back of my neck, under my breastband, and in the small of my back.

Tau pointed out poisonous and edible plants as we walked. 'You need to cook dry moss, otherwise it tastes just so, so bitter. What's the word in Trader's Talk? "Acidic"? Anyway, it attacks your gut like you wouldn't believe. But if you boil it for half an hour, then soak it in a few changes of water over two days, then it's quite nice. The right kind of moss, mind you. Not the medicinal ones. Oh, berries.' He passed me a handful of blueberries for a snack, and then shoved some in his own mouth.

I almost didn't take them from his hands, afraid to do so much as touch him, but the berries would have fallen otherwise, so I took them. I didn't like to waste food, even if I wouldn't normally have thought of this as food. The blueberries tasted sweet, only a little sour, and I smiled to myself.

When we rounded a bend and could see the volcano, the air thickened, becoming oppressive. It was like breathing soup.

I began to feel like I was dreaming, like everything was happening through a fog as I waited to see the volcano beyond the trees. I began hurrying, faster and faster.

The thumping of my heart was louder than whatever Tau was saying. *What is he saying?*

The volcano was beautiful today. Lush and green and waiting for me. I didn't stop until I was right at the edge of the mountain cliff, looking across at where the volcano's crater began. It was full of dark rocks with vivid grass growing between.

'Hey.' Tau grabbed my arm.

I jumped. 'You scared me.'

'I wasn't sure you were hearing me.' His eyes were dark mirrors searching inside me. 'Just look inside the volcano and check your own fires. That's the whole test. I don't actually want you awakening the volcano again.'

I exhaled shakily and nodded. Inside my head, my heart, my body, I looked for the little flame, the spark. It didn't waver.

Feeling more centred, I expanded my awareness outwards. Tau was there, standing close – close enough to kiss. *No. Why did I think that?* His full lips looked ready to kiss everyone in sight. *But I have a mate …* I tried to refocus on the volcano.

Little flame, came the voice again, deep and rumbling.

I shuddered and tried to turn to Tau, but my feet felt stuck.

Go to the water. My island is under threat. Look, little flame.

The voice dimmed, and I could move again. I took a deep breath. *Did it just happen again … was that the volcano's voice?*

But I couldn't help myself – that voice was compulsive. Compelling.

Frantic, I turned away from the edge of the volcano's mouth, looking for a place where I could see the water. I could still almost feel the threat it had mentioned – I had to find it. Protect the islands. It had to be part of why I'd come.

'What's happening? Fern?' Tau's voice sounded wary. With good reason. I must have looked like a crazy person, not listening to him, darting here and there.

I saw the ocean and ran. 'Come on!' I shouted over my shoulder.

At the edge of the cliff, he slammed into me, pulling me back. He must have thought I was going to jump. Probably thought I'd completely lost it. 'Fern, what—'

I just pointed, and he froze when he saw it. Four ships with no flags of allegiance – ships with red sails and black sails. They had wide bottomed-hulls, good for holding captives.

Tau swore, then swore again. 'More slavers!' He pointed. 'And there – those were our boats, the ones we sent after the slaver ship, trying to get the little girl, Maya, back.'

'Were' being the key descriptor. Our warriors' boats were sinking, and fast, and smoke was rising from the wood.

I started backing up even as he said, 'We need to get down, tell everyone.'

It took less than half the time to go down as we had coming up. My ankles and knees ached in protest during the long flight, thudding foot after foot down the uneven tracks, over rocks and mud and leaves and dirt. At the bottom of the climb down, Tau abandoned me without a word and ran to the longhut to find the chief.

I stood alone, shaking.

What exactly had just happened?

And just as importantly, what would happen now, with slave boats approaching? Was it safe here? Should I be telling Ayita and Grey so they could get the caravan people into ships and leave the island? Was it safer on the water than on the island?

I almost growled at my own thoughts. *Safe?* I didn't want 'safe'. The volcano had hardly been a successful test, but I had to do something. Instead of asking what was safe, I should be asking whether they would let me help fight off the slavers.

I didn't know what I would do next, but I just knew I felt like I had to help somehow, however I could. Without realising it, I'd become invested in this island, these people.

Chapter Eighteen

eing a mere guest on the islands, I wasn't permitted to follow Tau into the war councils and hear how they intended to fight off their attackers. But waiting outside the longhut with everyone else, I heard the proclamation as soon as the decision was made.

A warning-off fleet of war canoes was sent out in the direction where Tau and I had seen the slaver boats. The war canoes were different to the other boats I'd seen on the islands so far because they each had a figurehead at the front, a dragon's head soaring above the whitewater. There was no ceremony; they just went. No time to waste. The chief believed in sending a message once, immediately, and allowing no opportunity for any follow-up messages.

As always, as expected, we women were left behind. Many of them waited in the trees along the beach, where they would be able to see what happened. I walked up and down the treeline, hoping to find Dakota and Ebony, to find some solidarity and offer my own with my presence.

I found Peri and Roa. She nodded to me, and we stood silently together for a while, squinting out over the ocean, wishing we could see further, wishing we could see whatever clash was happening with the slave boats and the Aiatalei dragonboats.

'What a day,' I murmured.

Peri nodded, keeping her voice low so Roa didn't hear. 'Let's hope they catch the bastards and make them pay. The fewer slavers, the fewer they can send to harass us. Then Roa can grow up safe.'

'I can only imagine what it's like to worry like that. I feel stressed enough when it's just my own safety I'm thinking of, but …' I gestured to where Roa was playing with the sand, digging a hole.

One of the grandmothers walked down the shoreline, speaking in Aiatalei, maybe soothing people, I wasn't sure.

We heard the cannons when they started, a deep booming that shook the sand.

Boom.

Boom.

The grandmother's tone changed then; she shouted and began hurrying along the shoreline as fast as she could shuffle. I couldn't understand her words, as they were all in the Aiatalei language. But Peri suddenly looked around and grabbed Roa's hand, and everyone else was running into the jungle towards the village.

'To the longhut, Fern, come on,' said Peri to me, clearly realising I had no idea what was happening. 'If they've brought cannons, our dragonboats may not be strong enough to keep them away. We can defend ourselves better at the longhut if we need to.'

We hurried up the beach and through the village, Peri carrying Roa part of the way so we could move quickly. His feet jiggled against her stomach with each step, but she kept up with me.

The atmosphere of the crowd at the longhut was tense. Gulls cawed ominously in the sky above. The cool air whistled between us, and I couldn't see my other friends from the caravan.

Later in the day, the chief came to the longhut, and I could tell immediately that something was wrong from the grim look on his face. He had an arm around the shoulders of a weary-looking warrior standing beside him.

'I have some bad news,' the chief started. 'The fleet we sent out against the slavers this morning has been destroyed by the slavers. Of our hundred warriors we sent, only Noevo and his boat of ten men made it back. He will tell you of the battle later. For now, the enemy has retreated. We think they must have made a den for themselves on one of our islands; otherwise, how are they returning so often, and so quickly? We must grieve, recover our strength, and then hunt them so that we can strike them hard, and keep them from our shores for good. And if we cannot find them, we will go to Chidor, and make war for once and for all.'

'I don't know how we could possibly hunt them,' said Peri beside me, and I sensed her unease. 'They saw us coming last time.'

As I was leaving the longhut with Bear, Ebony nudged my arm and looked at both of us. 'The caravan is preparing to sail back to the mainland on the high tide tomorrow.'

I responded without thinking, 'Oh, no. I won't be able to join you. I must help fight off the slavers here. After more training, of course.'

Bear stared at me. 'How's that now?'

Dakota grabbed my arm. 'But Fern! Of course you should come back to the caravan with us. You can't leave us to dance alone, especially now that I've decided I'm ready to dance again. And we're heading north, so you'd get to see your family … And I'd miss you too much.' Tears formed in the corners of her eyes.

I felt like crying myself. My heart filled, realising I had friends who loved me. But I knew I needed more fire training. I'd barely begun what I needed to learn here. I wasn't ready yet to keep travelling the world. I needed to know that I was safe in myself first.

I looked into Bear's eyes and saw his anger. I shrank a foot.

Ebony looked at us awkwardly and said, 'Hey, I mean, if you want more training, it's up to you. You know the trainers would take care of you now.'

'I know.' I watched Bear's expression shut down, like a window shutting, and I felt more conflicted than ever. 'I just feel like I need to be here … if I can stay. If … it's all right with everyone.'

Dakota winced but gave me a quick hug, to show that she still accepted me as I was. That was Dakota for you – always loving. I didn't know what I'd do without her.

They left, and I touched Bear's arm. I took a deep breath and said, 'I'd been thinking, maybe I need more than just a few weeks of training here. Maybe, when the caravan goes back to the mainland … I could stay here, train more. Be with … people like me?' I didn't mean it to sound like a question, but it was. Why couldn't he just say what he was thinking? I *needed* to know what he thought, but I was afraid to ask outright.

He shook his head and blinked like he couldn't believe what he'd just heard. He stopped in place, eyebrows together, angry. 'What?'

'You're angry,' I whispered.

'Of course I'm mad,' he growled. 'I can't lose ye, but I can't stay here long-term. I couldn't do that; I can't lose my place in the caravan. It's my entire life, Fern.'

'Why would you lose your place?' I asked.

'If I stayed here with you.'

'But …'

'Where you go, I go, Fern. I said it before, and I meant it.'

It felt like a threat now, where before it had felt like a beautiful promise. 'Well, couldn't we catch up to the caravan on a later ship? I'm sure it won't be much longer.'

I didn't believe what I was saying, and I think he could tell.

Chapter Nineteen

At dawn, a score of canoes prepared to patrol the island, with Tau leading them. Before getting into the water, the warriors all gathered on the shoreline and got into a loose formation. The chief and elders gathered around, watching silently, and I wondered if some sort of ceremony was about to start.

Savan walked out in front of all of them, carrying two bowls of ochre paints – one red and one white. Each warrior dipped their fingers in, then marked a few distinct stripes and spots across their chests, biceps, and face.

Suddenly, Tau let out a loud roar, like a lion or a bull. I tried not to flinch, staring with wide eyes.

The warriors all echoed his roar, and I swore I could feel the breeze shimmer with it. Then they began a stiff kind of dance I'd never seen before, all kicks and punches and shaking their heads as if they were wild beasts tearing apart their prey. Every so often, Tau would lead them in another battle cry. They slapped their skin until it was pink beneath their tans, then scooped wet sand up and smeared it across their faces and chests, over their paint, over their tattoos.

Near me, Kazim sniffed and waved his hands in the desert demand. 'No fire. No fire, no breathing fire, no nothing?'

Ebony nodded. 'No fire while it's just a hunt. They save fire breathing for the war dances.'

Dakota's voice was light as she said, 'Well, then I'm glad we're not going to be hanging around here much longer, right?'

Ebony pulled Dakota in to her side and tucked her under her arm. 'Right. You don't want to see what happens if they go to war.'

I shivered as the men clambered into their canoes and splashed off into the surf. Then everyone got back to packing their belongings so they were ready to leave with the caravan.

I didn't tell anyone how scared I was feeling, about Tau leaving on the hunt and about Bear constantly leaving me and about the island children being at risk. I just let it all eat away at me.

Later that day, at the afternoon high tide, I walked my caravan friends to the beach, and the troupe and the ship's sailors packed the ship to the brim. Dakota gave me a warm hug before climbing aboard the ship, and my chest squeezed painfully in a way that felt like my heart would tear in two. I waved goodbye to everyone through a haze of unshed tears. I rubbed my eyes and shaded my face as if hiding from the sun. I gulped a few times, my throat tight.

I was grateful to have fire training to take my mind off the loss of my friends. As we were finishing our session later that morning, I saw Tau approach. He and the scouts had been absent since they left on their hunt yesterday morning. I came forward to greet him. Sweat was already glistening off his muscles and tattoos. His hunt markings were smudged.

When he saw me, he just said shortly, 'Let's get started.'

'Did you … find anything?' I asked.

'No.' His voice held a snap.

I didn't ask any more questions, and maybe I should have. But instead of joining the others on the fire training beach, he led me into the jungle, taking my hand briefly to guide me through the trees. The brush of his hand sent a thrill through me. My skin tingled where he'd touched me, not from the heat of fire wielding, but from the nearness to him and the tension running through him to me. Watching his broad back move ahead of me, I tried to copy his steps through the thick undergrowth. I found myself struggling to keep up with his striding pace.

I wondered if maybe this was a bad idea, wandering off into the jungle with him when he was in a bad mood. After all, I'd never seen him in a bad mood before, so I didn't know what to expect from him or whether he might lash out at me if he lost control. His eyes, whenever they caught mine, were dark and intense, like a wolf.

But I trusted him. I trusted him to take care of me, after the way he'd saved me from the volcano when I'd first come here, and the way he'd been so patient in training me to use my fire powers.

In spite of me thinking he was arrogant, in spite of Bear, in spite of him being the chief's son and my instructor, there was a tension between us I couldn't deny. I had no idea when my feelings towards him had changed from irritation and resentment to admiration and even appreciation … But they had.

Eventually, we arrived at a blue-green lagoon surrounded by walls of green leaves. The air was cooler, with a feeling that endless generations had come here to find peace, or inspiration, or courage. Tau stopped me as we were about to reach the lagoon.

'This place has *mana*,' he said. 'Spirit energy. So we offer it some of our energy by painting the rocks. This protects the place from our energy, because if our actions were to harm this place, it would be punishable by death.'

I gaped. 'And why exactly have we come here, where we might die if I do the wrong thing?'

He clenched his fists. 'I just need to be here right now, with everything that's happening. I need to find the strength to keep going when I don't know how I can protect my people.'

I could understand that, although I gave a frustrated sigh at the fact that he'd brought me along, risking my life if I accidentally did something wrong. And I'd done a lot of things wrong lately, it felt like. I dipped my hand in the mud and painted the rock next to Tau's handprint, before I could think about it.

We then stood beside the lagoon together, standing far apart so I could practise sparring.

The extra tension in the air did *not* help me focus on my training. I was trying to spark and practise the latest move I'd been learning, a sweeping arm movement that created a whip of flames. It was the move I'd made against Monu, when I dipped into the dark side, but now I was trying to create it using the light side of my flames. But I couldn't focus my emotions, and Tau had to keep saving me.

After the tenth time, he stopped to help me extinguish a line of flames erupting over my neck and shoulders. 'You're further along than this, and you know it,' he said. 'We don't have time to keep taking the same wave over and over; I need you ready to join us in the fight against the slavers.'

'What? Actually fight the slavers?' I sputtered. 'Like … battle? That's crazy!'

'*Nale*, you'll be a great fighter; you're so close to being ready.' He gestured in frustration. 'What's up with you today, why aren't you trying as hard as normal?'

'I *am* trying! *You're* in a bad mood today because of the slavers, but you just keep pushing!'

'Oh, you think I've been pushing you?' His eyes glittered dangerously. 'You think I'm being too hard on you?'

'No, not too hard … Don't twist my words; I'm grateful for your help in training me, really, I am. I just think, as chief's son, you're so used to getting thanked and praised and getting your own way, it's made you arrogant.' I regretted the words as soon as they were out of my mouth, but I didn't take them back. After all, he was the one who'd said I wasn't trying hard enough.

Tau growled at me. 'You would test the control of a saint!' He showed me his palm, lit it, and snuffed it out with a huffing breath. 'That's all I'm trying to teach you – control. You know you need it.'

I was so mad and frustrated and hurt all at once. Without any conscious thought, I fell into a fighting stance, and my fists burst into flame.

I realised what I'd done, stepped back, tried to refocus, pulled at the flames. But instead of pulling safely back into me, the flames grew. '*Huai dan*,' I swore, slipping into my first language.

Tau just laughed. He took two steps towards me, getting right up into my space, and touched my chin. I froze. Then he grinned … and kissed me.

The shock made my hands open, and the flames dissolved. I barely noticed, because the rest of my attention was busy registering that his lips were warm, full, soft … His body was all hard muscle against mine. His tongue teased my lips like a wild thing until I let it in. Then it played and swam against mine until I gasped for breath.

With Bear, kissing felt as natural as breathing. But this – this was teasing, tasting, playful. Desire lit a flame low in my stomach, just as it did when I was in Bear's arms.

Bear. I was supposed to be with Bear.

The thought was like stepping into a pool of icy mountain spring. I jerked back.

The way Tau was looking at me, he looked just as stunned as I felt. The absence of him, of his warmth, made my insides squirm, wanting more. Treacherous body.

But I couldn't just let him get away with kissing me like that, without my consent. My hand lifted, and I slapped him as hard as I could across the cheek.

Then I stepped back to see—

Bear? Oh, no.

Bear was approaching through the trees a few yards away, staring at us. His eyes were pained – I had never seen him look so hurt, confused, and angry, all at once. His fists clenched and unclenched at his sides. His jaw tightened until a vein popped in his neck. 'What is going on here?' he demanded.

'Bear, I – it's not – he started it!'

Bear just glared from one to the other of us.

I tried to walk towards him, putting some distance between myself and Tau.

But Bear took a step back. I flinched.

'And did ye kiss him back?' he growled.

'Well, I …' *Did I?* I stammered instead of answering clearly. 'I don't know.'

His eyebrows shot up. 'Ye dinnae *know?*'

Tau stepped forward, his shoulders tensing. 'She's right, it was my fault.' He shrugged. 'Not my fault if she liked it, bro.'

Bear snarled, 'I'm not yer brother.'

'Bear, come on, let's go.' I tried to move towards him again.

Bear stared at me as if he didn't even know me, then walked off into the trees. I thought about running after him, but he usually needed time to process things. And this … how would he process this?

I glanced at Tau, who was smirking at Bear's retreating back. 'I don't know *what* you thought you were doing,' I said, 'but next time I see you, you better have a damn good reason for it.' I didn't know what to say, and it was clear from the sparkle in Tau's eyes that he could tell. I strode away.

Knowing that Tau had kissed me on purpose to provoke either Bear or me – or both – wasn't going to help me try to explain it to Bear any better. I thought about how much I loved Bear, still, despite this rough patch we were going through, and how much I wanted to fix what was wrong between us. I felt sick to my stomach not knowing what he was thinking, or if he would ever forgive me … If only it was easy, and I knew what to do to bridge the gap.

I followed Bear to the horse training field. I watched as he rubbed down a horse and then untied its lead from the trees, and then let the horse out into an enclosed field. A brumby wouldn't put up with a pen or a stall until it was thoroughly tamed. Not without extreme stress. Horses could go mad that way, locked up when they were used to freedom.

When he was done, I approached him, feeling like I held my heart in my trembling hands as I put my hand on his bicep. He didn't shake me off, so I kissed his cheek and asked, 'Are you all right?'

'No.'

My throat closed until it ached, and I gulped. 'What can I do to fix this?'

'I don't know.'

'*Why?*' I was crying now, tears escaping me as my voice broke.

'Where I come from,' he said, 'it means something serious when two people are handfasted. I know I said we dinnae take our early couplings seriously, but we also don't sleep around once we've made our choice. And I chose *you*.'

'It means the same in my people,' I said, desperate to reassure him.

'Then why are you struggling to choose to be with me?' His face was so tense, but I could see he was trying to hold back his disappointment, buried under his frustration.

'I'm not,' I protested, but he scoffed.

'I saw how ye looked when he kissed you.'

'Then you saw me push him away, and slap him!' I cried. 'I'm not choosing between you – I already *chose* you, Bear. Tau just doesn't take love seriously; that's why he's always pushing the boundaries between us.'

'Ye let him,' he accused.

I reeled back as if struck. 'I did not. I've been trying so hard to relax around him so I can open up my powers and get trained, so I don't keep hurting myself, don't keep hurting *you*.' My chest was heaving, taking in gulps of air as if this were a physical fight, and at any second, I might need to haul myself up to punch Bear or run away from him. 'That's all.' My voice sounded unconvincingly pleading to my own ears. I shut my eyes for a moment, wishing this moment was already over. I knew how important honesty was to him – what if he didn't believe me?

And besides, this wasn't just all my fault. I put my palms over my eyes, and in the dark, spoke again without thinking. 'You keep leaving me on my own. If you were around more, you'd see that what I'm saying is true.'

When I opened my eyes again, Bear was looking at me coolly. He clenched and unclenched his fists again, clearly feeling as tense and upset as I was. He stayed silent for so long that I felt my throat closing up again, tears still leaking out of the corners of my eyes. I cleared my throat.

'I think we need to … take some time apart,' he said.

My heart shattered. A thousand splinters that I would never be able to piece back together without his help. I felt like throwing up. I felt like slapping him like I'd slapped Tau. I felt like kissing him in sheer frustration. I felt like dropping to the ground and wrapping my arms around my legs, curling into a ball and waiting to die.

'Oh,' was all I could stammer. 'Oh.'

Jamila was right after all, I thought in shock. *I should never have trusted him.*

I felt guilty even thinking that, but hadn't he just proven it true? He was rejecting me after promising me so much. After promising me forever. I felt like the most worthless worm. But I wasn't. I wasn't worthless. I knew my worth, and if he couldn't recognise it, what was the point of trying to please him?

Before I could give myself any more time to think about, I ripped the mating bracelet off my wrist and threw it at his feet. 'Well, if you're going to keep choosing horses over me, then yes, we shouldn't be together.'

For a moment, he looked so angry and sad at once that I couldn't believe he was still just standing there. Why wouldn't he do anything? He was losing me, and not doing a thing to stop it. Why wouldn't he fight for me?

Unable to bear it any longer, I turned and walked away blindly. All I could see was that he wanted me gone, so I left. I had no idea where my feet were taking me. I could see people in the village as I walked towards our hut – *our* hut – but they were only in the edges of my blinkered vision. I was barely aware of them.

That night, Bear didn't come to our hut to sleep. I didn't know where he was. Wracked with guilt, I began to cry in earnest.

Chapter Twenty

I couldn't find him the next day, either. The caravan had left now, taking my friends with them … what if Bear had joined them, and left me for good?

I heard a rooster crow in the village and realised I'd spent an entire restless night pacing the floor and tossing and turning on our bed. I'd already replayed a hundred times every word we'd spoken, until I wished I could just go back in time and redo the whole day.

What if Bear hadn't been in the caravan, and I'd met him somewhere else? Would I still have fallen for him? I knew I found him attractive, but would I still have approached, said something? If he'd just been another of the people we met by chance in the towns and cities we travelled to, if he'd just sat at our nightly fire for one night, would I have returned his interest?

It was so hard to look at him now and see what I had first seen there. I couldn't seem to separate the person he was from where we were now, this place of uncertainty and unmet needs. An awful feeling twisted in my gut.

And I couldn't help but wonder … He'd helped me keep going with the caravan after my powers had burned me out last winter. But what else did we actually have in common? Sure, we both loved to travel. We were both gifted performers when the caravan troupe threw a circus.

But I had powers, and he didn't. He had no idea what I was going through. He had no idea who I was.

What if I'd met Tau first? It was impossible, of course, but …

I wished Bear hadn't changed his mind about me. *Someone who promises 'forever' should stay forever, shouldn't they?* It was such a heavy, heady promise we had made.

Before we'd gotten handfasted, he'd imagined a future together for us already. He'd been sitting next to me on the bench, driving his van together, when he'd said, 'We'll be visiting my family when we go to the far north, next year. You should come with us, meet my folks.'

I turned to him and said, 'Wow, that's a long time away. Are you … certain about that?'

His eyes were steady as he said, 'Aye, I'm certain.'

I just said again, 'Wow.' My heart was racing, palms sweating, and I could barely keep my head in the present as we kept following the other vans down the road. He hadn't even questioned my powers much, but I was starting to think surely nobody with powers like mine could ever end up with someone normal, someone like him. Surely he wouldn't want to risk staying with someone like me, once he'd had his night of fun.

When dawn broke, our hut felt empty. Forlorn.

I walked along the beach for a time, unable to pace any longer, full of too many memories and regrets.

I regretted being so angry at him, now that everything was over. I wished I'd kept my handfasting bracelet – at least then it wouldn't feel so final, like everything between us was over and done.

Surely we weren't *done*, not yet, not truly …

But he had kept abandoning me, leaving me to go chase horses on other islands …

I looked for him at the horse field and the training rings, along the main beach, at the breakfast hut … When I checked the village, I spotted Eli leaving his hut. When I asked whether the healer had seen Bear, the older male gave me a look of such pity that I almost wilted where I stood.

'Oh, Fern. He's off on another trading trip. They sailed on last night's tide. Funny time to go, eh? I thought he would've told you, but … hey, you know men, they gotta roam.' He patted my shoulder awkwardly, the beads in his hair clacking together as he shrugged. 'I'm sure he'll be back soon. You all right?'

I shook my head, tears welling up in my eyes, sobs welling up in my throat. I swallowed and uttered, 'Thank you.'

I left, sadness and disappointment quickly dissolving into anger. My feet sped up, kicking at small rocks as I stared down. My hands had been wrapped protectively around my waist, as if I could hold myself together, but now I dropped them and clenched them into fists.

How dare he? Leave without telling me?

Was this his petty revenge for Tau kissing me? Or even more, was he copying me, after that one time I'd fled the caravan during a sandstorm because Jamila had lied and told me my family were in trouble and Bear's clan were responsible?

What a coward.

How could he not even care enough about me to tell me he was leaving again? He owed me that much, didn't he? But there was nothing I could do.

And now that the person I'd thought I wanted most in the world had left me, there was nothing I wanted to do.

My hands unclenched, the strength leaking out of them.

Everyone was leaving me. First Dakota and the rest of the caravan; now Bear wanted to leave me. Maybe I should have gone with the rest of the caravan troupe after all.

With no one left to hang out with after fire training, I went swimming in the sea, just splashing back and forth in the waves until I was tired. The waves fought against my anger until I was emptied of anger, and all that was left was my empty shell, like our hut, empty and alone.

Then I just let the swell lift me up and down. I thought about letting myself go under the water. Just … slip away. What was there left for me?

Kicked out by my tribe.

Abandoned by my love.

Confused by my mentor, with his pushing me to try harder, and kissing me when I wasn't free …

Exhausted by it all, I felt almost numb; all my anger and grief and sadness rolled together in a hard knot in the bottom of my chest.

I closed my eyes and floated in the water, and did nothing else.

For the rest of the day, I barely knew what was happening around me. I got out of the water only to go to bed before the sun had even set, without eating. I was so waterlogged that I could hardly move, and I didn't want to.

My grief didn't keep me numb for long, unfortunately, before the sadness and anger returned. During the long night, I slept little, and resentment took over.

At least now that everyone I cared about was gone, I couldn't hurt anyone with my fire powers anymore. But at that thought, my chest crumpled again, my face dissolving in another flood of tears. Each drop stung, as if it was burning my face like acid.

I'd have kissed Tau first myself, if I'd known Bear was going to make such a big deal when I *hadn't*. In fact, I decided, I *would*. That would show him.

I could only thank my newfound control for the fact that my wild emotions didn't sprout flames into life all over my body. I'd never been so angry in all my life.

As I approached the fire trainers' stretch of beach early the next morning, thankfully there were no other students there yet. Tau was there, though. My skin tingled at the sight of him.

He took one look at my angry, sleepless face and said, 'Woah there. Are you all right?'

'I couldn't sleep last night,' I said shortly, still trying to decide what I was going to do. 'Kept burning the sheets.'

Tau said, 'I couldn't sleep either. Kept dreaming about the slavers. Fight it out?'

I shook my hands loose and adopted the island fighting stance, one foot forward and one far back, arms raised. 'Works for me.'

We sparred for a while, and I didn't burn myself once, in spite of my crazy emotions running roughshod through my heart, body, and mind. He caught each of my punches easily, so I was able to go as hard as I needed to, blowing off steam without worrying I would hurt him or myself. We both fought, shielded, and moved easily.

I was amazed that it could still be so easy between us, after what had happened yesterday. He was silent while my anger lasted, while my punches were fueled by rage, but soon he seemed to sense my mood shifting and adjusted accordingly. He let me relax and try a few of the new moves I was still learning, offering a word of encouragement or coaching every now and then.

He always made training feel more natural, and I was amazed all over again that with all his power and authority, he'd taken me under his wing and helped me master myself. I admired him, now that I saw past his confidence, which I'd misread as cocky arrogance. He knew who he was, and he knew his own strength, and he seemed to recognise something in me as I matched his strength with my own.

'Good,' he said after a while. 'Back in your stride. I was worried about you for a moment there.'

'You were?' I said, stunned. *He cares?*

'Of course.' He said it like it was the most natural thing.

That's what made me kiss him.

It was so easy to step in, take his hand, and kiss his mouth quickly. He saw me coming but he didn't try to stop me, and he returned my kiss with one of his own, deepening the kiss and pulling me against him while my heart thundered. I tasted coconut and salt on him, and it was so distractingly attractive that I nearly went back for another taste.

He stepped back then and laughed. 'You're just trying to get back at me, eh. Or maybe you're trying to get back at Bear.'

'What if I am?' I shrugged wildly, swinging my arms.

He paused. 'What happened?'

My arms fell, the numbness washing over me again. From head to toe, I suddenly felt so heavy. 'Bear broke our ties.' Tau looked confused, so I added, 'I don't know how you would say it in your language, but he left me.'

Tau's expression became a mix of surprise, then anger. 'His loss.' Desire entered his eyes. 'Why, because he saw me kiss you?'

'Yes. No. There's more than that. He said I want you more than him.'

Tau's eyes held mine while I blushed, feeling the heat of it between us as I admitted to myself that it was true. I did want Tau more than Bear.

I covered my flushed cheeks with my hands, trying not to drop my eyes.

Finally, he said, 'If it helps either of you, I honestly didn't know Bear was there, or I wouldn't have done it. Kissed you.'

I stopped, lowering my hands. 'So if he hadn't come along, you would've kissed me in secret?'

He shook his head. 'No, I just … I wanted you to know you have options.' He lowered his head, then met my eyes again. 'But I definitely wish I'd done things differently. I wish I didn't kiss you then.'

'Oh.' I knew I looked crestfallen. I had to; my heart was sinking and my shoulders couldn't help but sag. I'd wanted Tau's kiss, both in that moment and again now.

'Hey.' He took a step towards me. 'I mean because it was the wrong timing. In front of the wrong person. While you were still with someone else.' He shook his head, looking embarrassed. That was something I thought I'd never see. 'I did it all wrong. I don't know what came over me.'

I took his words to heart. I believed he meant it. He'd flirted with me, sure, but he'd never been dishonourable, until that moment he kissed me in a fit of frustration because they hadn't found the slavers on their hunt.

He waved a hand. 'Well, you can kiss me if you want to kiss me – but later. For now, we need to focus. We need you ready to help take down those slavers.'

All the tension drained out of me, and I was – yet again – embarrassed at how I'd let my emotions run away into action.

I'd seriously been thinking that since it was over with Bear, I should try something new with Tau. It seemed crazy, one night after we'd broken up. *If the others knew, what would they say? Would they call me fickle, or a slut, or worse? Or would they say it was fine?*

I was annoyed, but more than a little relieved by Tau's reaction. He was the one who kissed me first – and now I knew he hadn't done it just to annoy Bear … But he wanted to get back to training instead of kissing more – really? Maybe it was just a fleeting thrill for him, and now that I was no longer with Bear, not 'forbidden fruit' anymore, he was less interested.

My fellow students began arriving, boys and young men eager to spar, even though the sun was rising, bringing more heat into the air.

Despite struggling with sleeplessness, rage, and a whole crate of new and tempting feelings towards Tau, I stayed for the whole training session with the boys. Hopefully they couldn't tell what a complete mess I was. We learned more about creating smoke to send signals to our hunting partners, or making smoke walls to hide us from our enemies, or using smoke to cook our food.

I tried to listen to Sefa's teaching, and not think about how close Tau sat. How I could reach out with my fingertips and brush his hand …

He turned his head and caught me looking sidelong at him. He winked, and then looked back to the front.

I laughed at myself for blushing again, clenching my fists in my lap.

Chapter Twenty-One

Throughout the week, I thought about Tau and Bear often. I couldn't stop replaying the two kisses with Tau in my mind, his lips sliding over mine. Every time, I felt a wave of intense desire, butterflies dancing in my stomach. But it was immediately followed by a surge of guilt, turning the butterflies to a lump of coal in my gut.

What was I going to say to Bear when he came back? Would I tell him about the second kiss? Was I the worst woman in the world for wanting two men at once? How much of it was Bear's fault, for leaving me alone so that I was faced with temptation, when I was so new to loving him?

And why should I feel guilty at all? We had, for all purposes, been separated when I kissed Tau that second time.

I tried to tell myself it didn't even matter whose fault it was, if our relationship was over and done with. But I couldn't find it in myself to believe that things with Bear were truly finished. I had loved him with my whole heart; maybe I still did. If I gave him time, perhaps he could forgive me.

Maybe he would take me back.

Part of me thought that if we were talking about 'forever', I was a traitor to both Bear and Tau. Because when it came down to it, I didn't actually want to leash myself to Tau, either. In his culture, the couple lived with the man's family after they married, and his family was, well … He was island royalty. Living with the chief's family? I just didn't think I could do it. I couldn't take that kind of pressure.

At lunch, Tau made a point of being near me, touching my arm to get my attention.

'You want to be eating more of these ones,' he told me, pointing to the spiced fish and fried rice. 'Some foods are helpful for building up your inner fire, making it stronger.'

My skin fizzed where he'd touched me, and I just smiled up at him. But I worried, because what was I supposed to think? Some of his actions, like selecting food for me, made it seem like he genuinely cared about me. Otherwise, why would he be doing it? Was this flirting in his culture? It certainly would have been considered flirting in my home tribe.

I moved away from him to try and get some physical distance and some mental space from the thoughts running circles around my mind.

Sefa approached me after lunch. 'You're all right to patrol, Tau says.'

I looked over, but Tau was talking with the chief and didn't see. Tau must not have told Sefa what I *really* did during our 'test' with the volcano. But if he had confidence in me, I should have confidence in myself. I nodded to Sefa.

'This is Rafafei, he'll be patrolling with you.' Sefa waved over one of the older students.

He wore a shell necklace that he twirled around his neck

constantly, as if fidgeting was as necessary as breathing. 'Call me Rafi,' he said.

I smiled, glad that he didn't seem to be one of the boys who wanted nothing to do with me.

Leaving from the fire training beach, we made a loose loop of the island, a solid four-hour trek that followed the shoreline. Where the beaches were separated by rocky outcrops, we clambered over the rocks and walked among the trees until the sand opened up again.

I knew these patrols were mostly a device to keep the villagers feeling safe to stay on Aiatalei, but I couldn't stop myself searching as if our little patrol could actually find a real threat. My eyes darted constantly between the horizon and the treeline, expecting at any moment for slavers to sail into view or leap out at us from the jungle.

Rafi suggested we break up the walking into three stretches of a little over one hour each, and I was more than happy to agree. He knew the island infinitely better than I did, having grown up on these stretches of beaches and rocks, mountain cliffs and mangroves.

Our first stretch took us past the main port where we'd arrived just a few weeks ago, a calm bay, and the secondary port where the rum and *hava* traders preferred to come ashore. We stopped at the beach entrance to the markets for a snack of fried plantain fritters. Sweet and spicy at once, they were delicious.

I asked Rafi whether he'd been afraid of the slavers when he was younger.

'Well, yeah, I think everyone is,' he said.

Rafi told me he'd been planning on taking the trials this season, although he was only fourteen, not quite as old as the fifteen- and sixteen-year-olds who usually competed.

'What's the point in waiting?' he said. 'There's nothing I can do locked up here on the island. I want to be out there, exploring, fighting, where I can do some good.' He looked at me sideways. 'Like you did, with those slaver bastards who tried to take that boy.'

I was flattered that he admired what I'd done, and that he didn't hate me for being a *fafine* with fire powers. But I knew I couldn't take him too seriously; he reminded me of a younger me, full of a desire for adventure and an optimism as-yet-unquenched by the world. I hoped his bright, hopeful spirit wasn't altered too much by his first real encounters with war. The inter-island battles that Tau had described sounded brutal and bloody, and I could only imagine the battles to come against Chidor would be even worse. After what I'd been through recently, I wouldn't wish violence on anyone.

But Rafi was a young man. I wouldn't say anything to try to deny him his freedom. He had every right to explore and fight, if his elders judged he was ready.

As for me, the longer we walked, the more I felt the challenge that faced Aiatalei. Nobody could patrol this island constantly, day and night; the island was simply too large. And the fact that I and my fellow students were included in the patrols was enough proof that the islands couldn't afford to take many warriors away from their real roles.

On the far side of the island was the rubbish dump, where the island's waste was either burned or recycled. Everything that could be burned had to be burned, or all their waste and rubbish would have had nowhere to go but the jungle or the sea. In terms of recycling, anything that could be recycled or reused was either stripped for its materials and parts or transformed into something new. Nothing that could be repaired made it to the dump;

anything that could be fixed on this island or another island was fixed by whoever had the skill, and the chief always made sure that resources were apportioned to repairs.

A few beaches past the dump, we found the island cemetery, accompanied by a temple to one of the island gods. It was an open-air temple with no walls, only pillars made from palm trees that held up a thick roof, providing wonderful shade. The floor was tiled with a vibrant blue-and-green mosaic of Hualeilei, the dolphin god who rescued fishermen and those who were shipwrecked. Here, we stopped and sat in the shade of the sanctuary for a while, just breathing and resting. I prayed to the God I believed in, that our efforts would help to keep the island safe.

Finally, we arrived back at the fire training beach, and Rafi gave me a pleasant farewell. I returned to my hut for a well-earned rest, feeling like I'd finally achieved something here on the island.

Chapter Twenty-Two

The next day of battle planning seemed more heightened than ever. Everyone felt the spectre of the slavers, and the pressure to be better, stronger, faster. Fights broke out all up and down the beach over nothing. Men and boys alike were picking any excuse to burst into flames against each other. Even the gulls cawed more loudly and raucously than usual.

When I showed up at dawn for patrol, I put my hand on Sefa's arm and said quietly, 'Teacher, would you patrol with me today? Please?' I didn't want to be partnered with any of the 'fired up' boys, or even Tau; I just couldn't take it today.

Although surprised, the elder agreed.

I soon regretted my decision, though. He didn't let us take frequent breaks like Rafi had; we walked for almost four hours straight, with only short breaks for me to drink water and catch my breath.

After my four hours of patrolling were done, I sat on the beach staring aimlessly at the water until I saw Peri walking with Roa. Roa was collecting shells along the shore. Apparently, he'd bitten another child, so Peri had disciplined him and was now giving him his space by keeping him away from the other children and letting him play within eyesight. I joined them, and we all walked together along the beach, slowly.

While Roa was out of earshot, Peri approached and asked me, 'Are you all right?'

'Sure, of course,' I said automatically. Then I stopped. 'It's just all this business about trying to hunt down the slavers. And – well …' At last, I couldn't stop myself; I felt I had to let it out. 'I kissed Tau.'

She gaped at me. 'You what?'

I groaned and clapped my hands over my eyes, so I wouldn't have to keep seeing her staring at me. 'I know, and I feel so guilty about it, but I also feel so happy and … and … I don't know *what* I feel!'

'Oh, Fern.' Peri looked at me askance.

'What?' I could feel my feet slowing already under the weight of her judgement.

'Well, I mean … you *do* need to pick one of them, though … right?' She held her hands up as if asking me to be reasonable. 'We don't have multiple lovers here in the islands. I know it's different on the mainlands, but … Well, and Tau is special, hey. He's not like the other men, or even the other chiefs. He could do great things, bring new changes. He doesn't need anyone holding him back, and he definitely doesn't need anyone stealing him away from our island girls. One of them should marry him, have his babies, help him build a strong island.'

I ached. I felt myself getting mad, but I couldn't have put it into words if I tried. I was mad at myself, at Bear, at the situation, at Peri for judging me, even at Tau for making my life more complicated. When I couldn't think of anything good to say in response, I just nodded and waited until Peri had started to walk off following

Roa. It felt like I was doing that an awful lot lately, but hopefully a polite nod was better than starting a fight.

I mean, really, what could I have said?

She was right. I was horrible. Worthless. Only good for burning things.

I threw fire at a rock near me. Just pulled together all my raw emotion and threw it into the rock.

The rock melted into a smoking heap. I stared at it, all red and smoking, blackened rock. For a second, I was filled with a delicious swell of my own power and pride. Look what I could *do* now!

Then I looked up, and froze.

Peri could still see me, and she stared at me in what looked like real fear. Her hand clutched at her throat, and then she started running back towards Roa, half-crouched.

'Oh!' I cried, and my voice caught. 'I didn't mean …' I couldn't find any words to explain.

I felt awful that I kept hurting people I cared about, by not controlling myself, not learning fast enough, not being there at the right time. I turned and tried to reassure Peri and Roa, but it was too late. Maybe I'd been wrong to seek out friendship for strength during this time of trial. Maybe, after all, I would have to stand alone to grow strong.

That night, I felt like I would be spending another sleepless night if I stayed in *our* hut alone, so I took myself out to lie on a rock under the stars. This time, I slathered myself in bug-away oil first. I remembered my mistake from my first night sleeping outside when I joined the caravan and didn't have the right repellent. The bugs had nearly eaten me alive there, in Tokseng. And here in the islands, the bugs only seemed to be bigger and hungrier.

My situation weighed on me like an iron weight. It felt like there was nothing else I could do now to improve the way I kept ruining everyone's opinion of me. But this time I actively chose to dwell on how I could improve myself and my situation, instead of just ruminating on how badly I'd screwed everything up.

If, as Peri had said, I had a choice between Bear or Tau, then each man was, I had to admit, quite different. Tau represented playfulness and joking, but also training and power. And everything he did was motivated by the privilege of his position. If I chose to stay with Tau, I would be giving in to the laid-back allure of the islands, where I would be working for the good of the island and myself. My goal would be to protect the island from slavers, sure, but also to enjoy every day, and to grow better control over my powers. My life desire to travel the world was decidedly not compatible with being shackled to one island ... but perhaps travelling between the islands like Bear did would be possible.

Ugh. It hurt to compare myself to Bear, but his goals certainly matched mine more than Tau's did.

In that way, Bear represented adventure to me, and he was always striving for a challenging life goal in terms of his desire to run a van of his own one day. I saw how he worked for the good of the caravan, always trying to improve things with Ayita and Grey's approval, never happy with a performance that was just 'good enough'. If I chose Bear and he allowed me to stay with him, I would likely be a van leader's wife one day. I would have the freedom to travel, perform, and try to do what I wanted with my life.

If I stayed with Tau, well ... I wasn't an Islander. Even Peri didn't think I was good enough for Tau, let alone – *gulp* – Tau's parents, the chief and his wife. I wouldn't ever be accepted as the wife of an island chief. I didn't think that was possible in the future I envisioned.

I wished I could stay here, belong here, with the fire warriors, the people who were like me. But I wasn't like them – I was always going to be a *fafine*, a woman, to them.

So, Bear, then.

After all, he had been good for me. He'd given me the love I needed to feel safe and included in my new life with the caravan. He hadn't even judged me or rejected me when I discovered my fire magic.

I'd been so in love with him, or at least with the idea of us, but when I thought about it, I'd said yes to becoming handfasted after a series of traumatic events. If I hadn't been looking for someone to help me feel safe, if I hadn't been so relieved just to be alive, would I still have said yes? I didn't know.

And once Bear had got what he wanted … Once we were hand-fasted, he'd stopped trying so hard. He'd let himself remain blind to how broken I was after the attacks, and he'd let me lean on him without actively trying to support me. He'd pitied me, and comforted me, but he hadn't understood that I needed to rebuild my strength.

And I couldn't rely on him. He kept leaving me on my own when I wanted him here.

That was the real problem – I'd been leaning on him ever since the first time I got burned from using my powers. That's why his leaving had been such a huge and difficult thing for me each time, because I needed him around to feel all right in myself.

As soon as Tau had begun training me, I'd begun to transfer some of my dependence onto him, leaning on him as my source of control. While I was proud of how far I'd come, I still knew I needed to learn to control my powers for myself, not to please him. And Tau had always encouraged that, from the start, telling me I needed to learn for my own sake, even though the others had initially refused to train me.

That was another big part of my problem, I decided.

Bear had brought joy and peace into my life when I first joined the caravan. I was still deeply connected to him in spite of everything we'd gone through recently. In contrast, Tau had brought temptation into my life at a time when I'd been at peace with Bear. Sure, Tau had helped me, but … maybe it was time to let go of my attachment to him.

Maybe now it was time to stand on my own feet.

So I could be strong alone.

So I could be an equal partner later, when I decided I didn't need to stand alone anymore.

As I was now … *Ugh. I don't deserve either of them right now.*

And I didn't want to depend on anyone anymore, but I also didn't want to be alone. Both of my relationships had started with an intense attraction, moving too fast for me to make sense of it. I needed to stop and think before I acted on anything right now.

I closed my eyes and prayed, as I had my whole life whenever I needed guidance.

Lord God, you know me. You see me and you know me. Please protect and guide me. Help me to make a wise choice, and a choice that honours me and my partner.

As I opened my eyes and gazed out at the dark horizon again, I felt so, so tired. I'd been kicked out of my old tribe because I couldn't commit to one path, couldn't pick a mate and a role in the tribe – and now here I was again. I'd joined the caravan, but now I loved two men and I couldn't bring myself to commit to either of them.

I prayed until I could feel myself falling asleep, but I didn't find any clarity.

*

Days passed. Bear returned from his horse trading trip, but he didn't come to see me, didn't even greet me. If he rested in a hut for his daytime nap, it was elsewhere in the village, far from the hut he had shared with me. Nevertheless, I couldn't stop myself being aware of his comings and goings now, as much as when we were together.

I was standing on the beach when I saw him approach the chief, greet him politely, and say he was leaving Aiatal to catch up with the rest of the caravan. The chief walked him to one of the waterbug canoes and waved another man over, presumably to help navigate for Bear as they passed between islands.

Bear and the chief touched their foreheads together for a moment in the Islander way, and then Bear turned to help his boatman. Together, they carried the boat down the beach and dragged it halfway into the water, ready to set off. Still, he hadn't acknowledged that I was standing nearby. Then, just for a second, he turned and met my eyes.

His eyes were steel grey and cold.

I froze. My stomach dropped like a stone. My heart ached.

He glanced away.

And then I was alone again.

How did I end up here?

I turned away, not wanting to watch them leave. A small part of me just couldn't believe that it was real, that he was leaving me for good, that he didn't love me anymore. Maybe he didn't even like me anymore.

I looked around to see if anyone was looking, before wiping the tears that were pooling in the corners of my eyes, as I began walking back to my hut.

Alone.

I saw Tau walking along the treeline with Sefa then. He lifted a hand to wave to me, then slowed as he saw my face. He looked down the beach, saw Bear and the boatmen still talking and preparing the boat, and stopped.

I just hurried away, not wanting to have to talk right now. Let Sefa keep talking to Tau. If that made me a coward, so be it.

Chapter Twenty-Three

One of my next patrol shifts was with Tau. Normally, that would have given me a bigger thrill, but everything felt dull right now, in the wake Bear had left. I barely felt the sun on my skin or the breeze in my hair.

Then I saw him, and gasped. 'What happened?' I demanded, reaching up to turn his face so I could see it better. He had a black eye the size of coconut on one side of his face.

'Nothing, kitten,' he said easily.

'You look like you walked into the pointy end of a canoe!' I said, hands on my hips.

He winked. 'You should see the other guy.'

I groaned. I was pretty sure I knew who 'the other guy' was. 'You didn't,' I pleaded.

'Kitten, he hurt you. I just made sure he knew how much.'

My wounded heart sang to hear it. But I kept remembering my conversation with Peri, and the guilt of her accusations was weighing me down. *He doesn't need anyone holding him back ... stealing him away from our island girls.* I knew the only way to get past the guilt was to admit it aloud. I rubbed my hands over my eyes, then admitted, 'Peri said I'm a bad influence on you.'

'Oh, why?'

'She says you're destined for greatness, and I'm going to pull you down. She said you could have your pick of island girls, and I'm not good enough for you.'

'I used to sleep around a lot in the past, it's true. You might say I *did* have my pick already. But I haven't … in a while. Maybe since you all came to the island.'

'Why not?' I asked, finding I was still curious about his feelings, even though I could barely bring myself to care about anything right now. Mostly, I think I wanted him to say 'because I met you' or something equally stupid and romantic.

He gave me a wry look, and I wondered again whether he could read what I was thinking. 'Just haven't felt like it.'

Then he offered me his hand while we were walking, and I took it without thinking. I even leaned into him like I would have if I was walking with Bear. It felt wrong, but only because I felt guilty, like it still should have been Bear's hand I held. The truth was, holding Tau's hand felt different, but so good at the same time.

My skin tingled, and my heart began to pound again, but a part of me held back, afraid.

Because honestly, what were we doing? He hadn't committed to me, and I hadn't committed to him. Was that necessary? Maybe we were just playing at being in love. Maybe this wasn't about love at all; maybe it was just about the sex we hadn't had yet.

When we had completed our patrol route twice, he said, 'I have to go to some meetings with the elders, you know.'

I nodded solemnly, reached out and rubbed his arm, admiring the muscle underneath his stark tattoo. 'I know.'

I couldn't decide why it had hurt like daggers when Bear had left me for days at a time to chase the horses he loved so much, but it didn't feel disappointing when Tau left me alone for a few hours at a time to do important chief-to-be business. Maybe it was because, based on his actions so far, I knew I could trust Tau to keep supporting me, keep showing up for training, even when he was busy.

He slid a hand up to stroke my cheek, and brushed back a lock of hair that had escaped from my braid. I smiled, breathing in his scent of salt and coconuts.

He leaned down and kissed my cheek. Then he trotted away, throwing a grin back at me. I sighed, feeling a thrill run through me, for once unaccompanied by guilt or regret.

That night, when I couldn't sleep – which was becoming the norm, unfortunately – I ambled along the same route we took when we patrolled the island.

The island was so different at night. Sounds that during the day sounded raucously funny, like the cawing of seagulls, turned into the wild screeching of storm birds, the flapping of bat wings. In the dark, I kept slipping and sliding in the sand because I couldn't see where the shadows of each dune began and the dune itself ended. More than once, I found myself falling backwards onto my butt, or forwards onto my hands and knees.

I wondered why the warriors hadn't been able to find the slavers' den on the islands yet. Maybe they'd already left. Or maybe there had never been a den, and now, having stolen some Islanders, they were headed back to Chidor.

Pausing for a moment, I squirmed my toes in the sand and looked out over the water. I prayed that God would call the thunder eagles, that they would come help us hunt the slavers and drive them from our shores. They would be able to see things, flying around the islands, that we couldn't spot from the ground.

Towards the end of my walk, I was blinded by a flash of gold and red fire overhead. A trio of thunder eagles flapped above me, a few feet from my head. The heat of their tails brushed my scalp as they beat their wings and rose far into the sky, flying out over the water.

I stopped in my tracks, staring until I saw their flames wheel away, around the island and back over the volcano again. I clapped a hand over my scalp, checking I wasn't actually on fire.

What just happened?

Stunned, I tried to reason with myself. *I'm sleep-deprived. I'm probably imagining things. Thunder eagles do not come when I call them. Definitely time to go back to bed.*

I went back to lying under the stars, feeling as if I was floating above the sound of crashing waves and rustling palm trees. The sun had set hours ago, so the mosquitoes and sand midges didn't touch me. There was no breeze; the cold night air tickled my bare face. I fell asleep gradually, feeling like I was sinking into the sand, deeper with every breath.

Around noon the next day, I began to feel that something was wrong, although I didn't know what. The sky seemed dim after a morning rain shower. The birds in the trees and on the ground were rejoicing in an abundance of grubs to eat in the damp, but I could barely stomach my own lunch, my belly too heavy with anxiety. I couldn't figure out if I was feeling guilty, or just anxious, or what was going on.

At the shore, I happened to be there when a boat ran up onto the sand in a big hurry, and the boatman came running straight up the shore looking for Eli. In the boat, I saw Bear slumped in the front, barely propped up against the side. His arm was bound against his side.

I knew then that the anxiety I'd been feeling was about more than just myself. I rushed to meet the boat, not thinking about why I was going, barely aware of my feet slapping through the sand. *How is he hurt? Didn't he manage to reach the caravan troupe's ship?*

Eli and some others arrived on the beach just after I did, and I was thankful, since I was barely coherent with worry for Bear, and Bear wasn't talking much. I gathered from their chatter that the boat hadn't fared well on one of the outer reefs beyond Aiatal. The canoe had overturned – which was no big deal for the Aiatalei boatman, but Bear, unlike me, hadn't let Ebony teach him how to swim on the voyage over here. He'd been injured on the reef coral and nearly drowned. I could tell from his expression as they all talked that he was at his very grumpiest about the whole thing.

My heart clenched; my gut churned. I couldn't stand to be so close to him, not knowing what was wrong, but knowing that he was hurt. I almost couldn't believe that after being together, I now didn't even feel like I could approach the boat to ask him if he was all right, to hold him, to check him all over for more injuries. It felt wrong to even want to know if he was all right, now that I was with Tau, if I could say I was 'with' Tau, which I still wasn't sure.

'It'll take about six weeks to heal fully, if he doesn't do too much heavy lifting,' said the healer.

Bear finally met my eyes. He must have been able to see how much I wanted to come close to him, to see for myself that he was all right. His eyes softened, not like they had the other times he'd avoided my gaze or looked at me so coldly.

'Aye, Fern, I'm fine,' he said simply.

'All right,' I said.

But he coughed and then winced with the motion, and his whole face went pale.

I frowned with worry. 'Thank goodness you were so close by, so you could come back quickly,' I said.

Apart from his arm, which was fractured in only one place, he had some bruising along his ribs, but thankfully he hadn't hit his head on the coral. Eli said he would need some help to wash the grime of the day off him, and Eli tried putting cool compresses of willowbark on his arm and ribs, but Bear didn't tolerate that for long. Other than that, Bear just seemed crabby about being in pain and needing to rest, so Eli left him with the boatman, with instructions to carry him carefully up the beach.

'Cannae catch my breath lying down,' Bear complained to some of his fellow horse hunters, who had come to see if Bear was all right. 'Healer Eli said not to spend too long laying about, anyway.'

'Good luck with that,' one of them said with a laugh. 'If there's one thing we've learned about this guy, it's that he doesn't stay still.'

Another agreed, 'We'd have to tie you down.'

As they left, I sorted through the thought creeping around in the back of my mind: that I was glad we were apart, because now he couldn't make me his nursemaid. Taking care of him would have meant I could do fewer patrols of the island hunting for slavers, less training in my fire wielding, less dancing practise. I couldn't stand the thought of being sidelined again, not after pulling myself out of the pit of despair I'd fallen into. I was finally actively swimming through my life again, not just dragged back and forth by the current of my fear and trauma from the winter. I didn't want to slow down my progress, although I felt guilty that I didn't want to take care of Bear.

And yet … I still loved him. I ached inside every vein, every heartbeat painful, because he wouldn't let me near him, because he had cast me aside, and because he had spoken to me at last, had acknowledged that I cared for him.

Chapter Twenty-Four

The volcano awakened shortly before dawn. I woke in the dark without knowing why. Deep in my bones, I could feel the magma rising. It filled me with panic from my eyebrows to my toenails. I was even more panicked this time than the last time I had felt the mountain rising, because I could tell I hadn't started it.

The subtle, insidious scent of rotten eggs was infiltrating the air, thickening it like goo. Somehow, I knew that I would have to get the volcano to stop making the gas, or it would slowly kill everyone on the island.

The ground trembled.

I leaped out of bed and pulled on my boots, my hands shaking. My stomach felt like churning waves breaking on the shore over and over.

Outside my hut, I could see villagers all running through the trees towards the beach. We'd talked about volcanic fires in our training on the beach. The island wisdom for what to do if a volcano erupted was to either get to the beach and escape by boat, if the winds were in your favour; or to get to high ground, away from the flows of lava and out of any valleys where poisonous volcanic gases might pool. I couldn't tell if the winds were in our favour, but I could tell from the direction people were running that they had chosen to escape by sea.

But where should I go? If I was going to stop the volcano, I needed to be close to it. Could I find my way to the base of the volcano in the dark? I doubted it. And the jungle had a thousand traps for a mainlander who didn't know her way – things like quicksand, or wild boar dens, or ocean sinkholes that were giant holes in the ground that appeared out of nowhere and dropped down yards and yards to underground ocean paths.

But I could probably find my way to the river, and that led to Tau's hut, and he could show me the way to the volcano. I knew I couldn't stop the volcano on my own – I would need the help of at least Tau, and the elders and fire trainers if we could gather them in time.

As I hurried down the path to the river, I spotted someone hobbling down the road ahead of me, leaning on the trees as he passed. The shape of him looked so familiar, and as I got closer, I saw his hair and realised without a doubt that I was right. It was Bear, his progress hampered by his injuries.

There wasn't time to worry about what he would think. I could help him move faster, get him to the beach, and leave him with the others. It would slow me down, but he was going so slowly that he might not make it to the beach otherwise, and we all needed to be out of the jungle before the gases reached the jungle floor. I touched his arm, said, 'Bear, lean on me. We need to get you out of here.'

'Do ye know what's happenin'?' His voice was groggy with sleep and the medication Eli had given him.

'We have to get out.' I held out my arm to him, gesturing for him to lean on my shoulder so I could help him walk faster. 'The volcano. Something's happening. We have to get to the beach; the water will keep the air clearer there for a little longer.'

He was moving so slowly from his injury that I felt like shaking him, even though I knew he couldn't help it. We were going to die from sulphur poisoning just because he couldn't get moving! I held back a groan.

By the time we got through the trees and the village to the beach, thin ash was already starting to fall. Like black snow, it clogged the air. People had carried what they could to the beach: food, water, children. What should I have brought? Bear leaned on me, and I tried to calm my breathing. I'd got Bear out. So, I guess I'd brought something that mattered, although he wasn't the only one who mattered to me now.

At the sand, I helped Bear to a seat and nearly cried in relief when I saw Eli come running up to us.

'Boy, this is not how you take care of a rib injury!' he scolded.

'No choice,' Bear said with a grunt.

I stepped back, adrenaline flowing through my veins afresh as I prepared for my next step. 'I have to go,' I managed. 'I have to see if the fire wielders can stop the volcano.'

Bear just stared up at me; it cut like glass shards in my heart. I wasn't sure what he was thinking or whether he even understood.

'I'll be back,' I gasped, and ran away.

On the treeline, I found Tau herding villagers down to the beach. I grabbed him by the arm. 'Tau! The volcano—'

He interrupted me. 'The elders say this is the strongest they've ever felt it. We have to get everyone off the island, right now.'

'Yes, yes, but Tau, we can stop it together. I need you to show me the way, but I know we can do it.'

He shook his head so quickly I knew he hadn't even considered what I'd said. 'Women don't touch the volcano, only men.'

I grabbed him. 'Women don't wield fire, either, but I do! We need to get up there, together, and stop it from erupting.'

His eyes widened, and he nodded fiercely. 'You're right. We must try. Sefa!' He got his second to take over herding the Islanders, then turned and clapped me on the back. 'Come on, follow me!'

As we passed the creek on the way to the volcano, he stopped and ripped both the sleeves off his shirt.

'What are you doing?' I asked. 'The one time you wear a shirt, you rip it up?'

He shot me a quick grin and stepped into the shallows to soak the torn cloth in the water. He handed one of the sleeves to me, dripping water all over me. 'Keep this over your nose and mouth when we get closer to the volcano, all right? It'll protect us from breathing in tiny bits of ash as we get into the danger zone.'

I muttered.

I could tell he was grinning at me through the cloth covering his mouth.

We raced back through the village, black ash coating our feet, dodging people on every side. Above the treeline, in the pre-dawn sky, I could just see a faint glow at the top of the volcano. The sky was no longer black; it was a haze of grey ash and yellow and red light.

A thought niggled at me: *Why is it erupting now?*

The jungle was a malevolent mess of vines and shrubs and plants that tried to grab us as we hacked our path through them. I felt thorns attacking my skin as I ran. Little beads of blood formed all over me, but I barely registered them. The air was getting hotter, and I made sure to hold the wet cloth over my nose and mouth.

At the base of the volcano, we sat and sparked together, connecting our scattered minds to the power and calm of our inner source. As I closed my eyelids and breathed in deeply, I didn't need to go looking for the volcano's spiritual presence. It was a raging mass of heat and darkness in every part of my mental vision. It took up the whole world, crushing us. We were ants before it, burning under its heat.

I gasped, struggling to breathe.

Tau grabbed my arm to steady me, and it worked. I sucked in air, slowed my breathing to let in less sulphur, and looked inwards to my own spark again. *Beautiful. Strong. Powerful.* I could do this.

Then I focused my mind on Tau's spark – a vibrant, ever-moving flame that called to me.

'Together, now,' he said.

Our sparks linked as easily as holding hands. I took a deeper breath, and we looked up into the heart of the beast. It was big. It was mean. And it was definitely out of control.

The volcano was so much more than the mass of rock it sat on, I realised. With fire vision, I could see the inner structure of the fiery mountain: a narrow mouth, dark with ash, led down in a funnel to a series of tunnels that were slowly filling with heavy, crimson lava, almost like blood in veins. The vent opened at its bottom into a massive pool of liquid gold, so dark and hot it was almost black.

'Where does it go?' Tau whispered, watching it. 'It flows so far and wide – is it under *everything?*'

I shook him mentally. 'Focus!' I didn't let myself look at that pool of liquid. 'We need to calm it down, stop the gas escaping, and stop that liquid rising!'

We tried. We linked our sparks, built them to a fever pitch, and then reached out to the volcano.

Peace, we called. *Calm. Cool the flame. You are embers. You don't need to rise.*

It didn't work.

Little flame, I heard the voice rumble. I shuddered. *Go.*

'We're not close enough to the source,' said Tau, opening his eyes.

I nodded and stood on shaky legs. 'Let's move.'

We ran up the volcano faster than I would have ever thought wise, or even possible. I slipped and fell a hundred times, and the ground was hot beneath my hands. Ash fell in our hair and coated our skin, so I used a small portion of my spark to make sure the ash didn't burn either of us. As we went higher up the slope, the ash didn't have as far to fall to reach us, so it was falling hotter on us with every foot we climbed. The air began to burn in the back of my throat despite holding the damp cloth over my face, but still we pushed on through the trees and over the rocks, ever upward.

Some of the foliage was catching alight from the lit ash. I tried to ignore it, saving my strength for the big challenge ahead. But I did worry that the bushfire might be out of control by the time we controlled the volcano – if we *could* control the volcano.

I saw the strangest thing as we climbed, and pointed it out to Tau with a hoarse, 'Look!'

The cloud of smoke rising all around us from the volcano was heating the water's edge to a bubble. I could only hope that once everyone was in their boats, they could get far enough out into the sea to be safe from the heat and ash … and pumice, if Tau and I weren't strong enough to stop the volcano before that stage.

At the peak, our eyes watering and blurring with smoke, we stood at the edge of the volcano's mouth and stared into the groaning, blistering depths. It looked nothing like it had a few days ago, when I'd stood on its neighbouring mountain and gazed across at the volcano's black rock layered with green vegetation. Together, Tau and I reached out again into the perilous heat.

Little flame, the volcano taunted. *I will eat you up.*

Tau roared in pain and jerked back, breaking our connection. Lava had bubbled up while we were concentrating, and burned his foot through his sandals. I pulled him back from the lip of the volcano and the seething lava. He beat the burning stuff off, to not let his skin burn any more, but it must have still hurt, because he winced as he straightened.

Then his eyes widened, and he swore. He grabbed my shoulder, pointing.

Five big slave boats were on the rear side of the island. And all the people of the island were gathering on the shore, so easily within reach of cannons, harpoons, arrows, or other weapons. I didn't know how the slavers could have thought they would survive being this close while the volcano erupted, but they didn't seem to be trying to turn around. Maybe they'd even seen this as an opportunity, to attack while we were at our most vulnerable.

Maybe they already had. One of the ships wasn't sailing towards the island, but away from it, and moving much slower than the others. They might have some of our people, our children, already trapped in their hold. My gut clenched.

'We have to warn everyone, or they'll just be waiting on the beach, ready to be picked off by those bastards.' My mind raced, trying to remember my lessons. 'Can we send a smoke flare?'

'Who would see it, in all this?' He waved an arm.

I shook my head, feeling helpless but knowing I couldn't let it overwhelm me. We didn't have the luxury of wallowing in fear or being weak now. If I hadn't learned enough, or if I wasn't strong enough – then the people who had saved my life by training me, like Sefa and Tau; the beautiful people who had accepted me, like Rafi; and the people who'd brought me joy, like Peri and Roa – would all suffer or die. This was a real test of how I'd adapted to the changes in my life. If I chose to remain too laid-back, not striving enough, the volcano would overpower us and kill everyone. If I was still being too rigid and unable to burn *with* the fire, the volcano would burn me up instead. I knew we couldn't stop now. Not yet.

I thanked God we hadn't yet reached the stage of the eruption where the rock of the volcano itself would be thrown into the air as pumice. There was still time to turn this around, I was convinced of it.

'We have to redirect or stop the volcano,' I said. 'Then we can help the others fight the slavers.' I didn't recognise the hard tone in my own voice.

Tau just nodded.

We sparked together and looked again into the maw of the beast. It was louder than anything I'd ever heard, as if the earth itself was groaning. Rocks crunching, melting, like the sound of teeth grinding. Fire sizzled and gas roared, hissing. Heat tried to choke and smother every part of us.

And it was definitely 'us'. Tau was fully connected to me in that moment, in a spiritual way. I'd never been this close to another person in my life. It was different to anything else I'd tried before. It wasn't intimate, like my love with Bear, but it was complete. I could sense every part of Tau's power and vulnerabilities, and I knew he could see every piece of me as well, not just physically but mentally.

Tau stared at me as if he'd never seen me before. The golden glow of my spark was so much brighter than I'd ever seen it, just as large and strong as his orange flame was.

Please, God, I prayed. *Please, guide me again.*

Seeing the two of us so clearly, I fit together our powers closer than before, and sent us into the fire.

It was everywhere.

Everywhere.

'Too much,' I shouted over the roaring mountain. 'Push it down, back where it came from.'

'You can't,' a voice shouted from behind us.

I whirled, opening my real eyes as well as my spiritual eyes. A burned, twisted figure was barely illuminated by the light of the gathering lava. His eyes were dark.

'Hanini,' said Tau. 'You? You woke the mountain?'

'I can't let you stop it,' said Hanini. 'You couldn't if you tried, now. It's too strong, too far past us.'

'Why?' I shouted, but I felt sick, as if I already knew what he was going to say. I recognised the look in his eyes, the delight at his own power and shame that it was unacceptable to use that power. I knew that look because I'd felt that way myself, every day since I first lit those fire fans in the ring, every day as I'd trained and hated myself for not being perfectly in control yet. Every day until today.

'I burned, and they mocked me,' he hissed. 'Said I didn't have enough power, enough control. But I have more power than any of them. And now all of them will burn.' He raised his arms, and the lava began to bubble up again, out and over the rim of the volcano's mouth.

In the cloud of smoke above us, lightning flashed with a deafening clap. I didn't have time to notice my fear; I just moved.

I tackled Hanini to the ground and grabbed at his legs as he pulled away from me. His skin was warped from his old burns. Then Tau was there, pinning Hanini's arms behind his back.

Through my hold on Hanini's leg, I linked myself internally to the black rope of power that was Hanini, and I *pulled* at it. I pulled until I could feel it trapped beneath mine. It felt like a stray dog straining at the unfamiliar sensation of a leash. It felt feral, and dirty, and vicious. I almost immediately wanted to drop it, let it slither away from me. But I had to hold on.

I felt like I could pull the power right out of him if I tried, so he could never use it again. Or I could pull his power into myself, and become stronger than ever …

But I didn't.

I already knew how power could be twisted, turned around to the dark. I'd been healed; I wouldn't corrupt myself with his dark power. So I pulled on the leash, until Hanini was fully restrained, both physically and magically.

'There's still time,' I said directly into his good ear. 'You can help us turn this around. Help us stop the volcano.'

I motioned to Tau to let him up.

'My power,' Hanini said hoarsely. 'You took my power.'

'And we'll take a lot more if you don't help us stop this thing,' said Tau. 'You owe the village your life, man! They could have had you killed, but they didn't.'

Hanini curled his twisted lip. 'What life?'

'Please,' I tried. 'Forget about the village. Some of our island's children are on those slave ships, and unless we can stop this volcano, their lives will be lost, too, like yours was.'

Hanini's eyes flickered, uncertain.

The ground rumbled, but I stood firm. I was only half there. Part of me was hearing a whisper, like a small, still voice that I couldn't quite hear. I didn't know where it came from – the air? My bones? The God I'd prayed to for so many years? The whisper held an idea.

'We can open up the vents,' I said. 'Let the magma out the sides of the volcano. It will release the pressure. Maybe even direct the flow so it hits the slave boats. Give the warriors time to reach the boat that's got our children, and to fight off the other boats. Give everyone else time to get in canoes and escape to one of the other islands.'

Both of them stared at me.

'Come *on*. We can do it.'

The next seconds were a blur. Hanini grabbed my hand in his twisted, clawed hand, and I felt his leashed power submit itself to me. Tau must have seen, because he took my other hand, and we crouched together beside the lava.

I gathered the collective strength of the three of us and sent it forth, united, into the flow of lava.

The volcano surged, as if sensing us coming for it. A wave of heat hit me, stronger than I was ready for. My vision, both physical and mental, greyed, and I nearly passed out. My lungs began to burn from the hot smoke I was choking down, and from sheer exhaustion. I felt my nose begin to bleed, and I realised with an acute sense of terror just how in over my head I was.

But I was more stubborn than that.

I spoke to the heat. *Big flame, flow out, and flow away.*

Little flame, why? it rumbled. *I am awake. At last.*

Lightning flashed again, all around me. My skin prickled with it, and for a second I flinched, afraid I might be burning alive and not realise it. I took a beat, and breathed in through my nose, trying not to cough from the smoke.

You belong underground, in the warm, I tried. *Not out here in the cold.*

The air around us began to clear.

Tau blinked, peering down at the shoreline. 'Eli,' he said. The water healer was using salt water in the air to wash the sulphur gas away. 'Thank the flames.'

I sensed the mountain weaken, distracted by the water healer's power, and I gave a shout. 'Now!' I pushed with all our combined might, and so did Tau and Hanini.

Our pressure forced the magma out sideways, burning through the rock veins of the mountain. The pressure grew and grew until it had nowhere to come but out. Lava poured down the sides of the mountain in a slow-moving stream that was as tall as a man and as wide as the longhut.

With the pressure released to the sides, the rain of ash from the mouth of the volcano stopped immediately.

I swayed on my feet, dizzy with relief and from using so much power at once. 'Now,' I said, catching myself on Tau's arm to keep from falling. 'Those slavers, the boat that was sailing away, with our little ones. Can we direct the lava flow towards them? Send fire after them? Something?'

Tau gave me a keen look, letting me know it hadn't escaped his notice that I'd said 'our' little ones. 'We need to stop the ships without sinking them or hurting any children who are still on board. As long as we avoid the hull, we might be able to do something.'

Hanini didn't say anything, just stared at the two of us as if we were Tuatahi reincarnated – the first man to touch fire. His twisted body showed fear, but also awe. I wondered if it was enough to turn his anger around.

Tau and I focused together again, this time not on the giant that was now subsiding into slumber, but on the heat it had left behind. The slave boat that was leaving was just crossing the reef. We gathered heat from a stream of lava and shot it like a cannon across the mast of the ship. As their sail burst into flames, the ship's crew burst into action, trying to put it out.

Then we turned our attention to the other boats, and soon had their hulls burning.

Satisfied, I gasped out, 'They'll be kept busy for a while now.'

'Perfect,' said Tau, wiping sweat from his brow. 'Our fighters will send a fleet by and clean them up, and then bring home any children they've stolen.'

'Oh, good,' I said, and tried to suck in some air. My vision was greying at the edges again, and Tau and Hanini seemed to swim in front of me, looking down at me.

Swamped all at once by a sense of being drained, I dropped to my knees, wobbling.

Tau grabbed my hands, and hissed at the burn, but held onto them, gritting his teeth. 'You're still clinging to the volcano, Fern.'

Heat made everything sway before my vision, as if Tau was a mirage. 'I'm all right,' I mumbled. 'I'm just tired.'

He shook his head and rubbed my hot hands in his. 'All right now, kitten,' he purred into my ear, so I could hear it over the sound of the volcano. 'Let go of the candle, and we can go have a rest.'

I knew he was right, even through the foggy heat.

Thank you, I whispered to the mountain, and I wavered my spark away from its pooling inferno. A cool breeze hit me instantly as I let go, and I sagged with relief to the ground.

Chapter Twenty-Five

I must have stayed there on hands and knees, not saying anything, for more than a few minutes, but I felt myself rising back to awareness again to find the heat in the air was dissipating. My skin felt clammy, and my heart was racing. Stars danced across my vision, everything too hazy to see. I gulped in a breath and looked up, trembling all over.

Tau's face staring over at me instantly lightened with relief. 'We need to go,' he was saying.

I nodded weakly.

Somehow, the two of us staggered down the mountain. The air was still thick and hard to breathe, but it only stank faintly of sulphur now. I was covered in sweat; the droplets sizzled where they fell onto the rocks. The soles of my boots were completely burned through, so my feet were flinching against the hot ground with every step.

Old Man Hanini had disappeared, but I could still feel him as a tiny tug on the heartstrings of my power where I had leashed his powers. I tried not to think about what might happen to him now.

What could his life possibly be like, with his powers leashed unless I released them? Could the Islanders ever forgive him for trying to kill them all?

I didn't have the energy to ask Tau whether the chief would let Hanini live or not. My whole body felt like it was made of lead. I nearly stumbled and fell with each step. My head ached, and I was so thirsty.

When we neared the base of the mountain and found a stream of warm water, I tested the temperature, thinking about dunking my whole head in to cool off and shake this headache.

'Don't drink it,' Tau warned me just in time. 'Not until we've boiled the water. The sulphur is poisonous, and most of this water will be contaminated.' He looked around wearily as if seeing more than the trees around us. 'I don't know what we'll do. If we stay, we'll need to wait until Eli is able to purify all the water sources on the island with his water wielding. Until then, everyone would need to boil all their drinking water.'

I nodded, and as I went to stand, I saw something shining in the water and I stopped, startled. 'What the—'

Tau smiled wearily at my reaction. 'Noticed it, have you?'

I waved my hand in front of the water, and then stuck it in Tau's face. 'How could I not notice? Tau, I'm glowing!'

From my fingertips to my shoulders, my skin was shining slightly, the glow swelling and dimming in waves, in time with my pulse. It was subtle; it kind of looked like I was standing next to a campfire. I could feel myself start to tremble.

He waved a hand. 'It's just *mana*, don't worry about it. It'll fade by the time we get off the mountain.'

'Don't worry about it?' I echoed, still in shock. I didn't know if I wanted to laugh or cry. 'I can barely remember what you told me before about *mana*, only that it was some kind of … spirit energy?'

Tau nodded. 'Yes, looks like the island approves of what you did.' He patted me on the arm. 'Consider yourself blessed.'

The sun rose as we reached the beach.

When they saw us, everyone cheered. I laughed, almost hysterical with tiredness. It was so vastly different to how people had been reacting to me lately, afraid of my untamed power. And it was a whole world apart from the response I'd received this past winter, when I saved the caravan from the witch doctor. Then, people had just looked at me in shock and fear.

But I was different now.

I owned myself and my power. I owned my fears and the strength I'd used to get past them. I had borrowed strength from Bear to cross the ocean, and borrowed courage from Tau to brave my training, but not anymore.

I knew what I was, and I wasn't ashamed of it anymore, and I wasn't afraid of it, either. I'd used more power even than I had, and the dark side hadn't consumed me. I was strong.

Around me, I heard other voices.

'Mountain calmer,' they were saying. 'Fire whisperer.'

They didn't seem to be afraid of me. They didn't seem angry now, that I was a *fafine* who had wielded fire – while standing on their sacred volcano, no less!

I mused over what it would mean if I decided that this was my life's purpose, or at least the purpose of my powers: to keep others safe from the violence of the world. I saw a little more clearly now, and I wondered in my heart what my next step should be. How I would find it, how I would make it happen, I wasn't sure, but perhaps I would figure it out if I travelled north with the caravans.

I couldn't think about that now. First, I wanted food, and sleep, not necessarily in that order.

When the children were rescued and brought back to shore by the warriors, some of the families came to thank me with tears streaming down their faces.

I stopped short when I realised one of the children the warriors had rescued was a boy I knew from fire training, Ualesi. He was the kid I'd seen get thrown into the ocean on that first day when I showed up on the beach to ask Sefa to train me. I couldn't imagine how the slavers had got him, although I knew he didn't have as much control over his powers as the others had.

When he saw me, he began running towards me. At first, I didn't realise he was running to me; I thought he was running to his family. But the warriors must have told him I was responsible for stopping the slavers, because he grabbed a few of the other boys and they threw themselves on me like a dog pile, shouting their gratitude at me.

I didn't even know where I found the energy, but I managed to stay standing under the weight of their embrace. I talked with them, although I have no recollection of what was said. And I listened as they all shouted at once, just hearing their gratitude, hearing their shock, hearing their anger at the slavers.

Ualesi told us all about how when he'd been trapped, he'd suddenly found himself unable to use his powers.

'Fire deadening rock, and steel, in their weapons,' he said. 'They didn't even have to hit me to disarm me. It was like they'd just poured sand all over my fire, stuffed it down!'

A few moments later, Peri found me and without hesitation, wrapped her arms around my neck in a warm hug.

'Fern,' she gasped, 'I'm so glad you're all right!'

My heart swelled – so we were still friends, even after I'd

scared her. I burst into tears of joy and relief. The pain and fear and confusion of the past weeks all jumbled together, and I wept into her neck. She held me, rocking me back and forth, reassuring me with her closeness that we were all right.

The celebrations and repairs wore on into the setting of the sun that evening, drums and tambourines, singing and dancing and feasting, and I danced along with all of them. I danced until my feet reminded me I'd raced up a mountain that morning.

But despite the celebrations, there was a tense mood among the Islanders.

'So much here was burned to ash. We will rebuild, farther from the volcano,' the chief said as we all sat around the supper fire. He was downcast, and seemed smaller than the giant, larger-than-life man he'd been before. He still radiated the same fire, but the events of this season were clearly wearing on him physically. 'I cannot ask our women and children to live in a ghost village, not when our men must wage battle against these slavers. So as your chief, I will stand guard here on Aiatal, and organise the rebuilding in a new location. I will send messages to the Emperor of Chidor on behalf of my people, demanding the release of our young people, and we will see if he is a reasonable man. And in the meantime, Tau will be your war chief and bring our warriors to the mainland, for the reconnaissance and to lead the war against the slavers of Chidor. He is ready. He can lead us to victory. We will find where they have hidden our people, and we will rescue them from the slavers, and then we will burn their whole civilisation to the ground!'

I wondered how Tau felt about that. I looked over at him, talking with the other warriors. Leading was what he was raised for, although I doubted going to war against the most bloodthirsty nation on the mainland was how he'd expected to start out. He was probably excited. All those scouting parties he'd been on, all the battles fought against other islands for rights over fishing, and land, and women … War chief. It was the best of both worlds: a taste of real leadership, with his father still around to be the island's chief and guide him. This was probably everything he'd been waiting for.

And if he hadn't told me how he dreamed of being a different kind of chief, if everyone hadn't told me how special he was, how he was going to change things for good in the islands … then maybe I would have believed he was pleased to be going to war.

He must have sensed my eyes on him, because he looked over to meet my gaze. I found heat and determination in his eyes, and I felt a delightful shiver.

With a pang of grief, I remembered that I would probably be leaving him soon. Surely, calming a raging volcano would finally be enough proof that my powers were controlled enough to return to the caravan troupe. So … I would soon be asking around for a sailing ship that was headed for the mainland, either from Aiatal or from one of the other Golden Islands.

I hoped I would be welcome among the vans once more. Some of my fellow travellers might still look at me with fear, but my performances and my powers would bring them coin and protection at once. And I had friends there, true friends, like Dakota and Ebony. If some people didn't know the value of my power, they would know it in time. The world wasn't safe. The caravan wasn't safe. They needed me now, just as much as I needed them.

I just didn't know if I really wanted to return to them. I'd been feeling so much more at home in the islands, after my challenging start here.

The thought of leaving Tau … my gut twisted with the

uncertainty of it all. I wouldn't know how he fared, what he would do next, whether he would even live or die in his island's war against slavery.

And wasn't that crazy? How could they be going to war against slavery, and I not going with them to help?

But I'd chosen to live in the caravan, to serve the caravan, and now that I was trained, there was no rational reason for me to stay here.

Confused and despondent, I walked out to the shore. I found myself a nice, cool spot in the sand, a hollow that the sun hadn't touched in many hours. Dune grasses prickled my arms, keeping my mind sharp, even though I was beyond exhausted. I watched the water, the ripples of black and gold as the sun sank below the horizon.

Up there, on the mountain, I had heard God's voice. I just knew it. I knew it like I knew the name I'd chosen, like I knew how to eat or sleep or breathe. I knew it with a fearful certainty, an unconscious but vital knowing. I felt it in my bones and the pounding of my heart with each breath.

And I had loved the sound of that whisper. I wanted to hear it more. Follow where it might lead me. Do whatever was needed. I wasn't afraid to follow, even though I knew it might mean once again stepping out of the path I was expected to take.

I was excited.

Maybe that was the answer, I said to myself. *Maybe I should go with the warriors. Learn more about how to use my fire from those who know it best.*

I had wandered off on my own in the dark when I felt it coming.

One moment before the punch hit me, I felt – or maybe heard – the *swoosh* of a fist through the air. It was enough that I half-turned, and the blow glanced off my shoulder.

I gasped, pain rushing through my shoulder, the shock tingling all the way down my arm. My arms were sensitive, even after being healed.

I turned, lifted my other arm to shield myself. I couldn't see who it was yet, just a dark figure against the dark beach.

My first instinct was to run, but I had other tools now. If someone was attacking me with their fists instead of fire, maybe I had a chance – I could use my fire to defend myself against them.

'Fire bitch,' they said roughly, and I recognised the voice. 'Give me my flames back.' He reached with both twisted hands for my throat, and I backed up, wrestling his hands down.

'Hanini, no.' Afraid, I tried to persuade him. 'I'll give them back.'

'You didn't have any right to take them! I'll kill you to get them back!'

'I couldn't let you hurt the village.' I could tell from his face that reasoning with him wasn't getting me anywhere. I fell into a defensive stance.

He just snarled, then swung at me again with a wild punch.

I was only just fast enough to back up a step. He was faster, more desperate. His hands clenched around my throat, the palms rough, the fingernails ragged, tearing at my skin.

Oh God, help.

I gasped and began frantically pulling away, trying to remember the self-defence moves I'd learned in my first few weeks of fire training. But the strength was slipping out of my arms with every moment, until I couldn't manage to fend off his wiry arms. I could see my death in his feral eyes. His ruined lips pulled back in a snarl over dark, rotting teeth.

He squeezed, and things began to go spotty around the edges of my sight. I wheezed, panicking.

Flames burst all around me, but not from within me this time. Hanini pulled back. I gasped in a giant breath and staggered further away from Hanini.

All around me, covering me from head to toe with their wings, like angels, shielding me from him, were three thunder eagles.

One was behind me, its wings stretching over my head, blocking my ears so I couldn't hear Hanini's terrified curses.

The other two stood at my sides, their wings curled around my belly and legs. Their eyes were locked not on me but on my opponent.

They gave me the moment I needed to remember who I was.

I was strong.

And I had a strong fire within me.

No crazy man was going to take away that power. I'd already put him in his place once; I could do it again.

Then the thunder eagles opened their wings in unison.

I blazed, fire roaring out of me, controlled but unshakably powerful. Undeniable. Hanini had only enough time to lift his hands before him, not even enough time to draw another breath to scream.

With the strength and speed of wildfire through underbrush, the flames whipped out from me in vines that wrapped around him from head to toe. I breathed out steadily, no longer afraid, and clarified the vines into ropes that held him fast, trapping his arms and legs against his body.

The flames weren't actually touching him, but if he moved so much as an inch, he would be burned alive.

If he stayed still, he would survive, to face his deadly trial at the hands of the villagers he had tried to kill.

I took a shaky breath, relieved. I could have so easily eaten him up in the flames, turning him to ashes, like I had killed the witch doctor. But I didn't want to kill anyone else. And I hadn't; I had held back, my power in my control.

A well of sadness rose in me – not exactly regret – after all, at least I hadn't killed him. I only wished human nature were different. I wished Hanini hadn't been exiled, and gone mad, and tried to kill everyone, and then tried to kill me. I was disappointed that after I'd been able to calm the volcano yesterday, I hadn't been able to calm Hanini.

I looked up at the thunder eagle beside me, and whispered, 'Thank you.'

They waved a wing, and the blinding flash of flames had me shutting my eyes tight. When I opened them, the thunder eagles were flapping into the dark sky.

I left Hanini shouting and screaming on the beach while I went to tell the two chiefs that one of them would need to organise a trial.

Chapter Twenty-Six

The next day, I was waiting as a small boat was loaded up with food and other supplies, ready to take me to the mainland to catch up with my fellow caravan members. The boat would only hold me and the few sailors who had been on the island before the eruption.

The sailors were all nervous, repeating their superstitions every few minutes to ward off evil. One man kept throwing salt over his shoulder; another kept spitting; another kept making a praying gesture with his hands on his forehead.

The chief said that by now, everyone on the sea and along the coastline of the mainland would have seen the eruption. A passing ship this morning had already made it clear they were checking things out, not coming too close. They must have felt the earth tremble and seen their own shore tides grow larger and more violent.

Tau approached me, the swagger in his walk tamped down compared to normal. Red, raw lines marked his collarbone where Savan had added a war chief *tatau* to his other markings. I lifted my fingers to the red and purple bruising around my own throat, a violent echo of his new tattoo. It struck me as odd that we'd each been marked in the same place on the same night. I tried to think of my bruises as marks of my success, instead of seeing them as another failure.

My heart leapt to see him, although I tried to squash it down. I was leaving, I reminded myself. I was literally standing in the shallow water, waiting for them to say it was time for me to walk up the narrow plank and board the ship.

And he was war chief now – he would have so many responsibilities. It was his big chance, everything he'd been training for his whole life. Only more reason to try and keep some distance in my heart.

But as soon as he was close enough, he pulled me into his arms without checking to see who could see us.

In spite of my fears, my whole body sighed into him, drawing us closer. 'People will see,' I whispered. 'They'll make you do even more purifications.'

'Let them see.' He pulled back to look into my eyes, his gaze sharp. 'If they think the woman who saved us from the volcano and from the slavers could possibly make me unclean, they're mad. Our island spirits wouldn't have let you anywhere near the volcano if they disapproved, and instead, they helped you.' The lines of his body tensed against mine as he paused, then said, 'You know they're calling you the Mountain Calmer. You were stronger in the end than I was.'

I couldn't believe he'd admitted that. His self-assuredness had been such a big part of how he presented himself to the world – where had it gone?

'You taught me well,' I replied.

He gave me a wink, but he looked tired. I knew he'd had a late night, with so much to organise.

I wanted to tell him so much. That I was glad to have met him, and thankful endlessly to him for training me. That I was more than a little in love with him. That I hadn't only been playing with him. That I was sorry I couldn't stay. That I was sorry if me coming to his island had awoken the volcano to begin with and caused all this trouble. But I didn't think it would help me to say those things, or help him to hear them.

So, I let go of him, stepped back to put some space between us, and said, 'I'll never forget my time here. Thank you for training me, and I'm sorry for all the trouble I've put you through.'

He waved it off with one hand, but he didn't give me any of the casual laughter I'd grown so used to hearing from him. 'No, Fern, I need to apologise to you. My father won't offer you the combat thanks he should. If I was more than a war chief, I would gather everyone and do it myself. But my father is still chief of the islands, and he even said – well.'

'What?'

'If you were any other warrior who had saved our island, our people … But being *fafine*, and a northerner …' He shrugged, and I could see his frustration. 'He wanted to blame you for what happened, wants you off the island.'

I scowled.

Tau lifted his hands. 'I told him the island woke the volcano, to warn us of the slavers' fleet approaching, and that it was only you and I working together that calmed the volcano again. I wasn't the only one saying we wanted you recognised. Even Eli stood up for you as well, but it wasn't enough.'

I gave a half-smile, picturing the mild-mannered healer speaking up for me. 'Well, I suppose it's no surprise,' I said, thinking of how the caravan troupe had reacted after I'd used my power to save them. Many of them were still afraid of me even now, after the training I'd undertaken. 'But I want to know what you're going to do now. Where will you start? How will you bring back your children?'

He shrugged. 'Begin our reconnaissance.' I didn't know that word in Trader's Talk, so he explained, 'Spying on Chidor. We'll look for where they have taken our young ones to, and look for places where they are weakest along their coasts. Try to decide where we could best approach to surprise them.' He reached for my hand, and I gave it to him, his touch lighting me up like it always did. He held my hand firmly and gripped my forearm with his other hand. 'Come with us.'

'Where, exactly?'

'Come with me and my warriors, as we find and fight these slaver bastards.' His eyes burned into mine. 'You know you can help us. You have so much strength. And I know you don't want to let the slavers win.'

'Everything you're saying sounds right,' I said, 'but what use could I be as a spy? I don't have any experience doing that, and look at me – I'd stick out like a sore thumb no matter where we went.'

He looked so disappointed that I felt like I had to keep defending myself. 'And anyway, I committed myself to the caravan. I said I would stay with them. And they've left, to go north.'

'So that's it, then, eh?' He rubbed his thumb over my skin, still holding my hands in his.

Everywhere he touched me tingled. My inner fire was heating, trying to tell me something. I could feel how our sparks were twining together while we talked, getting closer and closer. But I was used to doing what made *sense*. My head felt heavy; my spark felt light.

Quietly, I said, 'I only came here for the month, to be trained, so I could be safe around others.'

'Be safe?' he scoffed. 'If you'd wanted a safe life, you would have stayed in the mountains and become a shepherd or a cheese-maker or something. You'll never live a *safe* life, Fern. You'd be bored stiff.'

I tensed. 'The caravan is my family. They took me in when I had nothing. I owe it to them to keep them safe, as well, no matter what I want for myself.'

'You already saved them once, Fern,' he reminded me. 'You don't owe anybody anything. And I know you don't owe me anything, either, but … I want more time with you.'

'I … I know. I do, too.' I blushed, wondering whether I needed to hesitate at all.

He was right. I was stronger now – I didn't need to cling to a real family or my new substitute family in order to survive. I'd find a way. I felt hope rising in my chest, an unbelievable lightness compared to the heaviness of only a few moments ago, when I'd thought I was saying goodbye. It didn't make sense to be hopeful when we were off to war – but I'd be doing what I could with my powers, to keep others safe.

Maybe this was the whole reason I had joined the caravan, and let it bring me here. Because I needed to be here.

And I'd have more time with him, this man I was so desperately attracted to. The man whose compassion was the whole reason I wasn't still burning myself. The man who'd taught me how to use my powers safely, and then trusted me to use them. The man who said I was powerful, and wasn't afraid of me.

But everything I'd said was true – I was no spy, and I'd already committed. I felt the agony of regret all the way through me, like a whole body ache. 'I want to say yes. So badly. It just seems crazy. Won't your people say this is a mistake? Especially if the chief … not …'

He took a step closer, so that we were almost body to body. He lifted one hand, and cupped my face. 'They have nothing to do with what's between us. And if they don't want to see us together, after everything we've both done for them, let me deal with them.'

His eyes were killing me. I felt like if I met his gaze for much longer, I would either melt in regret or I would throw myself into his arms and never let go. I knew which one I wanted to do, and I didn't want to have any regrets.

I held my breath for a long moment, then nodded in a rush. 'All right. Let's do this!'

He grinned. 'There's just one more thing.'

I laughed, letting it spill out of me with messy joy. 'What?'

He grabbed my waist and pulled me tight against him. He kissed me, and everything was right with the world. Sailors pushed past us, still getting us ready to leave. I barely noticed them, kissing Tau back with everything in me.

His strong arms lifted me, holding me with joy, without reservation. I pulled back enough to lock eyes with him again, smiling even though I knew others could see us and I was probably blushing by now.

One second, I was kissing Tau. The next, the ship was lilting away from the shore, and everyone was running around, shouting instructions to each other. The sails filled with air like a giant, gulping breath, and as oars slapped the water on either side, the ship leaped forward through the waves.

And I wasn't on it.

I stood next to Tau in the sandy shallows and watched the ship grow smaller and smaller, wondering whether I would ever see my friends again. I had no idea what the future held for me. But deep down, I felt I was in the right place.

Glossary

Locations featured

The Golden Islands:

Aiatal (main island)

Kamahimaihi (second island)

Fefine mohe (lesser island)

Lateilei (lesser island)

Lelena (lesser island)

Meanings of Aiatalei phrases

afi – fire

afio maligayang – welcome

afi toa – fire warriors

e ia – it was

faafeyai – thank you

fafine – woman

fafin tatau – female tattoos

fa ora – hello

hava – alcohol

kene – in the front
lou alofa – my love
malolo – rest/nap
nale – no
naniwala ka sa – are you convinced?
oe – yes
o e manuia – are you all right?
papan palusapa – private conversation
pase – in the back
peya tatau – male tattoos
sau ii – come here
tauta leleiya – speaking well
treleilehine – crossover child (non-binary human)
tuatahi – first
uma tagata – everyone out
witihai – sunrise

Acknowledgements

First thank you in this book has to go to my amazing editor, Michele Perry (Wordplay Editing Services), whose comments like 'LOVE THIS!!!' made me smile during a really dark time. And of course, those comments like 'I thought he went back to the mainland?' are the only reason this book now has fewer pesky plot holes.

Thanks to everyone who bought Book 1, or who said, 'Oh, my wife/friend/daughter would love this book, I'll have to tell them about it!' You're the BEST.

Thanks to my brightest and best cheerleader, Nikki. Love you!

I also dedicate this work to my little one, Zoe, who is no longer so little. I love you so much, and it trips me out to think that you might enjoy reading this book one day.

I acknowledge the traditional owners of the land on which I currently write, the Yuggerah people (or I've also seen it written Jagera, Yeggarah). I thank the elders past, present, and emerging, for their work in caring for this land. I am constantly looking for ways that my work can honour the first people of this big island,

Australia, where I was born, and the indigenous Filipino people of the islands in the Philippines, where I was raised.

Finally, thank you God for showing me unending love through this endless turmoil that is life. This story was informed by some of my own experiences with PTSD – although I will say, there are a lot more techniques you can use than just the few I was able to squeeze into Fern's story. For example, meditation is just not my jam, but I love dancing for mindful movement. So, mama/papa God, I pray you use this story to show us how we can grow stronger mentally, physically, emotionally, and spiritually.

Other books by TJ Withers-Ryan

Fire Dancers in the Sand (2021) – Fire Dancers Book 1

About the author

TJ published *Fire Dancers in the Sand*, the first book in her Fire Dancers series, in 2021. With a double degree in Laws with honours and Fine Arts (Writing), she worked in publishing for a decade in roles including editor, proofreader, and marketing before joining the corporate world.

In her spare time, TJ enjoyed more than a decade of serving the young adult community in Australia as a youth group leader, youth mentor, young adult group leader, and creative writing teacher. Before becoming a mum, she loved studying languages and travelling throughout south-east Asia, practising martial arts, and painting.

These days, you can find TJ on social media, working as a corporate copywriter, and generally trying to survive #mumlife.

For more by
TJ Withers-Ryan ...

read my rambling thoughts on my blog tjwithers.com

subscribe to my YouTube channel

or follow me on Facebook, Instagram, TikTok,
and whatever platform they invent next.